OTTILIE

Star of County Down

Ron Cassidy

Broomfields Publishing

First published 2013 by
Broomfields Publishing
19, Broomfields
Denton
Manchester M34 3TH
roncass_99@yahoo.co.uk
0161 320 6955

ISBN 978-0-9568 108-3-0

Cover design and photographic reprocessing by
Simon Pantling *simon@pantlingstudio.com*

Cover Photograph: Jim Hobden

My sufferings are the blossoms on the tree of my life.
The harvest is my understanding and acceptance of them

Ottilie Patterson

THE BLUES

Blues music was the musical sign and symbol of the Negro's emancipation. In its singular vigour and incisiveness it bore the characteristic sign of a vast social achievement. At the same time however it bore the mark of the social and spiritual agony of an emancipation that had brought relief from slavery without leading to social, economic and cultural recognition.

The Negro was now free to sing as he pleased - but all he could sing about was poverty, desertion and escape.

Yet misery and self-pity were presented in a lean, matter of fact manner which had the true ring of free men's poetry.

Ernest Bornemann, Jazz Critic
Preserved in her writings by Ottilie Patterson

CONTENTS

ACKNOWLEDGEMENTS

My grateful thanks go to all who have given me so much help in the preparation of this study, through invitations to their homes, through emails, letters, articles, newspaper cuttings and by their general encouragement. Including:

John Andrews, Comber, County Down.
Chris Barber, Bandleader and former husband of Ottilie Patterson.
Gerard Bielderman, Discographer, Zwolle, Netherlands.
Ron Bowden, Drummer with Barber Band, 1954-7, Greenhurst, London.
John Crocker, Reed Player with Barber Band 1968-2003, Southgate, London.
Louis Lince, Romiley, Constant encouragement and advice, and an absolute mine of information.
Walter Love, BBC Radio Ulster Producer, Belfast.
Amanda Martin, Information Officer, Ards Council, Newtonards.
Johnny McCallum, Banjo and Guitar player with Barber Band 1973-1994, Tonbridge, Kent.
Brian McAnoy, Architect and long time friend, Liverpool.
Stu Morrison, Banjo and Guitar player with Barber Band 1964-1971, Worthing, Sussex.
National Jazz Archive, Loughton, Essex.
Mike Pointon interviews for *Just Jazz* Magazine, 2007.
Udo Schneider, jazz concert promoter, Wuppertal, Germany.
John Service, Trombone player with Barber Band, 2008-2009.
Alyn Shipton, Chris Barber Biographer & Jazz Critic of the *Independent*, Oxford.
Dick Smith, Bass player with Barber Band, 1956-1966, Minehead, Somerset.
George Smyth, East Belfast Jazz Club, Belfast.
John Warner, Teddington, London, for copies of diaries and early programmes.
Lisa Watson, Care Nurse, Ayr, Scotland.
Albert 'Wild Al' Watt, Musician and Friend, Tampa Bay, Florida.
Erskine Willis, Historian, Comber, County Down.
Jen Wilson, Jazz Heritage Wales.

PROLOGUE

Manchester Free Trade Hall, September 1958

For four jazz-crazy fifteen year olds this was the biggest night of their lives so far. Having saved all their pennies for ages they were squashed into a packed Free Trade Hall in Manchester for a live concert with the Chris Barber Jazz Band. They shared their passion for the music by frantically swapping their meagre collection of singles, EPs and LPs between themselves and had found their enthusiasm growing day by day. Now they were to see their heroes in the flesh.

I was one of those fifteen year olds.

The moment finally arrived, and at the bidding of the Master of Ceremonies Graham Burbridge strolled languidly onto stage, immaculate in his pale blue suit, to take his position behind his enormous drum kit. He was closely followed by Dick and Eddie Smith, Monty Sunshine (could it really be him?), the bushy-haired Pat Halcox, and finally Chris Barber himself.

We were as "gone" at the sight as any latter-day groupies, except that we managed to suppress the undignified squeals that so often characterised those rock star acolytes.

The first bars of *Bourbon Street Parade* shook us from our trance, as we were reminded what our evening was all about. Those first marching strains set my feet tapping on a journey that would take me right through my teenage years and would become a life-long obsession, leading me eventually to visit New Orleans itself more than six times, involve me writing books and articles about jazz, and which would help me make wonderful friendships with people all over the world - friendships that have lasted. Jazz is like that. It is an infectious music that draws people together through irresistible collective toe-tapping.

And then there was Ottilie Patterson, strolling regally onto stage in an olive green dress and with immaculate, auburn hair. Sadly the ravages of time have had their effect on my memory, and I cannot remember a single word of any of the songs she sang that night. What I can remember however is the electrifying effect she had on the audience, turning rapidly from polite applause to thunderous acclamation.

We went out afterwards on a cloud. We had actually seen and heard our heroes in person. And yet there was no doubt in our minds who had shone as the brightest star. On subsequent visits to jazz concerts at the same venue we would go on to see legends of New Orleans such as George Lewis, Kid Ory, and the Daddy of them all, Louis Armstrong, as our musical horizons expanded exponentially.

But for us this is where it all started. Just as John Wesley had his heart "strangely warmed" in the Aldersgate Street Chapel many years earlier, subsequently launching out on a missionary venture that made the whole world his parish, so being in the audience that night, with the Barber Band in full swing, was for us to be a life changing and life redirecting experience. Many wonderful things would follow from this first encounter.

The interesting thing is that for many jazz fans their baptism into jazz music was not unlike mine. Many would point to a time and place when they heard a piece of traditional jazz that changed their musical lives. More amazingly still, more often than not, that introductory piece of music would turn out to have featured Chris Barber and his Band. He has been the gateway into jazz for literally thousands of people. These people have gone on subsequently like me to gain an appreciation of jazz in all its many forms. But for them Chris Barber and Ottilie Patterson were the beginning of their interest and participation in the music.

As we shall discuss later, the accessibility of Barber's music has often been derided over the years and dismissed as "commercialism", the selling of a musical birthright. To those detractors he might well respond, as indeed I would, that there is no point in playing music that no-one wants to listen to! Participation is a key element in jazz, and jazz music has from its very inception been music that has held performers and audiences together in a close bond. Jazz has never ever been a take it or leave it music.

The vitally important thing is that in popularising his music and opening it up to the widest possibly audience, the performer should not tear himself away from his musical roots. In my considered view Chris Barber has never done that.

It has also not gone unnoticed or unremarked upon by those with green eyes that he has made a good living for himself in the process! Those who are free from the clutches of the green-eyed monster however, might well say "good luck to him."

In spite of the foregoing, to consider Chris Barber and his Band simply as a "taster" for the appreciation of jazz music would be to do him a grave injustice. He is so much more. His restlessness, his thirst for innovation and trail-blazing has led to the introduction of many new forms of jazz music, not all of which have endured, though many have.

And one of his most significant innovations of all was the employment of the subject of our study, Ottilie Patterson. It would prove to be an incredibly significant day for Barber and all of us when a young Ottilie walked into that Soho Club in May, 1954 and boldly asked to sing with the Band.

The word "sensational" is an over-used and much abused adjective in the Show Business world. It is used frequently of artistes who in reality have no right at all to the description. In the case of Ottilie Patterson however it is a wholly inadequate word to describe the diminutive Irish girl with the big voice who swept away all preconceptions and defied all conventions governing what should be involved in singing jazz.

The firmest of these preconceptions was the idea that only black people could sing the Blues. Blues was *black* music in its very essence, and whites should keep their hands off it, so the critics lined up to say. The error of that statement was demonstrated by black people themselves, who were very ready to tell Ottilie directly that she sounded "just like one of us". As we shall later note, the compliment Ottilie prized more than any other was that she sounded "just like Bessie Smith", the black Empress of the Blues.

As Barber and those associated with him were later to acknowledge, with a mixture of reluctance and generosity, Ottilie was the making of the Band. She was the X Factor, the *something special* that made the audiences get up off their seats and shout for more. In reviews of Barber concerts, reviewer after reviewer would acknowledge Ottilie's appearance on stage as the high point of the evening.

We could ask, "would the Barber Band have risen to the top and survived the passing of the so-called Trad Boom without her?" That has to be open to question, and is a topic to stir much debate over a pint or two (or three) in the jazz clubs of the land. We hope our study will provide some fuel for that debate.

The biographies of many jazz greats, such as Buddy Bolden, Joe "King" Oliver, Jelly Roll Morton, Bix Beiderbecke and others reveal that their fame and their stardom usually came at a price. Bolden died after 24 years in a

Louisiana asylum. King Oliver died in 1938 working as a pool hall janitor in Savannah, Georgia, forgotten and impoverished. Morton died in poverty in Los Angeles in 1942, while Beiderbecke went to meet his Maker aged just 29. In all cases their much-acclaimed public personae masked private tragedies.

Ottilie was no exception to this particular rule. The bold, public, professional presentation hid a highly nervous and emotionally unstable personality. She was dogged with ill health all through her singing career, a situation made worse by her being subjected to the rigours of incessant touring. She endured the agony of divorce from a man she never ceased to love and who she hoped right up to the end would return to her. Because of the agony of unfulfilled hopes she ended up turning her back on everything in her life that had brought her fame and fortune, and followed the trend of those mentioned above by ending her life in ill health and relative obscurity.

In some ways, as we shall see, this obscurity was of her own making, moving as she did from the London Area, where it was all "happening" to the quietness of Ayr, where, with all due respect to the good people of the seaside town, nothing very much ever happened. As a result of this relocation she was largely forgotten. The world moved on, jazz moved on, and most assuredly Chris Barber's Jazz and Blues Band moved on. When her death and funeral eventually came along, few knew about them until afterwards.

Among those who never forgot her were many good and loyal friends who appreciated and loved Ottilie both as a person and as a singer. One of the things that has amazed and gratified me is the way they have lined up to offer their help in writing Ottilie's story. All of them are unanimous that Ottilie's story is a story that needs to be told. I am very grateful for all their encouragement in my attempt to tell that story.

To Ottilie, and to her many good and loyal friends this book is dedicated. I hope they will judge this a worthy tribute to one who made the Blues come alive to people who otherwise would have dismissed it as obscure ethnic music, and who gave so much of herself in so doing.

Ron Cassidy, Manchester, United Kingdom.

1

THE STAR OF COUNTY DOWN

Gleaming brightly in the spring sunshine, the blue plaque stood out proudly on the end house of a very unpromising row of terraced houses in a little street in the Market Town of Comber in County Down. I am ashamed to admit that this was my very first visit to Northern Ireland, and as I looked at the little house it struck me not for the first time how the most wonderful things can have very ordinary beginnings. The plaque in question marked out the house as the birthplace of Anna Ottilie Patterson, whose meteoric rise to fame in the jazz world was to mark Comber for all time as a distinguished location on the musical map.

Ottilie was born on January 31st, 1932, the youngest of 4 children, with one sister, Jessie, and two brothers, John and Jim. The experience of six people having to squash into this tiny house, with neither bathroom nor running water, was to give Ottilie an early insight into the later privations caused by touring the world with a jazz band and its entourage.

Whilst "Anna" was the name of her Latvian grandmother, "Ottilie" was the anglicised form of the Latvian name *Ottilja*, the name of her mother's cousin, Ottilja Redlichs. Ottilie would later say that whilst she preferred the Latvian transcription, she was not over-thrilled with the name itself. To her it was a neutral name, neither male nor female. She had even occasionally received letters addressed to "Mr. Ottilie Patterson"!

In spite of this she reversed the order of her Christian names. "Anna Ottilja" as she was baptised, became "Ottilja Anna" and then simply the familiar "Ottilie".

Comber is today a bustling county town in the west of Ulster, close to one of the many inland lakes, or "loughs", that populate that part of the country. It had grown from a small village to a significant township as nearby Belfast overspill, becoming established as a fashionable place for the better off residents of Belfast to commute to and fro.

One of its major claims to fame is that it was the birthplace not only of Ottilie

Patterson, but also of Thomas Andrews, designer of the ill-fated luxury liner Titanic. Under the war memorial in the Town Square is a model of the bows of the Titanic, a memorial to the loss of life on that disastrous maiden voyage. Comber residents are very quick to point out, however, that the town quite understandably prefers to commemorate the *launching* of the ship rather than its sinking! Andrews himself, in traditionally heroic fashion, went down with his ship, so that there is of course no local grave to be marked.

Parents

Ottilie's father, Joseph Patterson, was an Ulsterman of Presbyterian Protestant background, whilst her mother, Julia Jager, a name later changed to "Jegers", was a Lutheran Latvian, from Tukums, in the former Soviet Union.

Joseph, oldest of six children, was car crazy. He would have loved nothing better than spending all his time tinkering with them. His mother however insisted on him getting a "proper job", in this case a position with the Belfast Co-op. The Co-op offered the sort of safe and steady option all mothers want for their children. On the day of the interview, Joseph duly took the bus to Belfast, but instead of going into the Coop for the interview, stood outside the building until it was time to get the bus back home. The story he concocted for his mum's benefit was that he had been turned down for the job. The real truth was he had seen another job advertised. A local doctor, Dr. Colwell, was looking for someone to clean and look after his brand new car. To the young, enthusiastic Joseph this offered a much better prospect, and so off to Dr. Colwell's house he went.

He learned to drive by watching Dr. Colwell, until one day, when the good doctor was not looking, temptation overcame him and before you could say Jack Robinson he was off on a jaunt around Belfast. It was only later, once the excitement had died down, he realised that life would have turned out very differently if he had been stopped by the Police in the course of his unsanctioned journey. For one thing, he had no paperwork to prove he had not stolen the car! He got away with it on this occasion, and in course of time this excessive zeal for the motor car would prove very handy when the Army came calling.

In spite of this typically youthful indiscretion, Dr. Colwell, an enlightened man, saw lots of potential in the young Joseph. He kept him on, with the condition that he improved on his basic elementary education, not least so that Joseph would learn that actions have consequences!

However, the driving bug had well and truly bitten Joseph, and when he was called up in 1915 he naturally jumped at the opportunity of becoming a driver, being sent for his initial training to Reading as part of the Army Service Corps. To his delight the Army gave him plenty of opportunities to drive. These opportunities extended to driving abroad as well as in this country, as the Corps was posted first to to Egypt and then Salonika. These overseas ventures caused him also to see active service.

Julia's Story

Julia was born in Riga, Latvia, the daughter of Russian parents. Instead of Riga however, she was brought up in Tukums, where she worked as a lady's maid until the outbreak of World War I changed the whole landscape of Europe and caused many to reflect on their national and cultural antecedents. Julia's great-great-grandfather for example was German and had owned a flour mill in Lithuania. His surname was actually "Jager", but because of the possibility that he might have been thought to be Jewish, it seemed prudent to the family to Latvianise the name to "Jegers".

At 3 a.m. one summer's morning in 1915 they were all awakened by the disturbing news that the Germans were on the outskirts of the town. Rapidly they gathered a few possessions into a bundle and fled their home in the face of the invading army. On the family's horse and cart along with these possessions were two little pigs (not three!), with a pair of dogs to complete the party. They all headed for Riga, the Latvian capital, travelling like gypsies along roads swollen with fellow refugees, with stray cattle roaming around them along the way.

They were not in Riga for long, however. Approaching winter presented its difficulties, and so they moved on to Petrograd (= Leningrad = St. Petersburg). In Petrograd they attained a measure of settlement, and Julia began training to be a nurse for the Front. Julia's brother had been at college back home, and so it seemed that Petrograd presented an opportunity to continue his studies, joining one of the many classes set up for refugees.

Their relative peace was shattered by the outbreak of the Russian Revolution in 1917. Petrograd was in the thick of it, and pretty soon got its name changed to the more familiar Leningrad. If Petrograd was in the thick of the Revolution, then Julia was in the thick of Petrograd. From there she witnessed some serious pieces of history, including the storming of the Czar's Palace.

Once the initial revolutionary excitement had died down, the reality of the "glorious" Revolution was that for combatants and non-combatants alike there were food shortages and other privations. People had to queue for basic necessities such as bread, sometimes queuing from 2 a.m.

For Julia then it was time to move on. The prospect of the hard Russian winter was a major factor in making this decision, as Julia had a bad chest, and with only a samovar to keep her warm, knew in advance that she would find the freezing winter temperatures of Petrograd unbearable.

Providence smiled on her, however, so that she was given word of a woman in Southern Russia who wanted a lady's companion and someone to look after her children. Her move was not a moment too soon, keeping her as it did just ahead of the advancing militants. Frequently she would find herself leaving one end of a town just as the troops were burning the other. But on she went to Batum, on the shores of the Black Sea., arriving there at the end of an exhausting nine-day journey.

History repeated itself, as it often does. Julia found a measure of contentment in Batum, only to have it snatched away once again when the hills became alive, not with the sound of music, but with the sound of advancing troops. This time instead of Germans, or Russian revolutionaries, it was the Turks threatening Julia's idyll. So - you've guessed it - on she went again, this time to the city of Tiflis (modern Tblisi) in the Georgian Caucasian Mountains. Here, in the most unlikely of locations, her life really did take a decisive turn, one that would take her on her longest journey so far.

Joseph and Julia meet

The 1918 Armistice had not meant a swift return home for Joseph. Along with his mate, he had been sent across the Black Sea to become a designated driver for a colonel and a major. Although the War had officially ended, there were still things going on in Southern Russia. He was no James Bond for sure, but nevertheless Joseph was sent to engage in secret operations in the Caucasus Mountains. These secret missions earned Joseph a Mention in Dispatches (to Churchill) for gallant and distinguished services. Whatever precisely it was that he did, his service was apparently sufficient to gain himself the nickname of "Mad Paddy", although his fellow soldiers often asserted that this was more for his reputation as a joker than for his daring.

One very tangible, lasting result of these Caucasus missions was that they brought Joseph and Julia together. Julia had aspirations to be a nurse, and had been working in a field hospital for the Allies when she and Joseph met. The "Joe and Julia Story" was a classic tale of wounded soldier falling or his nurse, and has all the elements of romance you could wish for. In July 1919, in the Garrison Church on the Mikhailevsky Boulevard in Tblisi, they were married.

A flavour of what it was like to be married while in the Army is seen in the letter written by Joseph to his C.O.:

Sir,
I beg to apply for permission to get married in Tiflis as soon as possible

To which his C.O. replied:

The General Officer Commanding-in-Chief has no objection to the marriage referred to taking place, as long as the lady in question is of good character. In the event of the husband leaving the Caucasus however, passage at the public expense cannot be provided for the wife. Attention is drawn to King's Regulations para 1360 *et seq* as regards marriage of time-serving soldiers.

General Headquarters A   Signed: T.H.Veasey
Constantinople   Major D.A.A.G for D.A.G.
7th July 1919   Army of the Black Sea

I don't think that particular officer was famous for his charm!

Back to Ireland

After honeymooning in Constantinople in transit, Joseph and Julia arrived together in Comber on New Year's Eve, 1919. Joseph arrived wearing his British Army uniform, something that was perhaps not the wisest thing to do while Ireland was in the middle of a civil war! It was guaranteed to make him distinctly unpopular with at least one section of the population. What saved the day was the Irishman's well known capacity for drink, especially on occasions like New Year's Eve. Before anyone could sober up enough to notice, Joseph and Julia had slipped through and were safely in Comber in civvies.

While for Joseph it was a homecoming, for Julia it was a new adventure altogether. She found herself in yet another new land with a new language to learn and new ways to which to adapt. But at least one thing remained the same - social and political upheaval! Phrases like "out of the frying pan into the fire" come readily to mind. Julia had come through revolution and war in Russia, with all its hardships, only to land in a revolutionary Ireland, with the 1917 uprising fresh in the popular memory, with partition a new reality.

This was actually not so difficult for Julia to cope with as one might suppose. Ottilie tells the story of how her mother and her friends had been quite interested in politics, and how they used to dress up poor so that they could sneak into the Communist cinemas and not look out of place. Newspapers and journals from revolutionary days in Russia were found years later, yellowing in the bottom of wardrobes where they had been carefully kept.

Although Julia had a genuine interest in politics, she had no stomach for war. At one point she had a boyfriend in the Latvian Army, and frequently told him of her desire to be a nurse at the Front. As they were walking home one evening in Petrograd, they heard a shot close by. Julia's immediate reaction was to jump into a doorway, as anyone would do, only to hear the teasing comment of her erstwhile boyfriend that maybe she wasn't as suited to the front as she imagined!

Joseph landed a job with Lord Chief Justice Andrews, becoming a tipstaff at the Royal Courts of Justice. The good Judge had previously had a gardener, to whom he had given a small cottage in Comber. It came to pass that the Judge no longer needed a house for his gardener, so Joseph, who seemed to have a happy knack of being in the right place at the right time, was allowed to live in the Comber cottage. In the 16 years the Patterson family lived in the house all four children were born.

However, as we have discovered already several times, for Julia at least no happy situation seemed to last for very long. The good judge took on a gardener who did need the cottage, which meant the Patterson family had to move out. After a temporary period in Scrabo Road, Newtownards, they finally set up the family home in Avondale Gardens in the same town. Ottilie later commented that while the family had to leave Comber, their roots never did.

It was in Newtownards that Ottilie began her schooling, at the Model Public Elementary School, before gaining a scholarship for three years education at the local Grammar School, Regent House. Ottilie recalls it as being an extremely good school, with a sold reputation, and so was delighted when in 1947 she gained a further scholarship for two more years there, as in fact sister Jessie had previously done.

Her brothers were not so fortunate, their parents' money entitling them only to one term at Technical School. It is good to be reminded however that such setbacks need not be disastrous, with brother John ending up holding several prestigious posts in Engineering.

A Precocious Child

Ottilie had always been a remarkably precocious child, and, like her brothers and sister, could speak coherently at the age of one. She gained her own distinction within the family however for being able to sing current songs in tune with amazing accuracy at the age of two, and at four being able to pick them out by ear on the piano. Assistance was needed for little Ottilie on the piano however, since lifting the piano lid unaided proved for her to be an impossible task! Once that had been done, her parents were constantly amazed by her ability even at this tender age to pick out the melodies of many contemporary pop songs. She had in fact been singing some of them from the age of two, but now she obviously felt it was time to go on to the next stage.

The logical progression was for her to have piano lessons, which she did from the grand old age of nine. Ottilie remembered her first teacher as being a sweet old lady, but far too lenient with her, not insisting as she should on Ottilie practising hard, something Ottilie regretted in later life. This leniency came apparently from the teacher's own experience, being forced to practice endlessly as a child, instead of being out playing with her friends. As a result, she was therefore unwilling to be too forceful on her own pupils. As Ottilie herself confessed, she did not learn as much as she could have done in this period.

These lessons stopped when the old lady died, and there was a gap of two years before lessons could be resumed. Her second teacher turned out to be the young Church Organist, one Mr. Houston Graham. In contrast to her previous experience, the two years she spent with him transformed her whole understanding of music, particularly in the classical field. Although Mr. Graham was only 20, Ottilie recalls him as being a great teacher. Two examinations that she undertook under his tutelage saw her gain first place in the whole of Northern Ireland, with marks of 95% and 89% respectively. This wonderful progress ended abruptly when Mr. Graham upped and got married and moved away. Like Ottilie, he was clearly destined for great things, and progressed to become organist at St. Anne's Cathedral, Belfast. For a very young Ottilie getting married seemed a very poor reason for ceasing to carry on teaching her the piano! Undeterred by this setback, Ottilie tried another local teacher, but found her far too "square", and not a patch on the departed and now married Mr. Graham.

For later reference it should be noticed that all these lessons concerned playing only. There was no training for singing, and when the young Ottilie sang at all, it was entirely impromptu at home, for her own amusement.

The extent to which Ottilie's family were musical is a matter of some debate. One view sees Ottilie as heiress to a lot of musical traditions within her family. It suggests that Ottilie's father and grandfather were natural musicians and between them played fife, violin, melodeon and bagpipes in local country style. The Latvian side was said to have contributed several fine natural singers, including her grandmother, a concertina-playing aunt, and one Sofija, an Opera singer who had sung in Opera companies from Riga to Vladivostok. From time to time Joseph would twiddle the knobs on the old radio to find Armenian stations, so that they could enjoy some of the music they enjoyed back in Tblisi back in 1919.

It's a good story, but in her 2007 interview with Mike Pointon for *Just Jazz* Ottilie seems to suggest that this was not the case, and that her parents and siblings had only a general interest in and appreciation of music:

> *Mike Pointon*: Was your family musical ?
> *Ottilie*: Not particularly. Just average. We weren't musical as such, but we liked music in an ordinary sort of way. My mother bought a piano, some second hand thing she bought in Belfast.[1]

We can't argue against Ottilie's own words of course. And yet we can safely assume that Ottilie's talent and enthusiasm for music did not come out of a vacuum. We must be grateful at least for the vision of her mother in buying that old piano. The family was sufficiently musically aware to at least see the

[1] In interviews with Mike Pointon for *Just Jazz* Magazine, published March-May, 2008.

possibilities it created for the young Ottilie.

In addition to the inspirational purchase of the piano, there were several other incidents from Ottilie's childhood that tell the story of how life was pointing her in the direction of public singing performance. She recalls for example making her debut at eight years old her local Church, singing *Looking Upwards Every Day,* with the organist constantly whispering in her ear, "don't keep jazzing it, dear".

Then again, every year the Sunday School to which she belonged held a social for the congregation. The clever ones were expected to do something attractive musically.

Naturally "the clever ones" included Ottilie. As she says:

> The organist had put me through a minuet, the Paderwski minuet, as my offering for the congregational social. Well I got up and did it, but when they asked for an encore I was stuck, because I didn't have one! I looked at the audience applauding and went over to the piano to play *Boogie Woogie Bugle Boy,* singing on the chorus. The place nearly went down because of that, and I was asked to do still more. What did I know that came easy? Oh, I know, *The Dying Cowboy.* I was quite broadminded you see. And it didn't seem strange to me, because it was all music. In a strange way it was getting me into, for want of a better word, the Trad stream. It also began to narrow my focus as up to then I had been playing everything under the sun.

Yet another incident stems from the age of sixteen, when she was asked to provide suitable interval music at a local Beetle drive. After a while, finding a diet of Strauss Waltzes, tea and buns a bit tame, she relieved her feelings of boredom with an impromptu vocal and instrumental attack on *St. Louis Blues.* Her performance was accompanied by hysterical off-stage shrieks of "bring the curtain down!" In spite of these protests Ottilie played on like a trooper. We don't know to this day whether the curtain actually came down. What we *do* know is that on that occasion the house certainly did!

A significant day for Ottilie's journey towards jazz was the day that the film *Birth of the Blues* came to Belfast. She pestered her parents to take her to see it, even though they said it wasn't really a film suitable for little girls. They would attempt to put her off by saying things like, "I believe it isn't on any longer", and so on, without success. In the film there was a funeral scene in which lots of black people were singing with a strange, fantastic quality that made a great impression on the young Ottilie. This was in spite of the fact that, as Ottilie herself recalled, that she came back from the film not aspiring to be a singer, but wanting to become a clarinet player! Fortunately for the world of jazz her parents couldn't afford to buy her the instrument.

The impression gained from the singing choir was all the stronger because Ottilie had in fact never actually seen a black person until the age of 19. The first she encountered was "Prince Monolulu", a racetrack tipster at the local point to point meetings.[2] He was an African student at the University, and was often given to parading at the racecourse in bright costumes and feathers.

Another part of the film that resonated with Ottilie was *Melancholy Baby*, already a favourite song of hers, as she thought of herself as something of a melancholy baby. Naturally therefore Bing Crosby's rendering of the song to a young girl in the film was for Ottilie once of its highlights.

Another milestone on Ottilie's Blues odyssey came with a shopping trip to Belfast. Ottilie recounts:

> We were in a place called the North Street Arcade. I had 5 shillings to spend (a lot of money in those days when I scarcely had more than two and sixpence in my purse at any one time). While mummy was looking in one shop window I was looking in the window of the Music Shop. And there I saw something called *Handy's Blues Folio*. And so, in my blue Sunday coat, my matching hat, my grey knee socks, and my hair in four blonde ringlets, in I went. The whole five shillings went in one go on that book - no ice cream, no chips, no nothing. The transcriptions were in fact very "white", but at least it gave me a foothold on the Blues. My performance repertoire for congregational socials, etc began to expand and feature increasingly songs like *St. Louis Blues*. But when I sang something like *I hate to see the evening sun go down* only to get the response "very nice, dear" I knew they couldn't take it!

The folio of Handy's blues was a precious possession until the 1950's, when as

---

[2]   This tipster modelled himself on *Ras "I Gotta Horse" Prince Monolulu*, a West Indian racing tipster whose career started at the Derby in 1902.

she says a certain Mr. Barber borrowed it, for some reason of his own. That turned out to be the last she saw of it, something that always rankled with her. In her music collection that had shared pride of place with another book she bought the same year, a collection of *Novelty Piano Solos,* amongst which we included *Bugle Call Rag, Creole Love Call* and *Sophisticated Lady,* the last piece of which she recalls as being too hard for her at that tender age.

On another trip to Belfast with her mother, Ottilie spotted in the same shop window *Eight to the Bar: Teach Yourself Boogie Woogie,* by Frank Paparelli. Bang went another three shillings and sixpence.

Ottilie recalls that at the time Mr. Paparelli had also published *Eight to the Bar: Teach Yourself Blues,* something that would have been of immense value to her. However she couldn't get hold of it. She couldn't get hold of it because she thought she could buy it only in Belfast, not realising that she could have ordered it from her local Newtownards shop! Ottilie had nevertheless settled firmly into the pattern of spending any spare money she had on buying sheet music.

She was saved from early poverty by Santa Claus, who was very good to her that year. On Christmas Morning 1944 she came down to find sticking out of her Christmas stocking *Chips from the Woodchoppers,* five piano solos featured by the Woody Herman Orchestra. Of course at eleven going on twelve she couldn't play them. What however she could do was pick out the bluesy sounding passages and learning them if she could.

However there were some ambitious jazz pieces she *could* master even then. Among them were *Cow Cow Boogie,* a piece she bought with money she saved up herself, and the celebrated *Boogie Woogie Bugle Boy of Company B,* a piece that was in a book loaned to her by a neighbour.

Throughout her teens her enthusiasm for good music accelerated and the ends to which she would go to listen to it grew more numerous. On Saturdays she and her friends would take the bus to Belfast to hear whatever noted pianist was in town before dashing back home to listen to the Jack Jackson Show on the Radio. Ottilie liked Jackson because he played what she described as "interesting" music. Readers who remember him will recall that he always presented his show with a lively enthusiasm and energy, "Oh it's Saturday, yes it's Saturday !" being his signature tune.

The War Years

In the Forties the residents of Ulster were all involved in the War effort. The

Patterson family were aware of the War and involved in it to some degree or other. Ottilie's brothers were in the R.A.F., though Jim was invalided out because of his pleurisy. John served for four years, from 1941 right through to 1945.

There was no conscription in Ulster, because of the "Troubles". The Patterson family were volunteers, four out of six serving. Joseph joined the R.A.F. in 1943, while Jessie, Ottilie's sister, joined the women's R.A.F. Just Ottilie was left with her mother at home.

There were air raids, though thankfully not so many. The blaze from the Belfast Shipyard bombings could however be seen clearly from the house in Newtownards.

At school Ottilie helped to knit scarves, balaclavas and hoods for the men at war. Among the items of school uniform for her and her schoolmates were their gas masks, slung over their shoulders at the ready. They were rationed for food and clothes, but milk was plentiful, because of the agricultural make up of Ulster.

Like everyone else, Ottilie would pray for the War to end, although she admitted that her prayers always ended:

> Please God, let *us* win the war. Thank you. Amen.

Entertaining the Troops

What Ottilie was of course very suited to doing as part of the War Effort was to entertain the soldiers and airmen. So she found herself in a Concert Party set up to entertain the Americans at Camp Clandeboye, just four miles away from her home. For young Ottilie this was tremendously exciting, as the Americans treated them like Lords and Ladies, introducing them, among other things (!)[3], to such delights as Apple Pie.

Ottilie takes up the story:

> I had prepared to sing the Alice Faye song *You'll Never Know Just How Much I miss you*. I knew the song, but its setting was in G, and much too high for me to sing comfortably. The pianist unfortunately couldn't transpose it. So I wrote out the melody by hand in my own key (which

---

[3] Better not look too closely as to what those "other things" were.

was D), and left the pianist to busk the left hand.

The American soldiers must have liked it, because they called for an encore. My encore was too much for the pianist, and so I sang it unaccompanied. You can picture it - a child in her last year's Sunday frock, made by her mother - white artificial silk with pink rosebuds from black market material - giving out with *Whistler's Mother in Law*. Well it's quite a picture. Because I had no accompanist I just swung my body in time and tapped my foot to the offbeat. I wasn't conscious that my timing *was* offbeat - it just came naturally.

The follow up to this is that while the other boys and girls were rushing round the room playing games, young Miss Patterson was sitting at the piano, playing her party piece *Boogie Woogie Bugle Boy*. After a while a young American came over to listen, and then after a further pause asked politely if he could play. Of course Ottilie agreed, to find herself immediately enchanted.

He played real Boogie Woogie! I was so excited I couldn't speak. I knew I was hearing the real thing. I didn't know what to say to this grown up man. What I did know was that I was listening to someone playing with *musicality* and *authority*.

Ottilie never did discover who this Boogie Woogie GI was, although she did discover some years later that at a nearby camp another young American pianist called John Lewis was based. Illinois born Lewis was to go on to become the creative genius behind *The Modern Jazz Quartet*, and would go on to become a good friend of the Barber Band. His meetings with Ottilie were memorable in that he could never fail to express his surprise that the Blues could be sung effectively not only by a white woman, but a white woman with an Ulster accent! He would amuse Ottilie also by constantly asking her for some soda bread, a delicacy so peculiar to Northern Ireland that even the English, never mind the Americans, don't know about it!

It is I suppose of the essence of conditions in wartime that people move around all over the place and make connections accidentally that gain significance only in later life. Certainly Ottilie's journey on to a career in Blues singing was, as we shall see, characterised by many such "accidental" connections all over the world.

2

I GOT THE BLUES

Just as two heads are better than one, so two scholarships are better than one. The young Ottilie was bright enough at school to gain further scholarships, or in her case, *two*.   So successful was she at school that she was in the privileged position of actually having a choice of Further Education, University or Art School.   She chose what she describes as the "Bohemian life" of the Art College in Ballymena, rather than the sterile intellectual life of a University.

As   an artiste she was by no means without talent.   The *Belfast Telegraph* reports how the Belfast Art College students were decorating the Belfast Central Hall for the annual Arts Ball with Mardi Gras themes. It reports that these designs were taken from

designs by Ottilie Patterson, a student at the College [4]

The same paper reports on a public exhibition by the students during which he commends a piece called

The Gossips (Exhibit 44) by Ottilie Patterson.

Whether or not the Bohemian in her ever came to fruition we don't know, but certainly her artistic skills never left her. They came together in a number of sketches she made of Blues artists, especially the sketch of Big Bill Broonzy featured in this book. What did unquestionably flower was her interest in and passion for singing the Blues.

The Art College had a long lunch hour, one and a half hours. This would leave the piano-mad Ottilie plenty of time to wander round Belfast, searching for piano showrooms. When she found one, she would often slide up to an adjacent piano and start tentatively playing it, quiet and mouse like, until the

[4]   From a cutting kept by Ottilie from the Belfast Telegraph, sometime in 1950.

salesman's voice rang out like the voice of doom with: "can I help you madam?"

One day in college she made a wonderful discovery. No, not the answer to some long standing philosophical problem, but the presence in the Concert Hall of a grand piano! As Ottilie recalls it was just standing there unattended, just begging to be played. She couldn't believe her luck and made regular visits to the keyboard to play - what else? - the Blues. One day, as she was playing, a man came and stood beside the piano, listening. She describes him as a "Mr. Cool", although she then confesses that she have never met any "cool" people before and didn't really know what they looked like! He asked if he could play, and Ottilie immediately stepped aside. What she heard was Albert Ammons and Pete Johnson, a new and impressive sound for the young Irish student. It was Camp Clandeboye all over again!

"Mr. Cool" turned out to be one Richard Martin, popularly known as "Derek". Quite unwittingly and unintentionally, he was to change the course of Ottilie's life forever. From the moment she heard his rolling Albert Ammons left hand, Ottilie and Derek became firm friends. She had been managing well enough on her own, eagerly grabbing any song sheet that had "Blues" in the title, whilst picking out bluesy bits in other compositions, all in a desperate attempt to obtain that indefinable and indescribable sound she was seeking. But it wasn't until she met Derek that any kind of cohesion became possible.

As well as giving her a master class in Boogie Woogie, he also lent her a number of 78s, featuring such artists as Bunk Johnson, Louis Armstrong, Bessie Smith, Jelly Roll Morton and Muggsy Spanier, as well as the celebrated "Chicago Three" - Albert Ammons, Pete Johnson and Meade Lux Lewis. Ottilie had heard Louis Armstrong on the radio, usually playing and singing popular songs. Now she was hearing him play songs with mysterious titles such as *Willie the Weeper, Struttin' with Some Barbecue* and *Cornet Chop Suey,* recordings that presented a different sound altogether.

Taking home the records she had been loaned was one thing; playing them to listen to was quite another. The only record player available to Ottilie was one her brother John had acquired in the Air Force. It was an old, clapped-out thing which of course needed to be wound up every time. Even that wasn't straightforward. If you happened to put a 12-inch record on it to play, you had to rewind it even before it had finished playing one side!

The first record she played on this dilapidated player was Bessie Smith

singing *St. Louis Blues,* with *Reckless Blues* on the other side. Words are often all too inadequate to express the effect that first hearing of the Empress of the Blues had on Ottilie. Philosophers and theologians use terms like the "numinous" to refer to experiences we as human beings are not able to describe in words. "Numinous" would not be too strong an expression to describe the effect on Ottilie of hearing the wailing, note flattening sound of Bessie Smith. It was a sound like no other she had ever heard before.
Ottilie describes this as a life-changing moment:

> It was momentous, shattering, awesome. I was transfixed, elated, in a near trance. *This* was the sound that echoed and expressed something way deep down inside me - the music I'd been groping to find, the cadences I needed to make sense of everything in my life - the Blues out and out, nothing less.
> I ignored my mother's voice calling from the kitchen to tell me my dinner was getting cold. The Blues. Not to be found in *Chips from the Woodchoppers* or anything else you could buy on paper for 3 or even 5 shillings.
> The world had changed since Bessie's opening phrase "When I was nothing but a child". I was seventeen and would never be the same again. I knew I would never rest until I had discovered all that was possible about this woman, this music, and these soulful, suffering black people. My pursuit of the Blues and Jazz had begun in earnest.

Ottilie describes the care she took of this record, to the point almost of being reluctant to play it, for fear of spoiling the memory of this first hearing experience By its very nature it could not be repeated. Although Ottilie went on herself to make very fine recordings of both songs, including those on her debut performance at the Royal Albert Hall, she always had a sense of the inadequacy of her own attempts to match up to what she heard in that first hearing of Bessie Smith.
Much later in her life Ottilie would reflect that she could not work out whether she got hold of the Blues, or whether the Blues got hold of her. My guess is it was something of both.
To accompany her on her journey Mr. Cool also loaned her a copy of Mezz

Mezzrow's autobiography, *Really the Blues.*[5] In the same way the sound of Bessie Smith's voice had shattered her perceptions, so Mezzrow's book, with its graphic images of early New York scenes, had a mesmerising effect on her:

> I was caught up: I was high as a kite for three days. No sex, no drink, no drugs - only the music. You didn't need "stuff" to make you high in those days. You just read it and your mind made you think of all that. Mezzrow had no dangerous side-effects except that it gave us a new world of imagination.

In case readers begin to worry about the picture this might present of Ottilie's private lifestyle, it should be understood that her remarks were shaped by Mezzrow's well known connection with the drugs trade, and the seedy side of New York life in general.[6]

Ottilie begins performing

In the light of that unique experience it was inevitably only a short step for Ottilie to develop the desire to go beyond listening to the Blues, on to performing them.   It wasn't long before opportunities began to present themselves at College.

There were relatively few active jazz musicians in Belfast at the time, and fewer still who had organised bands. One of these was Ken Smiley, and Derek duly took Ottilie along to hear him. Ken was a great enthusiast and a true pioneer of jazz in Belfast.[7] Ottilie was sufficiently impressed to organise a booking for Smiley's band to play at the College Arts Ball, in her capacity as 1951 Student Representative. It was at this event she heard her first rendering of *If You See Me Coming,* rendered by trombonist "Wild Al Watt", startlingly dressed in white pants, red and white striped blazer, and straw boater. In fancy dress, as Alice in Wonderland, and a little too full of celebration drink, Ottilie herself sat in with the band, rendering a slightly tipsy version of *Careless Love.*

Ken Smiley, who had cut his journalistic teeth with the Belfast Telegraph, left

---

[5]   M.Mezzrow & H.Wolfe, *Really the Blues,* (New York, 1946)

[6]   "Mezz" in fact being one of several slang names of cannabis. See p. 178-9 below.

[7]   Brian Dempster pays full tribute to Ken Smiley's contribution to the development of jazz in Ulster in his book *Tracking Jazz: The Ulster Way* (Belfast: Shanway Press, 2012),23-28.

shortly after that in 1952 to take up a job with the Daily Mirror in London. Once in London Ken lost no time in seeking out the best of the jazz locations, finding a niche in a Fleet Street bar alongside fellow jazz loving journalists. After a spell working for the media in Africa, Ken returned to settle in Eastbourne, involving himself in the local jazz scene there (of course).

After his departure, the leadership of the band was taken over by Smiley's trombonist, Jimmy Compton, a young but already extremely mature musician. After her "memorable" rendering at the Arts Ball, Ottilie was invited to sing regularly with the band.

However this was not the meteoric take off of the Ottilie Patterson career that she might have hoped for. After only two weeks Ottilie had a major "musical" difference with Jimmy. Jimmy wanted her to sing a current pop song, *Anytime You're Feeling Lonely*, to keep the audience sweet, but the idealistic and stubborn Ottilie refused - it was not jazz. It was *commercial* (the 'c' word) and Ottilie was not to be turned from the True Path.

Jimmy got angry, not, in Ottilie's view, because he cared about the music, but because he was focussed on the thirty shillings he would get in his pocket at the end of the week. He informed Ottilie in no uncertain terms that if she didn't like it, she knew what she could do. Ottilie knew exactly what to do. She walked out.

It would be very interesting to know if, when reflecting on the huge audiences Ottilie would go on to perform before, how often Jimmy reflected on that intemperate exchange, and what he had lost for the sake of thirty bob! As is the case so often in life, as one door closes, another opens. Just two days after the showdown with Jimmy, Derek Martin came to Ottilie and invited her to join a band he and Al Watt were forming, called *The Muskrat Ramblers.*[8] The band, under the leadership of trumpet player Glen Clugston, played its first engagement in August of that year at the Ulster Rhythm Club in the Ulster Civic Hall in Belfast. Their "residence" was a gig one night a week at the exotically named *Chalet d'Or,* in Belfast, a restaurant by day but available for hire for any entertainment purpose in the evening.

A beautiful piece of calligraphy in one of Ottilie's scrap books lists the Ramblers' line up as - Clugston (trumpet), Derek "Haggis" Martin, the leader (clarinet), Al Watt (trombone), Norman Watson (piano), Stanley Clugston

---

[8] No connection with the Muskrat Ramblers Jazz Band of today with Bill Phelan.

(bass) and Tony Scarisbrick (drums). As the listing shows a pianist already in residence, Ottilie became the band's Blues singer instead, but, to her delight, was allowed to take over the piano during the interval. Her joy would know no bounds when, in Norman Watson's absence she was deputed to play piano at rehearsals. There she would sit, plonking out the chords for tunes like *Riverside Blues*, dreaming of one day having a band of her own and playing like George Lewis's pianist Alton Purnell.

Ottilie also had opportunities to sing with other local groups. One such group were the White Eagles, with Ulster jazz legends Billy Bryson (clarinet), Hugh Logan (trumpet), George Hayes (banjo) and Tony Martin (drums) among their ranks.[9]

In spite of his interesting sounding nickname, "Wild Al" settled down to become a very distinguished Ulster musician, combining trombone with the banjo. Impossible even for Wild Al to do at the same time of course, so he confined his banjo playing to the intervals at concerts.

Wild Al regularly won trophies at Musical Festivals, including those at places like Derry (Festival of Britain Cup for Operatic Solo), Belfast (The Ulster Cup, The Rose Bowl, and the Judge Thompson Memorial Trophy), Carrickfergus (Baritone Solo), Port Stewart and Bangor (The Bangor Cup). Ironically, all those triumphs were not so much for his multi-instrument playing, as for this classic operatic singing. Wild Al is a versatile and talented man with many musical strings to his bow. He later emigrated to the USA and now lives in Tampa Bay, Florida.

Belfast to America appears a well-trodden road, Derek Martin also going transatlantic, to settle in Seattle. Norman Watson however stayed in Ulster, in Donaghadee, and kept up a friendship with Ottilie over many years, sometimes accompanying her on her tours.

Although Ottilie was extremely excited by the new venture, it was undoubtedly a struggle. There simply were not enough jazz fans in Belfast to sustain more than one or two bands. Most of those fans were already devoted to Jimmy Compton, though he had in truth inherited them from Ken Smiley. But on they soldiered, finding premises where they could, and playing for those, however few, willing to listen to them.

The above reference to Alton Purnell points to what at this stage was the

---

[9] My thanks go to George Smyth of East Belfast Jazz Club for that piece of information.

interesting thing about Ottilie. What we have said about her encounter with Bessie Smith notwithstanding, for Ottilie singing was only a time-filler until she could reach what at that stage was her ultimate ambition - to get a job as a piano player in a jazz band. Although Bessie Smith continued to be an idol and role model, she represented only one strand of Blues tradition and singing. Ottilie's horizons needed to be expanded; and this expansion happened through, of all people, the aforementioned Jimmy Compton.

Expanding the Horizons: Gerry McQueen
Jimmy introduced her to Gerry McQueen, a local record collector who possessed thousands of 78 rpm records, representing a wide range of jazz and Blues artistes. Gerry used to have parties at his house at which a select number of invited friends would listen to the latest of Gerry's record acquisitions and subsequently critically discuss them. Becoming one of Gerry's elite was not easy, and sometimes necessitated passing spontaneous tests set by Gerry on the threshold. Not everyone by any means would pass the test. Eventually Ottilie managed to gain access to this elite circle, and would henceforth spend her Saturday evenings having her mind blown and her horizons expanded by the people she was privileged to listen to such legends as Robert Johnson, Leroy Carr and Big Bill Broonzy.
What was of special interest to Ottilie was the fact that they sang a kind of Blues different from those of Bessie Smith. Where Bessie sang songs that were accompanied by Jazz Bands, these Blues artistes accompanied themselves, or were accompanied, on the guitar or piano. It gave Ottilie further impetus to the development of her own piano playing, and soon accompaniments in the style of Jimmy Yancey and Big Maceo Merriweather began to be heard from her piano.

Ottilie gets a job teaching
On graduation from Art College Ottilie took a job teaching Art part-time at *Ballymena Technical College*. Not a lot is known about her actual work there, although one former student of her comments that she was such a stunner it was difficult to concentrate on work. That is entirely believable!
The economic climate and the situation in the teaching world was such that Ottilie was hired only part-time, teaching just a single period a week in fact, and would inevitably find it difficult to make ends meet on her salary. And prospects for the future were not good, so that she was entirely justified in

exploring other options, although the one she did explore was something of a surprise to her friends and family.

Ottilie gets to hear of the Barber Band
Ottilie tells how she, Derek and some others from College were invited to a friend's 21st Birthday party, where they would have jazz records. One tune that immediately stood out was Ken Colyer's *Goin' Home*, from the classic *New Orleans to London* LP of 1953. Ottilie said she liked it, as did Derek. Ottilie liked what she called the "simple charm" of the song, and was struck strongly by the general sound of the band. On enquiring she was told that the singer was Ken Colyer and that his band was based in London.
Strong-minded Ottilie decided immediately that she had discovered *the* sound she wanted to follow, and that that band was *the* band with which she wanted to sing. What she didn't know at the time, indeed what nobody could have known at the time, is that when Ottilie arrived in London, all those musicians apart from Ken would have metamorphosed into a new entity, the Chris Barber Jazz Band, with whom Ottilie was to go on and have such a strong association.

The Parting of the Ways
The actual circumstances of the break up between Ken Colyer and Chris Barber are still much debated, many years later. With the passing of time memories fade or become distorted and tend to favour those who on other grounds have supported one protagonist or the other.
All but the most ungenerous of Barber fans would acknowledge that the newly-deported Ken Colyer played a key role in establishing the new professional band that carried his name, and that without him it would never have reached the prominence that it did in a relatively short time. Colyer was the name that appealed to promoters and fans alike. His deportation from New Orleans for overstaying his visa had virtually deified him in the jazz world. His stay in Orleans Parish Prison had been for him an apotheosis.
Having said that, it has to be acknowledged unfortunately that in many ways Ken Colyer was a disaster waiting to happen, and that the god had very obvious feet of clay.
Like all geniuses (and undoubtedly that's what he was) he was very temperamental and at times difficult to get along with. Mike Pointon and Ray Smith deliberately entitled their biography of Ken Colyer, *The*

Uncompromising Life and Music of Ken Colyer.[10] Their book is in fact more than a conventional biography - it goes beyond the facts of his life to assemble a collection of points of view of their subject.

George Melly for example summarised Colyer thus,

> Awkward as an old bear, often too drunk to play properly. He played as he wanted to from the very beginning.

Chris Barber himself describes him as

> A marvellous musician who became a pain in the ass

whilst Diz Disley takes the very opposite view when he says

> He wasn't a very good player, but he was a great bloke.

You pay your money and take your choice. One might only conclude that if Colyer were the hard-drinking roustabout that many claim, then he stood squarely in the best tradition of New Orleans heroes, some of whom were rarely sober and not often inclined to be careful about the sensitivities of their audiences or their fellow musicians!

The point is that any band of motivated individuals with Colyer in the mix would be likely to reach a crisis point sooner or later.

This crisis duly arrived on one warm May evening in 1954, just a year after the professional band's formation. British journalist and radio DJ Brian Harvey, part of the club management team that evening, describes it graphically:

> Even though it was a fine night there was an almost thundery electricity in the air, however, and out on the pavement for a break I wondered if it might thunder. And then, back at my desk listening to the band, I began to wonder whether the almost tangible electric feeling of oppression, of tension, I was experiencing was not the weather at all but something subtly psychological that I'd sensed but not understood - a near

---

[10] M.Pointon & R.Smith, _The Uncompromising Life and Music of Ken Colyer_ (Ken Colyer Trust, 2010)

subliminal signal I'd received from someone, or a group even, but not been conscious of at the time.

The band was playing on. They sounded great, with their climaxes echoing round the room sounding for all the world like the Bunk Johnson band in San Jacinto Hall. There was a joy about them as they went through *Lord, Lord, Lord, You've Sure Been Good To Me*, with Ken's unique vocal twang being unmistakable, and yet the intervals between numbers were longer than usual. I went into the hall for a moment, leaving the cash desk to a helper, and there, it became obvious, was the source of the tension.

The bandstand itself and the musicians - they were arguing in whispers but with heat and waved arms. This was clearly not a disagreement about what to play next or who did what on the last number, but something more serious. I was worried, frightened even, that they would come to blows and I'd be lumbered with a club full of people and a band that didn't play - or even couldn't.

I'd better explain. Harold Pendleton, a pioneer London jazz entrepreneur, had given me, a college dropout, a junior managerial job in his attempt to create London's first seven-days-a-week jazz club, The London Jazz Centre, at 14 Greek Street. We had different bands every night, but Ken Colyer's Friday session was the star attraction and vital to the club because few other nights would break even financially. That night - if my memory is not now too blurred by age - I was mainly on the cash desk in the foyer.

The evening continued but the band became somewhat ragged and uninspired. The breaks between numbers became longer, and by the end of the evening the atmosphere on the stand was really bad. Chris Barber, Monty Sunshine, Lonnie Donegan, Jim Bray and Ron Bowden left, I think, together. Ken and Brother Bill followed later - all looked downcast - but being junior I didn't ask what had happened, what was going on. And then I was told the shock news - Ken had fired the band, sacked them to a man![11]

Harvey's account owes only a little to exaggeration. Colyer had not in fact

---

[11]   B.Harvey, *An Electric Night,* from the Barber website.

sacked the whole band - just the rhythm section! Chris and Monty could apparently stay, but the others were out. Ken's brother Bill had apparently approached Chris at some point in the evening to convey this message and to explain that, in Ken's view the rhythmn section were not at all on the right wavelength. Jim Bray apparently didn't swing sufficiently. Ron Bowden owed more of his style to bebop instead of New Orleans jazz. He had actually had the temerity to use brushes (very non-New Orleans) on one of Ken's favourite numbers *Breeze*.

As for Lonnie Donegan - well Ken hated Lonnie's guts generally. Harold Pendleton, in a recent interview with Walter Love on BBC Radio Ulster, says that the antipathy between Colyer and Donegan was in fact very real. But this was for entirely personal and non-musical reasons. Lonnie fancied himself as a Max Miller "cheeky chappie" type, often interspersing the music with wisecracks. As is often the case with such people, they make at least one wisecrack too many, and get up the recipient's nose. On one occasion this led to the bizarre sight of Ken chasing Lonnie around the rehearsal room, with very definite ideas about where he was going to put Lonnie's banjo. *Very New Orleans!*[12] One suspects that in any such contest the skinny, pallid Donegan would have come off worse against the gnarled old sailor!

In support of Ken at this point, ubiquitous recording manager Denis Preston, who engineered many of the early Barber and Donegan recordings, had Lonnie down as someone who could cause a major disturbance in an empty recording studio. One is here reminded of White Eagles' drummer Tony Martin's quip: why do musicians have an *instant* aversion to banjo players? Because it saves time in the long run![13]

Although personality clashes played a part, especially given what we have said above about Colyer's personality, the break up was without doubt hastened by clear musical differences. Colyer was often said to be single-minded to the point of stubbornness and obduracy about the direction he wanted to travel - the relatively loose, free expression of traditional New Orleans music, especially that played by those musicians who had stayed at home and not joined the Oliver-Morton-Bechet-Armstrong exodus from the Crescent City. For him therefore rehearsing and arranging music were to be

---

[12] That incident, confirmed by Chris himself and Harold Pendleton, sounds like exactly the sort of thing that happened many times in New Orleans!
[13] Quoted in Dempster, 46.

avoided wherever possible. He expected any musical shortcomings to work themselves out over time in performances, and accepted below-par evenings as all part of the natural order.

Chris Barber on the other hand was in the Jelly Roll Morton stream whereby free improvisation could be combined with the careful arrangement of music. Barber's early recordings provide ample evidence of this, whilst his modern incarnation as the Big Chris Barber Band carries careful arrangement to the ultimate degree. It seems fairly clear that Barber's approach would be too restricting for Colyer, and that for Barber, Colyer's approach would appear to leave far too much to chance.

To highly motivated people like Chris Barber and (especially) Lonnie Donegan, both with their eyes on the stars, Ken's approach could appear all together too laid back and unadventurous. Ken was happy just to play the music, whilst Chris and Lonnie had ambitions that lay beyond the narrow confines of the streets of New Orleans. It was perhaps clear that such targets as they had would not be achieved with Ken Colyer at the helm. It was not the case however that Colyer himself was without ambition - far from it. He was as concerned as anyone that people should like the Band and the things the Band played. But his ambitions were tied up with the promotion of the *music*, rather than of himself, whilst the horizons of the Barber-Donegan vision were much broader altogether.

It should be said that historians like nice, tidy theories. The idea that Chris and Ken represented widely different musical poles makes up one such tidy theory. In reality however both band leaders had much wider musical interests than is generally acknowledged. Colyer was a great fan of Lester Young of *Lester Leaps In* fame.   Although not represented among his recordings, Ken would include swing numbers in his live performances. And then the music of the New Orleans pioneers themselves was a lot more imaginative and inventive that is allowed by contemporary revivalist bands that fossilize it.[14] At the same time Chris would make much more than a passing nod to New Orleans, and would never at any stage in his career cut himself off from his New Orleans roots, a statement that we shall repeat later. Where there were "clear" musical differences therefore, they were more of emphasis than substance.

---

[14] The topic for a book in itself!

Linked to musical differences was the inevitable question of power and leadership. Officially the Band was a co-operative, as Ken had been told in the written invitation to join. I have to say at the start that, knowing musicians as I do, the idea of six highly-motivated people surviving happily together as a democratic group in the hard world of professional music does seem to me just ever so slightly fanciful. Colyer, in his version of events, echoes this by claiming that the band still regarded Barber as leader, whilst it is difficult to imagine Colyer, "the Guv'nor", bowing to a democratic vote on any issue! Ron Bowden, in his interview with Mike Pointon in *Just Jazz*, lets the cat out of the bag ever so slightly when he refers to the prospect of *Chris's* ideas being unlikely to be fulfilled with Ken in the Band.[15] As Ron himself recalls in the same interview being summarily sacked himself by Barber a couple of years or so later in favour of Graham Burbidge, he has perhaps personal reasons for recalling the proactive role Chris played in the leadership of the Band!

However that may be, the co-operative card was played and Colyer duly informed that *he* in fact was the one to be sacked, with immediate effect.

Dramatic though the actual events were, and exaggerated though the differences between the two men undoubtedly were, it is difficult to imagine that a Barber-Colyer partnership, the combination of two highly-driven people, could have had any significant longevity. Had "musical differences" not reared their heads then, they would have surely done so around the next corner, or the one after that.

From time to time it has been argued that there was a basic personality clash between Chris Barber and Ken Colyer, Barber being a public school boy and Colyer as rough as nails, with a known penchant for railing against all graduates of private schools. Pat Halcox, in his *Just Jazz* interview with Mike Pointon doubts this.[16] He questions whether there was any significant issue between Barber and Colyer, apart from the question of arranging and organising, or between Ken and Monty Sunshine for that matter. Whatever was the case, Halcox says

It worked - because the band sounded great!

---

[15] Ron Bowden, *Just Jazz Magazine*, September 2008.
[16] Pat Halcox, *Just Jazz Magazine*, January 2009.

Stu Morrison, sometime banjo and guitar player with both the Colyer and Barber Bands, suggests that the issue was rather with Bill than Ken, and that Bill often shaped the bullets that Ken actually fired. Ever since Aaron set himself up as spokesman for brother Moses such relationships have existed.

Unfortunately Ken is no longer around to ask, but in his writings he would later claim that he had been used by the resourceful and business-like Barber, who saw the name "Ken Colyer, Legend of the Orleans Parish Prison", as a means of gaining publicity (not to mention bookings) for the emergent band, only for the name and its bearer to be unceremoniously dumped once the band had become established.

One interesting sidelight on this was given by another observer. It is very much a "so-and-so said to so-and-so" Chinese whisper type of sidelight, so must be treated with caution. But our observer claims that a musical friend of his, close to the events of that time (whatever that means) told him,

> Yes, I remember it well. Ken fired the band - or the band fired Ken - depending on who you listen to. But I knew it was going to happen two weeks before. Pat Halcox had been earmarked to take Ken's place weeks before the actual row on stage. It was a conspiracy.

There are always of course conspiracy theorists that emerge whenever any big event takes place. What can be said in mitigation is that any sensible group of people would have a Plan B should the worst fears about a Barber-Colyer partnership be realised. And Chris Barber certainly was sensible, to the point of astuteness. In that sense "conspiracy" is far too strong a word.

It should be remembered that Pat Halcox was already well known to the Band. He had been with them during the tentative, exploratory days in 1952 of testing whether the road to professionalism was the right road for the Band. He had already played publicly with the Band at a Soho Club in December of that year, and was all set to go off to Denmark with the Band in early 1953, when, in Barber's own account he came and told them that his parents had persuaded him to stick with a career in Chemistry rather than take on the risky life of a professional jazz musician. One can only assume that sometime in 1953 Pat had changed his mind, no doubt influenced by the success of the Band under Colyer's leadership. It is equally likely that this change of heart was known to the Band.

Nevertheless, we should in fairness say that conspiracy, like beauty, is very much in the eye of the beholder, or in this case, the conspiracy theorist.

Was there any substance to Colyer's antipathy towards the rhythm section of the Band? To quote DJ Brian Harvey:

> I have gone back over the recordings to try and discover what Ken was unhappy about at the time. I think I know. It was the absence of that almost magical inner rhythm and balance that the Colyer bands at best achieved - and then not all the time. That was Ken's genius, his gift, his legacy.

Getting at the truth about the whole affair therefore will be an arduous task and will always depend on who you speak to. What is beyond dispute is that the mysterious workings of Providence moved in favour of *both* Chris Barber and Ken Colyer in the aftermath of their dramatic musical divorce.

And whatever the precise circumstances of his departure from the Band, one very tangible souvenir of his days with Barber was his band suit, which he retained, had dyed, and used as his wedding suit!

Within days local impresario Harold Pendleton had installed the new Barber Band as the resident Friday Band, with Ken playing another evening with a scratch band, a band that included one Bernard Bilk on clarinet.[17]

The difference in quality between the two bands was obvious, but then it was the difference to be expected between an established band and a scratch band. After gradual changes in personnel, changes that would include Ian Wheeler and Dick Smith, Colyer would go on to put together what the aforementioned Stu Morrison describes as representing "the most significant moment in jazz".[18]

Although unable to rival Barber in terms of longevity, Ken did continue to lead bands and play for a further 30 years, until ill health, no doubt linked to his lifestyle, forced him to retire in 1986.

For Chris Barber the parting of the ways with Ken Colyer was the launch pad for *The Chris Barber Band*. If Barber's eyes were already set on the stars,

---

[17]   *a propos conspiracy theories*. How could Halcox so quickly have made himself available to turn professional, considering his earlier misgivings, and the shortness of time in which to fulfil his stated aim of getting qualified?

[18]   In a conversation with me at his home on 30th October, 2012.

now he and the band were able to begin their meteoric rise to meet them.

Meanwhile, Back in Ulster….
Blissfully unaware of all these machinations, back in Ulster the youthful
Ottilie, with her own eyes set on the celestial heights, made up her mind
there and then at that Party that she would save up her teacher's salary and
travel over to London to see and hear in the flesh the band that had so fired
her imagination.

3

STREETS OF LONDON

A Significant Holiday

So a single-minded Ottilie saved up the princely sum of £21 and in the summer holidays of 1954 came to London to seek out the mysterious Ken Colyer, whose singing had so impressed her at that Birthday Party. At that point she was blissfully ignorant of the dramatic in-fighting that had only a few weeks earlier driven Colyer and Barber apart.

On arrival in London she made a beeline for Humphrey Lyttleton, as she said, "the only name I knew", to ask for an audition. She had read that Humph's office was in Denmark Street, in the heart of Soho. On asking two passers by for directions to Denmark Street, she was greeted by the startled question: "what does a girl like you want in Soho?". On being told that she was going to Soho because she wanted to become a jazz singer, they replied that the best advice they could give was that she should go home, back to her (safe) job of teaching. The advice was no doubt well meant, but was nothing like strong enough to put Ottilie off, having come so far.

The great Humph, on the crest of a wave of popularity, was understandably at the time inundated with such requests, and had no time for the eager Irish girl. What he did do, with unrecognised wisdom, was to give her a letter of introduction to Chris Barber, suggesting she go and see him. At the same time Humph introduced her to Beryl Bryden, who he informed her had a link with Chris Barber's Band. Beryl Bryden's claim to fame was not so much for her singing as of course her washboard playing on Lonnie Donegan's chart-busting recording of *Rock Island Line*, which had featured Chris Barber on bass.

Bryden duly promised to take Ottilie down to see the Barber Band the following Friday only to let Ottilie down and leave the diminutive girl the unenviable task of wandering down to the Greek Street Club alone. Ottilie recalls the sight of the street walkers of Soho being quite a startling one, causing her to imagine that she had somehow been transported back to Storyville, the red light district of New Orleans!

Ottilie joins the Band

When Ottilie arrived at the Soho club the band was in full swing. Having come a long way at great expense for this opportunity, Ottilie was not about to waste it, and lost no time going forward in between numbers to ask the musicians if she could sing with them. She was in fact labouring under the illusion that Beryl Bryden had told them she was coming, and thus prepared the way.

Bryden in fact had not. "How about Basin Street in B Flat ?" Ottilie would enthusiastically enquire. Ottilie said that she mentioned the key so as to impress the musicians, and to stop them from thinking she was just "a girl from the country", which in fact was exactly what she was!

Chris himself was absent in hospital with glandular fever, so that the band doubtless felt that in his absence they had enough to cope with without taking the risk of putting up front someone who might prove to be a disaster, because of her obvious inexperience.[19] In passing we might wonder how many talented stars have failed to get a break because of such conservative reasoning. As politely as any jazzman could, they declined her request for the time being.

In fairness to Ottilie, it should be recorded that they wouldn't ever let Beryl Bryden sing with them either!

The story goes that at the end of the evening, as the musicians were packing up their instruments, Johnny Parker, Humph's pianist and good friend of the Barber Band, was idly tinkling away on the piano, as jazz pianists often do. With the eagle eye of a predator, Ottilie spotted a weak link. Just a little persuasion got Parker to begin playing *Careless Love,* Ottilie very quickly joining in with the lyrics. At this point real life became Hollywood. The sound was so startling and arresting that the musicians hastily unpacked their instruments and began to join in with her. The effect was startling and time-halting..

In the mayhem that followed this impromptu concert,, Ottilie was conscious of an arm going around her and a cheerful, cockney voice asking "Hi, darlin', howd'ya like to join our band?" That voice turned out to belong,

---

[19] In conversation with me 83-year old Chris confided that this was the only major illness he had ever suffered. Definitely not your average jazz musician!

perhaps inevitably, to the aforementioned Lonnie Donegan. Before Ottilie could respond to Lonnie's unofficial invitation, she had of course to meet Chris, once he had recovered from his illness. This she did a few days later. Ottilie recalled that her first impression on seeing Chris for the first time was one of surprise at his appearance.

> The first thing I thought was that he was very lonely. I bet he was a clever boy at school, and because of that he has no friends. My maternal instinct began to come out.
>
> What really impressed me was that, although he was getting married at the end of that week, he was nevertheless up on the stand, playing his trombone. "There's a man for you" I thought, "he's got his priorities right!"

It would be interesting to know how many female readers would agree with Ottilie at this point, or even whether Ottilie herself in the light of subsequent events would maintain that liberal judgement!

To Barber's credit he saw that the story told to him by the Band members from that Soho night were not exaggerations, and that in Ottilie Patterson he had someone very special. Humph's loss would very soon be his gain.

Some later reports would tell of Ottilie being offered a contract on the spot. It wasn't quite as simple as that however, since of course Ottilie already had a job back in Ireland. She would at least need to work her notice in Ballymena. And, as Pat Halcox had already had to consider, a good living in jazz could by no means be guaranteed, and would always carry an element of great risk. The agreement they arrived at was for Ottilie to go back to Ireland, complete her teaching and then re-join the band after Christmas. This she did with reluctance, as she realised she could not hang around in London on the off-chance the call from Barber would come. With one shilling and nine pence in her pocket she boarded the ship, sleeping on deck to return to Ireland and work out her notice.

In October 1954 the Band came over to Belfast for a concert, and Ottilie again sang with them, supported in the audience by some of her local Irish friends, keen to see the new direction Ottilie was keen to take. But still it was back to school the next morning for Ottilie as arranged.

At the end of term her teaching contract was duly cancelled, but no call had come from the Barber Band. An anxious little period followed, as Christmas came and went without word from her potential new employers. Had she sacrificed her teaching career for nothing? What would she do if Barber did not come through?

Finally, on 28th December, 1954 to her great relief, a telegram arrived that read:

Ottilie Patterson, Avondale Gardens:

We would love to have you sing this Friday. How about it? Happy New Year. We will expect you this Friday unless you wire. Chris Barber.

Ottilie went straight to the local Post Office and wired back:

Coming even if I have to ride the rods

The expression "ride the rods" was apparently a line from W.C.Handy's *Atlanta Blues,* a phrase Ottilie had discovered in the book of Handy's Blues she had purchased all those years earlier in the Belfast Music Shop. She later confessed that she didn't have a clue what "riding the rods" actually meant, but that to join the Barber Band she would have done it, whatever it entailed.

Leaving Ireland was not in fact such a big deal as might be supposed. Ottilie's parents had long since given up on her before she packed her suitcase and went off to join the band. In any case there was virtually no work in Ireland to keep her there. She had only been teaching two days a week anyway, with little sign of any more teaching opportunities turning up. So she began her career with the Chris Barber band, at the princely salary of £10 a week. She exchanged the relatively safe, predictable job of teaching for the exciting but highly unpredictable life of a jazz singer in a professional Jazz Band.

Ottilie's search had proved successful. She was now engaged to sing with the Band she had heard (or most of the Band) at that celebrated 21st Birthday Party.

In later years, as the Barber Legend with its associated publicity machine began to grow, it would said more than once, without Chris' complicity, that Chris Barber discovered Ottilie Patterson. The truth is the opposite. By following the trail that began at that 21st birthday party, she had come across him. That his and her musical talents should discover each other was a combination of wisdom from Humph, determination from Ottilie, and good fortune for Chris. We should all have that kind of good luck!

Just as it is inaccurate to say that Columbus discovered America (which was there at the time), so the most that could be said is that Barber had the great perception to recognise the tremendous talent that providence had brought his way.

Ottilie begins performing with the Band

There is nothing like starting big I suppose, and so her first professional engagement with the band is generally reckoned to have been on the biggest stage of all, with a concert at no less a venue than the Royal Festival Hall on London's South Bank.

It is always something of a pity to spoil a good story (and a tidy theory) with the facts, but it would appear that the RFH concert was *not* in fact Ottilie's Concert Debut with the Band. That debut had in fact been made in Lewisham just two days earlier.

John Warner kindly sent me the programme from a "Jazz Band Show" in the Town Hall, Lewisham on Friday, 7th January, 1955. The Barber Band shared the Bill with the Dave Carey Band at this concert organised by Pete Payne, of Payne's Music Shop.

The programme notes mysteriously say,

> Rumour has it that Chris intends to feature a female vocalist in the future, singing in the Bessie Smith tradition; we are hoping she may sing in this concert.

This programme writer obviously knew a thing or two. His hopes were indeed fulfilled, and the petite Irish girl did in fact appear on stage singing with the Band. The Band's programme that evening included several numbers that were to find permanent places in the permanent Ottilie Patterson repertoire, including *St. Louis Blues, Trixie's Blues* and *Weeping Willow Blues*.

The Royal Festival Hall, January 1955

What *can* be fairly said without contradiction is that it was on the stage of the Royal Festival Hall that Ottilie Patterson truly "arrived", and came to the attention of the Jazz world, critics and followers alike.

The January 9th concert, under the auspices of the National Jazz Federation, was entitled "Jazz Scene 1955", and was constructed in two halves, modern and traditional. Like many cricket matches today it was a day/night affair, with the "traditional" segment taking place in the afternoon, and the "modern" section in the evening.

On the dot at 3 p.m. proceedings began with the Merseysippi Jazz Band, with stalwarts Pete Daniels on trumpet and Frank Parr on trombone. After playing a number of tunes they were joined on stage by Beryl Bryden singing *I've Got What It Takes, Young Woman Blues* and *After You've Gone.*

After *they* had gone onto the stage came the Barber Band, who, as the programme notes tell us, had generously given up the Finale spot to the emerging Alex Welsh Band. They opened with traditional stompers, *All The Girls Go Crazy* and *I Never Knew Just What Girl Could Do,* before moving on to the Big Moment. That moment was introduced in rather downbeat fashion by the phrase "our new singer."

The publicity machine had been up and running however, and Brian Nicholls' notes in the programme for the Concert state in very bold terms:

> The main function of the Band today is to introduce the latest, and by all accounts, the greatest blues singer to emerge on this side of the Atlantic. Ottilie Patterson is Irish and has been training until now as a teacher. Having completed her training, she has apparently decided to leave well alone and join Chris' band as a permanent alternative to work.[20]

This description of Ottilie gives encouragement to our earlier suggestion that this concert was not in fact Ottilie's first public performance with the Band. It is scarcely possible, even with excessive Harold Pendleton-type hyperbole,

---

[20] I doubt very much if many of the people who subsequently played with Chris' Band would regard the tough touring schedule as an *alternative* to work!

that such an accolade could never have been given to someone who had never been heard before in public!

What is undoubtedly true however, is that Ottilie had never done any performances on this gigantic scale before. She confesses to having been terrified at the prospect of singing in the Royal Festival Hall. Who can blame her? For a young girl from rural Ireland just walking into the awesome setting of the RFH would be terrifying enough, but to actually perform on the stage - well it doesn't bear thinking about.

At the appropriate time Ottilie came on to stage, wearing a long white dress which she came to nickname "My Wedding Dress", opening up with her idol Bessie Smith's classic *St.Louis Blues.*

The story goes that the response from the 3,500 people that made up the capacity audience was so enthusiastic that she rushed off stage again, too terrified to even announce her next number, that task falling to Barber himself. Harold Pendleton tells how on rushing off the stage she gasped excitedly to him "I'm really only an art teacher!", such was the contrast between her humble life back in Ireland and the starry environment she had now entered. Happily she survived the shock and went back on stage to perform and record other Bessie Smith numbers, including *Reckless Blues* and *I Hate a Man Like You.*

All that we can say is that any nerves she may have had at the beginning of the evening were well concealed in the strength and assurance of her performance. Indeed those two words, "strength" and "assurance" are keywords that go a long way to summing up Ottilie as a performer, strength and assurance which however, as we shall see also concealed a degree of frailty and vulnerability.

A Star is Born

The post-concert acclaim was instant and ecstatic. "Sensational" is is not too strong a term to describe how the popular press greeted Ottilie's debut.

The Daily Mail, the following day said:

> Miss Ottilie Patterson was a schoolteacher in Ballymena, County Antrim just before Christmas. Yesterday this shy girl was being acclaimed "the greatest blues singer this side of the Atlantic". For Ottilie, who sings with her eyes closed, captured 3,500 jazz fans at Sunday's concert in the Royal Festival Hall, London.

The Belfast Telegraph on the same day joined in:

> A 23-year old Newtownards girl, who until a week ago had never sung
> a note professionally, has been acclaimed "the greatest blues singer to
> emerge this side of the Atlantic". She is schoolteacher Ottilie Patterson,
> who sings with her eyes closed. She was "discovered" yesterday when
> she sang in front of an audience of 3,500 at London's Royal Festival
> Hall. Miss Patterson, whose parents live in Avondale Gardens,
> Newtownards, has been in England just over a week.
> After the thunderous applause that followed her first song *St. Louis
> Blues*, she was too frightened to announce the title of her next number.
> Chris Barber, the band leader, had to announce it for her.
> But when she sings, the voice that comes out of her is rich and
> powerful.

The Newtownards Spectator predictably is more fulsome still:

> Miss Patterson was "discovered" when she sang, swaying gently with
> eyes closed to a moody rhythm before 3,500 fans at the Royal Festival
> Hall, London. When her voice died away the audience nearly brought
> the house down. Her early love of jazz has now taken her to the top of
> the tree.

Brian Rust, a contemporary jazz writer says:

> The audience was completely bewildered, captivated and amazed by
> the sight of Miss Patterson, a tiny fairy-like figure in a white dress,
> looking as though she could just about manage *Bless This House* in a
> quavering soprano, but in fact moaning the Blues with a rich, sombre
> majesty that recalled the days of Bessie Smith, Sara Martin and
> Margaret Johnson.[21]

It was however not just the popular press that acclaimed Ottilie in those early
days. There is nothing better than the acclaim of fellow professionals. So

---

[21] Brian Rust, quoted in J.Godbolt, *A History of Jazz in Britain 1950-1970*, 132.

George Melly, a respected music critic as well as a Blues singer, wrote in his *Melody Maker* column:

> When Chris Barber announced from the stage of the Royal Festival Hall that he would like to introduce a new singer, Miss Ottilie Patterson, only a very small proportion of the audience knew what to expect. Those of us who knew what to expect waited tensely, whilst the rest, from what I could see of their faces, waited indulgently. But with her first notes - she had them.
> Out of that prim-looking little figure roared the fierce, noble voice of an enormous negress singing the Blues.
> When she left the stage at the end of her third number the audience were shouting for more. When assured that we would be seeing more of her later in the programme, one individualist shouted "we hope so!" He spoke for everyone.
> We who had heard her before were not of course so surprised. But for me at any rate the impact had not lessened. The *frisson* which never fails to ascend and descend my back on listening to authentic blues singing was hard at work.

An interesting tailpiece to the reporting of the concert comes with the news that Princess Margaret had been scheduled to attend the concert. On the strength of this rumour battalions of paparazzi had been despatched to the Royal Festival Hall. Clearly the non- appearance of the Princess did not cause the photographers to feel that their journey was wasted, as the next day's papers were filled with pictures of the new singing sensation. A happy combination of circumstances for Ottilie!

Common elements of these reviews
The first element is the tremendous impact Ottilie had on her audience. In spite of the limitations of the early attempts to record live performances, and the irresistible temptation for recording engineers to fade out audience applause, this impact comes across.

This impact came in part from the tremendous contrast between her relatively frail appearance and the power of her voice. This contrast is heightened by the stereotype of a negroe Blues Singer as a "Big Fat Momma" (*my phrase*) presented by George Melly. Big voices can only be produced by big people, so the argument runs. Whether this is in fact true or not, that would have been the perception of the audience that night. It is worth noting in passing that there is not shortage of pictures of the young Bessie Smith as quite a slender figure. There would be much debate later about whether this was Ottilie's natural singing voice, or whether it was a "performance" voice. The problems she went on to have with her vocal cords might well have fuelled this debate. But powerful the voice unquestionably was.

This impact led quite quickly to an unbelievable degree of hype surrounding the description of her as the "Greatest Blues Singer this Side of the Atlantic". I am certainly not saying that she didn't go on to deserve this accolade, for undoubtedly she did, but to give it to *anyone* who had been singing professionally for only a week and had sung professionally in public only a couple of times is an irrational hype of a degree that would serve only to lay an impossible burden on the performer in question. The description apparently derived from Harold Pendleton, and must therefore be accepted as an entrepreneurial ploy to put bums on seats at her next performances. Pendleton's further comment was that "I had heard that Ottilie was a wonderful find, but I never dreamed she was as exciting as this."

Finally, the reference to Ottilie's relatively humble beginnings (in contrast with Barber's relatively privileged origins) is important for the story. This new star was self-evidently an ordinary person, albeit an ordinary person with an extraordinary talent. The Ulster people valued that and never forgot it - as Ottilie herself didn't. A great talent in a frail human frame was always the base line for assessing Ottilie's contribution to music.

John Warner recalls being a typical hyper-critical teenager at the time and remembers commenting that while Ottilie's voice was good, she lacked something in personality, especially when compared to George Melly and Beryl Bryden who he considered at the time to be the ultimate in Jazz Singers.

> It took me a couple of years of further maturity to realise that the best singers concentrated on their voices and not cavorting all round the stage ! Unlike Melly, you never saw Sinatra fall on his face while singing *Frankie and Johnny*, nor Ella Fitzgerald playing the washboard ![22]

---

[22] In fairness John admits he always enjoyed Melly and Bryden!

John Warner fully recognises his comments about personality were premature. Stagecraft would come with experience. Ottilie would learn to be mistress of all she surveyed when performing. For now it was the *voice* that identified her as something very special indeed.

When a news reporter went round to the Patterson house in Avondale Gardens, Newtownards the week after the Festival Hall Concert, he found Julia, Ottilie's mother, almost as excited and swept off her feet as her daughter! The first news of Ottilie's overnight success had been brought to her by her next door neighbour, who had rushed round with a daily newspaper on the Monday morning. Julia's comment, "it's been an exciting start to the year", must rank as one of the biggest understatements of all time!

Return to Ulster - Thousands locked out
Further indications of the sensational impact Ottilie's Royal Festival Hall appearance had were seen when Chris Barber brought Ottilie and the band over to Ulster to let the people see what they would henceforth be missing.

So a concert was arranged for the 29th January, 1955 at the Fiesta Ballroom in Belfast. If the organisers ever entertained any doubts as to whether there would be sufficient interest from the Ulster public these doubts were blown away not only by the overnight sale of the 1,000 tickets, but by the further 1,000 people who turned up without tickets and had to be turned away. The Belfast Police had to be called in to control the situation, something that had happened all too rarely at jazz events, and which I suspect has rarely happened since!

Ottilie was understandably very moved by the reception given her and expressed to a journalist from the *Northern Whig* how pleased she was at the progress jazz was making in Northern Ireland:

> Even my mother, who used to frown at my frequent excursions to Belfast Jazz Clubs, has been won over.

Comparisons are Odious - Encountering the Critics
This young, impressionable woman, now launched into a new life in a new world, had to encounter a peculiarly savage species of *homo sapiens* that prowls around that world - the jazz critic. She had to learn the hard way that not everyOne who writes about her is from Northern Ireland, nor does every writer by any means feel obliged to write only nice things about her. She had

to learn to ride the blows and let critical comments bounce off her. She was not the first to suffer in this way, nor would she be the last.

The main point on which the critics fastened was the self-evident similarity of sound and style between Ottilie and Bessie Smith. Was Ottilie influenced and moulded by the Empress of the Blues, or was she deliberately setting out to imitate her? And even if the case for imitation could be proved, was such imitation improper? After all, imitation is indeed the sincerest form of flattery.

Ottilie and Bessie Smith

If any aspiring Blues singer were looking for an inspiration and role model, then they could in fact do little better than choose Bessie Smith, by general consent the greatest of the early Afro-American Blues Singers.

Bessie Smith, the "Empress of the Blues" as she was called at that time, was a powerful, strong-willed woman, who rose from the poorest of backgrounds, against all odds, to the top of her profession in the 1920's and 30's. The difficulties she faced in that journey were overcome by a fierce determination that caused her to back down before nobody. This determination could turn into a fierce temper, which in turn could become violence. At 6 feet in height and more than 200lbs in weight, she presented a formidable figure, someone you definitely didn't mess with. While no one was exempt from her wrath, she was at the same time fiercely loyal to her friends. And all her experiences and emotions came out in her songs and the way she sang them.

Although Bessie rose to the pinnacle of fame by gaining the admiration of audiences of all races and colours, she had been forced to do this in the context of the most bitter racial conflict and discrimination. No event in her life was more demonstrative of this than her death. She was severely injured in a road accident in Clarksdale, Pennsylvania in 1937. The story goes that she was refused treatment by a whites-only hospital in Clarksdale, and died in the ambulance in the course of the enforced extra journey to a blacks hospital. The dramatic story varies with sources, and even led to the writing of a stage play, *The Death of Bessie Smith*. What is not in doubt however, is that she did die during a long drive to a blacks-only hospital.

The first point to note is that comparisons between Ottilie and Bessie were not made by Ottilie herself, but were placed on her by others. They were not part of her spin or the basis of her advertising campaigns.

On the other hand, that Bessie Smith was her idol and the inspiration for performing the Blues Ottilie would readily acknowledge. And any of us, if were to nurse aspirations to become performers and entertainers, would absorb elements of our idols' performance, whether consciously or subconsciously. Incidentally, that was true of Bessie Smith herself, who was to a certain extent influenced and mentored by the very first Blues "star", the redoubtable Ma Rainey. Jazz historians disagree as to the extent of Rainey's influence on Bessie. Few would suggest that Ma Rainey actually taught Bessie to sing. What such historians believe as far more likely is that Ma Rainey taught Bessie some of the elements of stagecraft, and the art of projecting herself to the audience an art Ma Rainey demonstrated vividly. Nobody slept while Ma was performing. It would be going way too far to describe Bessie as Ma Rainey's protégé - but it would be fair for our present purpose to suggest that Bessie had her own musical ancestors who helped her become what she became. So there is nothing wrong with allowing yourself to be influenced by those you admire - it is natural. The wonder would have been if Ottilie had *not* shown traces of Bessie Smith's influence.

We might say also that there are only so many ways to sing the Blues. If Bessie Smith were in some ways archetypical, then how can any woman attempt to sing the Blues and *not* sound to some extent like her?

James Asman, *bete noir* of many jazz musicians, including Chris Barber himself, wrote in the *Record Mirror* in March, 1955 under the banner headline

OTTILIE PATTERSON IS NO BESSIE SMITH

with the sub-title *The Full-throated Voice That Is Only A Copy*. Whilst he damns her with faint praise by commending her intonation, delivery and accent as extremely faithful, he condemns her for, through inexperience, falling headlong into the trap of aping her musical betters.

> She sounds like Bessie. She tries to sound like Bessie. *But she will never have the Bessie's instinctive genius.* She sings without the authority of "the white folks yard".

It is worth noting that this is the same James Asman who, around the same time, predicted that the test of longevity would prove his view that the Chris Barber Band were not up to standard! Fifty years later we might feel that his judgement is at least questionable.

Comments about "instinctive genius" are of course subjective and are easy to make about people that most people in jazz have never heard either live or on record. Such arguments are by their nature therefore difficult to engage with. More pertinent is the comment about "the white folks yard". It prompts the important question. In order to sing the Blues, does the singer have to have personally experienced the things about which he is singing ? If we answer "yes" to that question, then we would have to say that a whole lot of Blues would never have been sung. Big Bill Broonzy for example had no qualms about appropriating to himself in his stories and songs feelings and incidents that originally belonged to other people.[23] What he was doing in his performance was deliberately identifying himself with a people that had endured all the things about what he sang and then applying them to himself and to his audience.

"Everybody gets the Blues now and then" says Jelly Roll Morton in the opening line of the verse to his composition *Doctor Jazz.* Blues is a way of expressing a universal *feeling.* The musical form may have originated with a particular people at a particular time, but the feeling belongs to everyone.

Can a white woman sing the Blues with authority and authenticity therefore? Certainly she can. And if in the process she sounds like her inspiration, Bessie Smith, does that matter? Certainly not. When, on one of the Barber Band's American tours Louis Armstrong famously said of Ottilie: "this gal reminds me of Bessie Smith" he was paying her a compliment, with no sense that the familiarity was improper. If that was good enough for Satchmo, it ought to be good enough for most of us, and perhaps even for James Asman! And when, on the same tour, a black woman said directly to Ottilie, "you sound just like one of us", she treasured that as one of the best compliments she had ever received.

To go back to "Good Time George" Melly:

> If the question is: how can a Northern Irish art teacher sing blues authentically, then the answer would be: she shouldn't be able to do, but does. Perhaps it is a case of "possession"!
> As for the rest of the aforementioned carping, yes she does sound like

---

[23] As Bob Riesman describes in his biography of Bronzy - B. Riesman, *I Feel so Good: The Life and Times of Big Bill Broonzy,* (Chicago: University of Chicago Press, 2011),

Bessie Smith, but why not? Bessie was the greatest of the Blues Singers, and the strongest influence is never imitation if it is felt and meant.

If the charge of being a Bessie Smith imitator could be made to stick at all, then it is certain that she was no *mere* Bessie Smith imitator. She had many other things to offer, such as her piano skills, than enabled her to include Boogie Woogie in her performance[24]; a repertoire than was rooted in the Blues but extended far beyond, to include Irish music and even Shakespeare. And, as far as I am aware, she never spat in the middle of recording songs, as Bessie was known to do occasionally![25]

Neither Ottilie herself nor I would ever claim that Ottilie was as good as Bessie Smith. We are reminded that such comparisons are always odious, and are entirely unnecessary. We recall precisely what Louis Armstrong said about Ottilie was: "this gal *reminds me* of Bessie Smith". Enough said.

Like all artistes on the way up, Ottilie had to learn the hard way that no one says good things about you all the time; that there are people out there who are paid to say negative things about you. But for a country girl from Ireland, largely unschooled in the ways of the world, such criticisms hurt deeply. Fortunately she had plenty of people around her to encourage her to take the rough along with the smooth.

Because of course jazz originated in America and not Britain, the natural assumption the critics made was that every British jazz musician must be copying on or other of the American jazz pioneers. So every leading British clarinettist, such as Cy Laurie or Acker Bilk *must* be copying Johnny Dodds. Outstanding trumpet players like Freddy Randall *must* be copying someone - how about Muggsy Spanier?

So it was all too inevitable that Ottilie would constantly have the odious comparison made with someone like Bessie Smith. Critics became like gramophones with a stuck needle - no review of an Ottilie performance could be written without some reference, usually negative, to Bessie Smith. Originality on the part of British artistes was considered inconceivable. It was as unfair as it was untrue. For Ottilie, being constantly tagged as "the

---

[24] For example *Bearcat Crawl* on *Chris Barber in Concert* (Pye Nixa NJL 6, 1956).
[25] As recounted in H.Jones, *Big Voice, Fallen Mama* (New York: Puffin Books, revised ed. 1995), 39,40."Bessie failed her test for Black Swan Records because she interrupted a song with "Hold on a minute - I gotta spit! The President of the Company immediately terminated the audition."

poor man's Bessie Smith" became exceedingly tiresome.

Critics were overlooking a crucial distinction. An artiste can be an *inspiration* without become a *model* to be followed slavishly. This would be a fair assessment of Ottilie. She would readily admit that her admiration for Bessie Smith spurred he on and gave her the burning desire to become a Blues singer. But as that career developed, Ottilie went way above and beyond the famed Empress of the Blues. The later influences of Sister Rosetta Tharpe, Muddy Waters and Ruth Brown would, as one writer put it, place Ottilie so far ahead of the critics that it would be as though they were writing about some other singer.

She would learn that those who can, do, while those who can't become critics, as we all know. She would not by any means be the last to confound such critics and prove them wrong.

4

EARLY DAYS WITH THE BAND

So Ottilie became a regular feature of concerts by Chris Barber's Jazz Band. A typical evening would see her come on stage towards the end of the first half to sing three or four songs, usually Blues, to the accompaniment of the band. She would appear again in the second half in similar fashion before joining in the finale at the end of the evening, often in support of any visiting "star" touring with the band at that time. One variation on this would be for her to accompany herself on the piano or even play a piano solo.

Examples of this are heard on the First *Chris Barber in Concert* LP (1956) where she performs *Bearcat Crawl* on piano to the (scarcely audible) accompaniment of Johnny Duncan on guitar. She then leads straight into *Lowland Blues,* with the same piano/guitar accompaniment.

This new life for the young Irish singing sensation became a magical whirl. She announced herself to a countrywide audience when in March 1955 she made her radio debut, singing *Reckless Blues* and *Trouble in Mind* for a BBC Programme in a "British Jazz Today" series.

There were concerts in all the distinguished halls of Britain in front of packed audiences. There were tours to all the European countries, and in time tours of the United States.

Ottilie recalls in her diary how in 1959 alone she had found herself in such diverse places as Berlin, Hamburg and Kansas City, with holidays in Monte Carlo, Northern Ireland and Denmark. They had played to 12,000 people in Berlin, and many hundreds in New York's Town Hall. That year the band had travelled 9,000 miles in America alone, and still seen only the North Eastern part of that vast country ! They had the stimulating experience also of singing and playing to 200 "coloured people" in Gary, Indiana, through the agency of Muddy Waters. The inclusion of this last point is appropriate that black artistes performing for white audiences and *vice versa* was still an issue in the States at this time.

And everywhere she went she was a sensation. The little girl with the big voice packed them in everywhere and brought them to their feet. Her humble origins were forgotten, as was the colour of her skin, as audiences came to realise, whatever the James Asmans of the world might think, that they were listening to someone and something that had the ring of authenticity. Wherever she sang they shouted for more.

Long time friend Ben Hendricks tells of how Ottilie made the hairs in his neck stand upright.

> She had a rich, dark brown contralto voice, fantastic timing, enormous volume, and such a tremendous blues feeling that I wouldn't have been surprised if she were fat and negroid.[26]

Stu Morrison, who joined the band on banjo in 1963, reports that while he was familiar already with most of the Band's repertoire, he needed a special rehearsal to get to know Ottilie's material. This was duly held at Barnet Jazz Club. Stu recalls how Ottilie made him feel very relaxed at once, chatting and joking away.

Stu takes up the story:

> I'd heard Ottilie in concert of course, but that in no way prepared me for what was about to happen. We played the first chorus, and this little woman, with no microphone, opened her mouth. Out came this stonking great voice ! It wasn't so much volume, as power and depth. The hairs on the back of my neck stood up, I can tell you.
> Prior to this I'd backed American Blues singers like Sonny Boy Williamson, and later, with the Chris Barber Band backed Howlin' Wolf. So I can say, perhaps with some authority that *never* before or since has anyone of European extraction come as close to producing the American Blues style as Ottilie did. Her singing never failed to give me a charge, and it was great when her health allowed her to tour with the Band.[27]

Report after report of Barber Band concerts, after being suitably complimentary to the Band as a whole, will speak of the appearance of Ottilie

---

[26] Ben Hendricks, *Lost in a Jazz band,* unpublished mss. Presented to Ottilie, 1994.

[27] Stu Morrison, *Barber Jazz Club magazine* .

on stage as the highlight of the evening. This was true of Souchon's review of the Barber Band's 1959 concert in New Orleans, as it was in Barber's own report of a concert before an 8,000 crowd in Washington in 1962, where he takes great pride in saying that she got a greater reception than anyone except the Duke himself.

A typical testimony from back home was that of Robert Foulkes, commenting on a performance for the Bath Festival of Jazz in the Regency Ballroom, Bath:

> What a gal that Ottilie Patterson is! She really stopped that crowd of kids jiving, and had them clapping and stomping as she gave them some of their favourites, *Blueberry Hill, Beale Street Blues* and *I got my Mojo Working*. Ottilie was the "crescendo" to the Barber session.

It is tempting, though probably mischievous, to ask whether the Chris Barber Band would have risen so quickly to the heights that it did if Ottilie had not wandered into that Soho Club years before. Without any doubt they were a talented group, well organised, well run and with a great eye for detail. They were professional in the best sense of the word. To accusations of being "commercial", they would simply reply that they knew what their audiences wanted and were providing it.

So yes, they were well on their way. But any entertainer who wants to get to the top cannot do so on competence and organisation alone. He or she has to have "magic", that little bit extra that makes everyone talk about them all the time. And Ottilie provided that magic. She was the "extra" that sparked everything else. She was the One who set the Barber Band above all its contemporaries.

Even Chris Barber himself admitted this. In an interview with *Woman* magazine her concedes:

> Ottilie is the making of our band. When I emerged on the scene nine years ago, every band had a pianist. I did without one, and before long all the other bands were copying me. So added a singer, and *that* checked them, because no-one can copy Ottilie.[28]

---

[28]   Interview with Jonah Barrington in *Woman magazine*, 1962.

Whilst generous to a degree, one might think this a simplistic and somewhat inaccurate explanation of how Ottilie came to join the Band.

Part of Ottilie's success stemmed from the fact that she had a very firm grasp on the material she was performing. She had thoroughly studied and researched the Blues. She knew all the songs, she knew all the artists. She knew how the artists performed the songs. You couldn't get by Ottilie with a loose factual statement. She would drop on you like a ton of bricks.

Other singers would sing the songs, but never really feel them, because they weren't immersed in the medium. They would sometimes even get the words wrong - a cardinal sin in Ottilie's eyes. Ottilie felt the material as she sang because she knew the material inside out. And it showed on the stage.

Not that things were all plain sailing with Ottilie and the musicians. There were some teething troubles. For example, at first she had some difficulty with the volume of the band's accompaniments. She had learned her blues by fiddling around on the piano, and found it difficult to cope with having to shout against a full band background.

In those early days of working with the Band she also had to overcome a natural nervousness and build up her confidence in her own abilities. She would sometimes say:

> What limits me is the fact that that I sing my numbers in very awkward keys for most musicians to play in. As a matter of fact I'm rather a useless person to have in a band.

Few would agree with that self-assessment. And indeed Ottilie soon gained self-confidence and developed a stage presentation of a real professional, whilst at the same time not losing her basic modesty.

Her Ulster vowels were a constant embarrassment to her, though not really, it must be said, to anyone else. She found them alien to the musical genre within which she was trying to sing. They would not "bend" in the way jazz vowels needed to.

In addition, later in her career she discovered that English was not her natural language, but that Latvian was, passed to her by heredity from her mother. She discovered this when living with her mother in St. Albans, she encouraged her mother to teach her to speak Latvian and, more importantly, to sing in Latvian. When she did this, she suddenly found that singing was easy and that there was no strain whatsoever on her vocal cords. So those critics who claimed that Ottilie did not sing in her natural voice were correct, though hardly in the way they meant!

As far as her early recordings were concerned, she proved to be a very hard performer to please. On four early recordings for Pye-Nixa, *Trouble in Mind*, *Sister Kate*, *Make me a Pallet on the Floor* and *Poor Man's Blues*, she was dissatisfied with the vocals-band balance. On *Ugly Child* and *Careless Love*, on an early Barber LP she was even more unhappy. Later she would declare that she hated nearly all her recordings, though this rather extreme opinion was governed largely by the unhappiness she felt about music and life in general she felt in her latter years. Things improved however, so that when her next EP appeared, in July 1956, even Ottilie was pleased with it. Chris had taken great care over the arrangements, and Ottilie was in extremely good voice. One of the tracks, *Jailhouse Blues*, stands among one of the best recordings she ever made.

On another track, *Shipwreck Blues*, she accompanied herself on the piano for the first time. Later the same year she would perform Meade Lux Lewis's *Bearcat Crawl* in a concert at the Royal Festival Hall.

She continued to play piano occasionally at concerts until 1964, when she ended it abruptly because of what she refers to as an embarrassing experience.

> We did a concert in Birmingham Town Hall. Sonny Boy Williamson was top of the bill. I also played piano that night, starting up with *Bearcat Crawl*. But when I moved on to a boogie woogie "walking bass" number my left wrist suddenly seized up and I couldn't walk the bass at all. It was a dreadful feeling, and I never played the piano in public from that day on.

Years later she was able to play it without the wrist seizing up in the house of writer Ben Hendricks, who succeeded in recording the event, a recording he kept as a prized possession.

Jazzing the Bard

Ottilie certainly shared Chris' innovative spirit, and was not afraid to follow her fancy and experiment. Ottilie tells of a constant inner tension that from time to time caused her to want to be away from the pressures of performing and touring, but which was at the same time afraid to do it. However she did take occasional opportunities to break away and do something different. One such opportunity came with the 400th anniversary of William Shakespeare. Ottilie was inspired to do something to celebrate this by the work of Cleo Laine and Johnny Dankworth. So, recalling her English Master's advice at school she put together a musical setting for *A Lover and His Lass* as part of her stage performance, along with poems set to music such as *Tell me Where is Fancy Bred, Blow Blow Thou Winter Wind* and *Ah Me, what Eyes Hath Love Put in My Head.*[29] Some of these settings began to appear in the Band's repertoire. But though the material was extracted from Classical English Literature, the Patterson treatment was unmistakably bluesy.

Another tangential adventure was an *ad hoc* session at the Marquee Club, singing *Up Above My Head* with Long John Baldry and an extremely young Rod Stewart.

The Pace of Band Life

To any outside observer, what characterised the band was the pace of its schedule. Reflecting the hyper-energy of its leader, the band were here and there constantly - never still apart from a few days to draw breath and to rehearse.

Justification for this would include things like: "it's a big, exciting world out there, waiting to be explored", "the Band member's are all young and energetic; to stand still is to go backwards and - life is not a rehearsal, you get only one go at it." "There is so much competition in the music field we have to keep being out there." Difficult to argue with any of that.

In the years 1955-62 Ottilie's travels with the Band would take her to major concert halls in Holland, East and West Germany, Austria, Switzerland, Denmark, Sweden, Finland, Norway, France, Czechoslovakia, Yugoslavia, Hungary and Poland. Include all the major English festivals and the regular TV appearances and you get quite a hectic schedule. And that is without counting 7 tours of America!

In parallel with all this was a penchant that Chris developed for sports cars, and fast sports cars at that. His connections with famour Formula One drivers such as Graham Hill gave Chris opportunities to drive on the Brands Hatch Circuit, although not competitively of course. One might speculate

29 Bielderman & Purser, 63.

that had he become a professional Motor Racer, he would not have been the worst by any means!

Pat Halcox reports that when he and the other band members arrived at the airport for the Third American Tour, Chris and Ottilie, who had gone out a day in advance, met them in a car they had hired - a Lotus Elite no less.

The world of fast cars has its down side of course. Like many drivers of sports cars Chris found himself building up quite a collection of speeding tickets, both in the UK and in America, as well as one serious crash in Switzerland. A more pleasant memory of Switzerland for the Barbers came with a presentation of a giant Cow Bell to them by Swiss fans on another tour of that country.

Unwinding in the course of a tour was not excluded completely, and one of the ways Ottilie found enjoyable was Ten Pin Bowling. Whenever the opportunity presented itself they would go along to the Rink at Golders Green, to swap the concert platform for the polished lane. Although she had represented Regents College at hockey, Ottilie confessed she was no sportswoman, but soon became a fanatic at what then was Britain's fastest growing sport. She soared to the heady heights of a score of 127, against a maximum possible score of 300. Not bad for a novice!

Her Political Concerns

The hectic round of touring and travelling the world didn't cause Ottilie to lose sight of or cease to be concerned about the upheavals in her native country. Although born and raised a Protestant, she was outspoken, as many fair-minded people were, and very concerned that all peoples of Ulster should live together in harmony and peace. "The best four-letter word I know," she would often say, is "love."

In practical terms it was impossible for anyone raised in Ulster to divorce themselves from the political scene. When you are a high profile Jazz Band playing in Ulster it is even less possible. One potential flashpoint was the inclusion or otherwise of the National Anthem at the end of a Concert, something that was routinely done by the Band at their United Kingdom gigs. Such an event would be anything but routine in Ulster! You will be way ahead of me in realising that on this issue Ottilie and the Band could not win. At some venues they would be damned if they did, and at others damned if they didn't. At some venues they would even be simultaneously praised and damned!

The *Belfast Telegraph* reports an concert in Derry in May 1960. On their arrival at the Guidhall the Police Superintendent advised them to omit the Anthem, because to play it would almost certainly cause a breach of the peace. The officials cited the trouble occasioned by another English band, the Ken Mackintosh Band, which was attacked by the audience hurling chairs at the stage for playing the British National Anthem.

So the Band followed that advice and omitted the Anthem, on the grounds that they were entertainers and not politicians, and as such did not want to be responsible for a breach of the peace. Unfortunately, as the Anthem was printed in the programme, at the appropriate moment a number of members of the audience stood to their feet ready to sing it. When the music did not materialise they went away muttering about a "gross insult".

Like many Ulster residents Ottilie was deeply affronted whenever the "Britishness" of her country was maligned. Among her prized cuttings is a quotation from Winston Churchill, who reminds everyone in no uncertain terms that because "Loyal Ulster" gave the free use of the Northern Ireland ports and waters, the free working of the Clyde and the Mersey was ensured. He goes on,

> But for the loyalty of Northern Ireland and its devotion, we should have been confronted with slavery and death, and the light that shines so strongly in the world would have been quenched.
>
> *May 6th, 1943*

She was not slow in putting pen to paper either in support of her message and to confront those who through ignorance or malice were making things worse.

To the Editor of BBC's *PM* programme she wrote:

> The last two letters about Ulster on yesterday's PM programme simply astounded me with their ill-informed arrogance and were most distressingly insulting to my already distressed and beleaguered countrymen in Northern Ireland.
>
> I should like to emphasise that there is complete freedom of worship for everyone in Ulster and has been for more than 100 years, ever since the Church of England was disestablished in Ireland and the crippling Penal Laws against Non-Conformist Protestant and Roman Catholic

alike were repealed.

The conflict over here is entirely political, but people outside Ulster are undoubtedly confused by the fact that the support for Republicanism is traditional among Roman Catholics people, while adherence to the British Crown is equally so among all Protestant denominations, so that the religions have become symbols of the political differences. The IRA attacks Protestants for their *Loyalism,* not their *Protestantism,* while attacks on Roman Catholics are similarly demonstrations against their *Republicanism* and not their religion.

I have always been proud to be an Ulsterwoman, but after the example of English intolerance shown in the two letters in yesterday's programme, I am perhaps not quite as proud as hitherto to be British.

Ottilie Patterson

14th June 1974

Not one to mince her words!

If letter writing was not always her strongest point, then the writing of witty lyrics certainly was, as is indicated by the following:

> Oh I'm in love with a nice young man
> Whose Christian name is Seamus.
> And Seamus he would marry me,
> But bigotry's again' us.
> The neighbours shout as we go out
> With insults meant to wrankle.
> And all because he's from the Falls
> And I am from the Shankhill.
>
> Our parents will not speak to us
> They say it's sheer disaster;
> For his father is a strict RC
> While mine's the Lodge Grand Master.
> And as for Priests and Protestants
> I care not for their anger;
> For we'll marry down in Dublin Town
> And honeymoon in Bangor.

Now I'm often seen to wear the green,
And sure, no colour's grander
To the sight of the eye on the 12th of July
As Seamus with the banner.
And we will always keep the peace
Whenever we do marry;
For he will sing The Sash to me
And I'll sing Kevin Barry.

Even the Troubles provided their lighter side occasionally. Ottilie told the story of how her sister discovered near to their London home a local florist selling Orange Lilies. So on July 12th, to celebrate the anniversary properly, they bought several beautiful blooms. On the way home Ottilie carried the flowers very carefully to avoid them being crushed by other shoppers. In the butcher's shop, however, her mind was far away from roast beef or steak, but was across the water in Ulster, visualising the Procession, with all the colourful banners, and hearing the bands play all the old tunes like *The Sash, The Lily-O* and *The Protestant Boys.*

Still lost in thought, Ottilie became suddenly away of a lady in the shop smiling at her. Thinking she understood the significance of the Orange Lily and its historical significance, Ottilie smiled back. But she could scarcely contain her laughter when the woman came up to her and said, "you look so solemn and serious with those lilies - just like a little Madonna !"

She continued to smile and look suitably complimented, without pointing out that neither of them would live to see the day when paintings would depict The Madonna, object of worship for countless Roman Catholics, clutching The Orange Lily!

The Other Pattersons

Not to be outdone by his sister, John had worked his way via Queen's College, Belfast to a Doctor of Philosophy Degree at the University of Birmingham before taking up an appointment as Lecturer in Mechanical Engineering at the same University.

His career would take him to Australia as acting Professor of Mechanical Engineering at Melbourne University, before returning to England to settle down as Assistant Rector at Huddersfield Polytechnic.

Just like Ottilie, John was not afraid to be outspoken. Concerned about teaching methods in Engineering masking a serious deficit of knowledge on the part of the teachers, he campaigned for the raising of the level of knowledge of teachers rather than the development of teaching techniques. He was fond of wheeling out the famous definition of the task of the University Lecturer as often being that of transferring information from his notebook to the notebook of the student without it passing through the brains of either. I know what he means!

Like brother John, sister Jessie was not content to bask in Ottilie's reflected glory, but was concerned to make her own mark in the world. In Jessie's case it was through championing the cause of adult literacy. At the time she became closely involved in the scheme she was Principal of an English Department in Hertfordshire. A colleague who had begun to teach some adults to read discovered that she had so many pupils on her hands she couldn't cope. She needed help. Jessie provided it and found herself launched into a new and worthwhile career.

She moved on at this time to the Dumfries and Galloway Region, to face the challenge of organising an Adult Literacy programme for an area stretching from Stranraer in the West to Castle Douglas. The biggest part of this challenge would prove to be the recruitment of a sufficient number of tutors to provide the essential element of the scheme, one to one tuition in the client's own home.

One of the main points that Jessie sought to hammer home through her campaigning was that the inability to read did not imply any lack of intelligence. People with literacy problems are, on the contrary, often highly intelligent, well capable of running their own businesses and contributing fully to society, although not as much as they could were they able to read well.

Meeting other artistes and being influenced by them

Whilst it was too late for Ottilie to meet Bessie Smith herself, it was possible for her to meet up with the stream of other legendary American singers that came over to perform with the Chris Barber Band. And when you are mixing with people at the top of their profession it is inevitable that some of their stardust will fall onto you. That was the case with Ottilie's encounters and collaboration with some of the greatest figures in the Jazz and Blues world of that period.

The agreement that existed in those days between the British *Musicians Union* and the *American Federation of Musicians* made it almost as difficult to bring artists over here as it was to go over there. However, the ever-resourceful and innovative Chris Barber was not one to be put off by a small amount red tape - or even lots of it. He noted that the restrictions on importing artistes were applied mainly to *musicians*, rather than singers. Musicians you couldn't bring in - singers you could. The reason for this was that most singers belonged to a different union, the *American Guild of Variety Artists*, who didn't particularly mind where their members went as long as they coughed up 2% of their earnings as union dues. And if the singer you brought in happened to accompany himself or herself on a musical instrument then - nod and a wink - you could get away with it.

The resourceful Chris quickly fastened onto this loophole and sought to smooth the path by (amazingly) sponsoring the visiting singers out of his own pocket. This demonstrates on the one hand his commitment to enabling British audiences to see the best of American jazz artistes live, whilst on the other being a pointer to the good living he was making out of jazz, something he was himself honest enough to admit.

Big Bill Broonzy

Ottilie describes Big Bill, with dubious syntax, as "Blues Artist *par excellence* - the Utter Greatest"[30] Big Bill Broonzy, one of the few jazz stars to whom the title "legend" could be legitimately applied, was the first to arrive to tour with the Barber Band.[31]

Big Bill toured with the Barber Band up an down the country delighting all his audiences, but the highlight of the tour was undoubtedly his appearance in November 1955 at the Royal Festival Hall, at that time the country's premier concert venue. *Melody Maker* reports that at the end Bill had 3,000 people stamping their feet and shouting for more.

John Warner tells of Bill's participation in the Second Festival of British Jazz in the Royal Festival Hall that same month:

---

[30] Email to Scott Yanow, 23rd May, 2004.
[31] Though this in fact was not Bill's first visit to England. See Riesmann, 133f for details.

It was possibly the happiest concert I've witnessed. Not only was the standing-room-only audience delighted to be listening to Bill, but the other performers, Chris Barber, Lonnie Donegan and Ottilie seemed overjoyed to be performing with him. Bill had just returned from Paris, and so was exhausted by the time he had finished his nine numbers.
Lonnie tried to do a number to give Bill a rest, only for the audience to shout for more Broonzy. The problem was solved by Bill singing *I Shall Not Be Moved* to Lonnie's backing, giving Bill a measure of rest. The fantastic evening ended with everyone present joining in on *When The Saints Go Marching In.* Chris, Ottilie, Bill and the whole audience ended the evening happy.[32]

Chris Barber himself reports a great missed opportunity. Bill's tour came hard on the heels of the success of *Rock Island Line.* Record Producer Denis Preston duly set out to record Bill in Britain, but would not allow him to be accompanied by the Lonnie Donegan Skiffle Group, preferring to have "real" musicians instead. Barber believes that had that had Bill be backed by the Donegan Group he would undoubtedly have had a world-wide hit on his hands and become a millionaire.[33]
Big Bill was not only a fine singer, with a haunting voice, and an accomplished guitarist with a unique style, but was also a great storyteller. He saw his performances as an opportunity to tell the story, not just of the Blues, but of an oppressed people in the Southern USA, treated as slaves even long after they had legally been emancipated. It didn't really matter, at least not to me, that Big Bill used to gild the lily and tell stories about himself and his family that really applied to others - it was the story of a *people* he was concerned to tell.   And in that sense his stories had the definite ring of authenticity about them.[34]
Back in the South segregation was still rife, and some of these visiting artistes were quite nervous about mixing with white people and being seen in public with them.
Big Bill was one such nervous artist, having certainly been on the receiving end of the oppressive segregation laws. He had suffered the outworking of

[32] John Waner, *Diaries.*
[33] Quoted in Reismann, 214.
[34] See Reismann, 10f.

racism even on his British tours. On one occasion, when entering a Nottingham Hotel, where a telephone booking had been made for them, he and his agent were stopped by the Hall Porter, who informed them that coloured people were not accepted by the hotel. On complaining to the manageress, they found her corroborating the hall porter's statement. The spirit of Jim Crow seems to have been alive and well in Fifties Nottingham.

They went to find accommodation elsewhere for the night. When a *Melody Maker* representative contacted the hotel, they tried to argue that the telephone booking had not been confirmed and, in any case, the hotel was full. However, two days later a letter arrived for Big Bill at his agent's office from a Mr. G. Davies, proprietor of the hotel, offering sincere apologies for what had happened. Ottilie recounts how she got to know Bill very well in a relatively short time, so well that he invited her out for a meal in The Great Wall Chinese Restaurant. As they were walking along Oxford Street Bill asked her, quite genuinely, "you're not ashamed to be seen out with me ?" Typically Ottilie replied, "I'm proud" and reflects that Bill's question almost broke her heart.

It is to Chris and Ottilie's everlasting credit that they were willing to welcome Black artistes like Big Bill not simply to share their stage, but also to share their home. Reading that now, so many years later, it seems unremarkable, but at the time it was a gesture of enormous significance for people like Bill.

Over the meal in The Great Wall Bill gave her a little sermon about how the Blues was not in themselves the expression of a particular view of life, but could be adapted to express many viewpoints and many approaches. He urged Ottilie to go on, in spite of the hurt that she continued to feel from the aforementioned negative reactions to her from some critics. The letter written to her by Big Bill in December 1955 was kept by Ottilie as one of her most prized possessions.[35]

Sister Rosetta Tharpe
If Big Bill's reaction to Ottilie was one of quiet encouragement, then it is safe to say that there was nothing whatsoever quiet about Sister Rosetta Tharpe! The title alone of her biography *Shout, Sister, Shout! The Untold Story of Rock*

---

[35] Though ironically, it appears now to be missing!

and Roll Trailblazer Sister Rosetta Tharpe gives you a pretty fair idea of what to expect if you went along to any venue where she was performing.

Ottilie had heard her on records, and couldn't wait to meet her and hear her in person, which she did when Sister Rosetta came to tour in late 1957. She went along with Chris to the press reception at the airport hotel, where a gang of reporters quickly gathered round her. At the time the memory of Billy Graham's visits to Britain were very fresh in peoples' minds, so that many of the reporters were anxious to know if Sister Rosetta was following in his footsteps on a soul saving mission. The way the reporters persisted along this line was clearly building pressure on Sister Rosetta, who was trying to counter by stressing she was simply an artiste expressing her musical gifts.

The pressure was released when, at Ottilie's suggestion, she broke into her characteristic piece *Peace in the Valley* there and then. Ottilie recalls that among those hard-nosed journalists there was not one who didn't have to wipe his eyes. But that was Sister - with her big voice and the way she played the guitar, you always cried.

Sister's concert performances were divided between songs on which she accompanied herself on a booming electric guitar, and numbers on which she was backed by the Barber Band. We should recall that these were the early days of electric guitars, and the smooth sound of The Shadows had not yet been perfected. One critic commented that

It was a shame to hear that long-admired guitar playing transformed through a jangle box into a shambles of slurring sound.[36]

It has to be said that in comparison with contemporary Rock Bands, the Sister Rosetta degree of amplification would be a mere pipsqueak. It was perfectly possible to hold a conversation while Sister was playing, something totally impossible in the discotheques of today!

The power and flexibility of Sister's performance had a stirring effect on the musicians around her. Her finger snapping offbeat and her rocking way with even the slowest of tempos edged the Band away from the stodgy rhythms that were once characteristic of traditional bands. As they gratefully went on to acknowledge, Sister showed the Band how to "loosen up a bit."

---

[36] Bob Dawbarn, *Melody Maker*, (November 30, 1957). Believe it or not, Dawbarn is basically positive in his review !

Her performances were infectious for the audiences also. I defy anyone to sit still and not join in the chorus on songs like *Gimme That Old Time Religion* and *Up Above my Head*. One newspaper reports her as throwing down a challenge to the then Bishop of Manchester, Ulsterman William Greer.[37]

> I'll get up in his Church and sing any kind of music any time he likes - and I reckon I'd have his people tapping their feet in no time at all.

And she would have done, without question!

> Feeling, that's what've you've gotta have boy! (*to the Reporter not the Bishop!*) I reckon everybody deep down wants to start tapping their feet if they've got the feeling, but they stop as soon as someone looks at them.

Again she is absolutely right. Speaking personally, Sister would have been welcome in any of my churches anytime!

Working with Sister Rosetta was a therefore a great experience for the young Ottilie and inevitably left its mark. The original plan for the concert tour was for Ottilie to sing her pieces in the first half and for Sister to take over (and "take over" is not too strong an expression) in the second half. However, that was far too neat a solution for Sister! Minutes before the First Concert of the tour in Birmingham she insisted on a hesitant Ottilie joining her on stage for *When the Saints go Marching In*, the classic New Orleans showstopper. She overcame Ottilie's hesitations, and, after a little impromptu rehearsal in the dressing room, they were on! Ottilie recalls how well it went, and how it made both of them pleased with each other. *The Saints* went on to be followed by *This Little Light of Mine* and inevitably *Peace in the Valley*, a piece that Ottilie recalls that she and Lonnie had done from time to time.

The young Ottilie could not have had a better mentor than Sister Rosetta. Ottilie would later comment that she learned more in three weeks working with Sister, as her name was affectionately reduced to, than in ten years of listening to records.[38]

Having said that, it is a point all too often overlooked that the relationship

---

[37] Someone under whom I myself worked.
[38] Email correspondence with Scott Yanow, 2004.

between Ottilie and Sister was actually one of *mutual* benefit. Ottilie's performances with the Band had in a very real sense paved the way for Sister Rosetta, so that when she arrived in Birmingham for the rehearsal that preceded the first concert, she was pleasantly surprised, if not actually amazed, that the Band knew all about accompanying a female Gospel singer. They didn't need the complicated band parts and orchestrations Sister had brought with her. They just began with Sister where they had left off with Ottilie, and it worked out fabulously! Although Ottilie would no doubt have been far too modest to acknowledge it at the time, the relationship between her and Sister was undoubtedly one of *mutual* benefit.

Sister was at the top of her profession, and was in a true sense a pioneer. Not only was she a great Gospel singer, she was one of that rare breed, a woman who could truly rock the place on the electric guitar.

Odette, herself styled "Queen of American Folk Music" says of Sister,

> Sister Rosetta Tharpe was a part of that history that is so valuable to young blacks, as we were coming along. She is certainly a champion where the guitar is concerned. My playing represented a fair rhythm guitar, but that woman could really PLAY the guitar!

To the shame of the people of Philadelphia, where Sister eventually settled, it took 35 years from her passing to get the money together for a headstone for her hitherto unmarked grave in the city's Northern Cemetery. Today a beautiful rose-coloured monument bears respect to one who was broadly acclaimed as one of the most influential American artistes of the 20th century. The prime mover in this long overdue tribute was Gayle Wold, Professor of English at the George Washington University. The headstone was nicknamed "The Rosetta Tharpe Stone", after the celebrated "Rosetta Stone", treasured by archaeologists.[39] Sister's stone may not have any archaeological value, but it certainly represents a landmark in the history of Gospel singing.

It's inscription, taken from the Eulogy by Roxie Moore read:

---

[39] Named as a parody of the *Rosetta Stone*, an ancient Egyptian artefact, inscribed with a decree issued at Memphis, Egypt, in 196 BC on behalf of King Ptolemy V.

> **SHE WOULD SING UNTIL YOU CRIED
> AND THEN
> WOULD SING UNTIL YOU DANCED
> SHE HELPED TO KEEP THE CHURCH
> AND THE SAINTS REJOICING**

As a retired Minister and Church Leader, I would be extremely proud to have things like that said about me!

Sonny Terry & Brownie McGhee
In contrast to the career shaping encounter with Sister Rosetta Tharpe, the relationship with the harmonica player Sonny Terry and guitarist Brownie McGhee, who toured with the band in 1958 was less productive. Ottilie recalls that Brownie found her singing too heavy and used to pass comments to that effect whenever he heard her sing.
The only sign of musical collaboration with them was the everybody-on finale number *Glory/I'm Gonna Walk and Talk with Jesus*, when Ottilie is in the vocal scrum along with Sonny, Brownie and Chris.

Muddy Waters
The next to visit these shores was Blues singer Muddy Waters, along with Otis Spann on piano. Ottilie, along with Chris, on one of their visits to America had heard him at Smitty's Corner in Chicago, and had been blown away by his big sound. The size of the sound owed a lot to the fact that Muddy was the first to use the electric guitar in Blues playing. The amplification effect led critics and (some) fans alike to say he was too loud, though Chris insists to this day that he was no louder than Sister Rosetta. I myself was present at his concert and Manchester's Free Trade Hall in October 1958, and have no recollection whatsoever of painful eardrums.
The encounter at Smitty's introduced a new element into the Barber Band's playing, and made Chicago Blues their default Blues style. Some would go on to say that Muddy's music laid the foundation of later Rhythm and Blues style, which was in turn the parent of several other musical styles. British musicians had heard their American idols at close hand, and needed no further encouragement to go ahead and copy them.

Because of her earlier bad experiences at the hands of the critics, Ottilie quite understandably hung onto and hoarded compliments from wherever they came, as she put it "hugging my little bouquet of compliments." She recalled how on one occasion, backstage at the Maltings, she was playing away at the rehearsal piano when she heard Muddy's unmistakable voice behind her, "If Spann dies I know who to get for piano". For Ottilie it was more important to note who compliments came from, people who mattered, than the compliments themselves.

Louis Jordan

Ottilie recalls Jordan, who came over in 1962, as being a very intense and energetic performer. He would rehearse the band rather like he would drive a Formula One car, except that he would allow no time at all for pit stops. Under him the band would typically learn 10 tunes and arrangements in an afternoon, and, to earn Jordan's approval, everyone of them would have to be "just right".

Jordan, from Arkansas, was the ultimate extrovert performer, blessed with a profound sense of the ridiculous, as indicated by some of his song titles such as *Sam Jones done snagged his Breeches* and *What's the Use of Getting Sober?*

He recorded prolifically in the 1940's, shouting blues-shaped vocals with something of the vigour of Pete Turner or Jimmy Rushing, whilst managing to sound like neither of them. He rode the wave of the Boogie Woogie craze, and usually had a boogie pianist laying down the beat for many of his numbers. One outstanding example of this was his million-selling *Choo Choo Ch'Boogie,* recorded in 1946.

It was Jordan who inflicted on Ottilie one of her worst musical moments. In the recording studio, with the limitations referred to earlier, they were going through *Taint Nobody's Business if I do.* The singer's curse struck, and Ottilie lost a note in her head. If you lose it there, you can't sing it of course. Jordan overheard Ottilie asking Chris "what chord's that on?" Anyone who has sung or performed in public knows that that is quite a reasonable question, but Jordan, losing patience, snapped "don't you know anything about chords?", a remark that reduced Ottilie almost to tears. Chris' own comment on Jordan was that working with him was like being dragged along by wild horses! We get the picture.

Louis Armstrong

Collaboration with the great Satchmo came in the form of a concert in the slightly unconventional setting of Ibrox Park, Glasgow (home of Glasgow Rangers Football Club for the uninitiated). In the finale of that concert the Barber Band joined Louis on stage for the last number, in all probability probably "The Saints". Ottilie recalls that she and Jewel Brown were jigging about doing a little dance at the back. Louis, becoming aware of this, suddenly shot them a "black look" (what other kind could Louis give?) over his shoulder, to remind them that he was the star, and they must not upstage him.

Ottilie found this a surprising reaction from Louis, arguably the greatest, and certainly the best known, jazz man of all time. To her it pointed to great insecurity.

> All of us tend to be insecure. That is why we have to get up every day and do it. Last night's applause is no good. It's like yesterday's dinner. You have to get approval again tonight.

Marriage to Chris Barber

From the first moment the applause rang out at the Royal Festival Hall Concert, Ottilie was sold on the new life. To use a phrase current at the time, she was "solid gone". A door had opened for her onto a new world, and a new life, and through it she rushed with great enthusiasm.

The bright lights, the aphrodisiac of rapturous applause, the press conferences, the fast cars, not forgetting of course the money, had her spellbound.

It would be quite wrong to portray Ottilie as a total innocent in all this. A genuinely shy and retiring girl would never have made the courageous odyssey from Ulster to London that she did. Nor would a wilting flower have dared venture out to sing to a mass audience like the one at the Royal Festival Hall. Nevertheless, the contrast with life in Ulster was obvious. And so Ottilie grabbed the spectacular upgrade with both hands.

A major part of this new world was Chris Barber himself. It is entirely understandable that she should be mesmerised by this dynamic, highly motivated young man who had his eyes on the stars and who offered an exciting ride for anyone willing to travel along with him. And this man was interested in *her* for her singing !

Not surprisingly the impact of this realisation and the enforced proximity resulting from touring together meant that the two of them became an item almost immediately, from virtually the beginning of their working relationship, while Chris was still married to his first wife Naida.

It is interesting that on their 1957 recording of *Moonshine Man* Ottilie sings "the man I love ain't nothin' but skin an' bone". The audience can be heard laughing at what would appear (in all probability) to be a side reference to Chris on trombone, standing next to her. If that is a reasonable conclusion to draw, then this suggests their relationship was well known at that time, three years before Chris was free to marry her. Maybe Ottilie was here sowing something that she would later reap as a harvest.

Ottilie and Chris Barber married at Paddington Register Office on 12th November, 1959. They had needed to wait until Barber's divorce to his first wife, the exotic-looking Brazilian girl, Naida Q. Lane, whom he had married at Hendon five years earlier, had come through. Female readers will doubtless be interested to learn that Ottilie wore a royal blue suit with white accessories and carried a dozen red roses, while Chris wore a "dark" suit. Ottilie's sister Jessie was Chief Bridesmaid, whilst Pat Halcox, never far from Barber's side for so many years, was appropriately the Best Man. Ottilie's father came over from Ulster, whilst also in attendance was her brother Joseph, at that time Lecturer in Technology at Birmingham University.

The wedding was to have been a quiet affair, so there was no media build-up. Press announcements appeared just the day before in the *Belfast Telegraph* (of course), *The Daily Mirror*, *The Daily Express* and *The Daily Mail*. The couple themselves dashed from a gig at the Marquee Club the night before the wedding to make the announcement on AR-TV's *Late Extra*, leaving saxophonist Wally Fawkes to deputise for Chris in the front line. So the press were there in Paddington in force. Even the BBC got wind of it, publicising it in their 5.30 p.m. news bulletin, though the newscaster went on to comment that only a few passers by witnessed the event.

Hell hath no fury like a pressman scorned, and so the *paparazzi* took revenge for having been kept in the dark until the last minute by publishing some rather strange and inaccurate accounts of the day. One such account told of them being pursued by angry fans shouting "squares" at them (the mind boggles at what those fans would shout today!) Mr. & Mrs. Barber were at pains to deny the charge of deliberately snubbing the fans, indicating that in no way did they wish to avoid them. It was, they said, the press they wished to avoid, a not unreasonable idea in itself, although considering Barber's natural predilection for publicity, even that explanation must be accepted with caution.

The *Daily Mail* ends its report of the matrimonial proceeding by stating that "there will be no time for a honeymoon, as the couple are both appearing tomorrow", whilst all the reports are at pains to point out that the wedding took place on the Thursday because it was the band's only day free of engagements. Hindsight is a wonderful thing, that none of us possess of course. With hindsight Ottilie might have taken the fact that the pressure of Band Business ruled out the perfectly normal experience of a honeymoon represented a warning sign of what was to come throughout the coming years of their marriage. Even then it was clear what the priorities were. But love is indeed blind, and the still starstruck and much in love Ottilie simple accepted that "the band first, everything else second" was the natural order of things. She would in time come to see things very differently.

Significant Early Recordings

Not only would Ottilie become a regular feature of Barber concerts, she would also go on to become a regular feature of Barber's early recordings. Amongst these the most significant were: 1955 *Chris Barber Plays:* Ottilie sings *Ugly Child* and *Careless Love.* 1955 *Echoes of Harlem:* Ottilie sings *I can't give you anything but love* and *New St. Louis Blues. When the Saints go Marching in* and *Just a Closer Walk with Thee* featured on *Chris Barber Plays, Volume 4.* On the live LP *Chris Barber in Concert, Volume 2,* issued in 1957 Ottilie sings *Lonesome Road* and *Moonshine Man.* On the 1958 live recording, *Chris Barber in Concert, Volume 3:* Ottilie sings *Georgia Grind, Careless Love* and *Strange Things Happen Every Day.* 1959 Finally, in the classic Deutschlandhalle Concert recorded on *Barber in Berlin (1960):* Ottilie sings *Easy, Easy Baby.*[40]

As well as appearing as a bit-part artist on the Barber Band recordings, Ottilie would in this period make the first of what would be highly significant recordings in her own right. The first such project came in the issue of two EP s, *That Patterson Girl* in 1956 and *That Patterson Girl, Volume 2* the following

---

[40] See Discography, Appendix One, for full details.

year.

A significant step forward then came in 1961 with the release of the *Chris Barber Blues Book, Volume 1,* which featured Ottilie on all 12 tracks, though the title still read the *Chris Barber* Blues Book.

Ottilie's Irish Night

Some comedian once said that there were no Irish people left in Ireland - they were all abroad, singing about it! Ottilie admits that while that statement is not completely true it is not away far from the truth, as after four years with the Barber Band she began to feel the pull of the "auld country". She had the irrepressible urge to forget Jazz and city life for a while and have the pleasure of singing a few of the old songs that all Irish people like to sing when they get together (with suitable liquid refreshment of course).

Ottilie showed her versatility therefore in departing from "straight" Blues singing in the 1959 recording of *Ottilie's Irish Night,* featuring many popular Irish favourites, including *Hello Patsy Fagan, Captain Fisher, The Magpie, The Ol' Man from Killyburn Brae, The Old Llamas Fair, Eileen O'Grady, Let Him Go, Let Him Tarry, The Enniskillen Dragoon,* as well as a number of instrumentals.[41]

To help her put the project together she recruited George Boyd, an old friend from back in Newtownards, who in turn recruited Holywood musicians Norman Connor (drums) and Martin Fitzsimmons (accordion). Ottilie recalls that she had taken them on trust from George, and had never previously heard them play. However, just a few notes were sufficient to persuade her that George had come through and provided two excellent musicians for her.

The next step was to persuade Denis Preston, Ottilie's Recording Manager, to sanction the project. He agreed, or as Ottilie put it "capitulated" under the weight of her enthusiasm (who wouldn't), and duly set things up.

The original intention was to record Ottilie's bare vocals with minimal accompaniment from Norman and Martin. However, hardly had they got started when Ottilie realised it was not enough and didn't capture the right atmosphere. A few phone calls later other Irish friends had been enlisted until a motley crowd of assorted Irishmen had been formed and, after suitable lubrication, a genuine Irish night could be created.

What followed was, in Ottilie's own words, "two hours of madness", the disc

---

[41] Bielderman & Purser, 30

being full of organised spontaneity. There is no motley crowd quite like a motley crowd of Irishmen! There were no takes and re-takes. So voices heard singing out of tune were left on the recording rather than faded out. In similar fashion much hilarity and "Irish rowdyism" was left on.

Long John Baldry and Rod Stewart

Although undoubtedly Ottilie felt most at home singing the Blues, the above examples serve to show that she was not afraid to break new ground. In March 1964 some unissued recordings were made with 6' 7" Long John Baldry, with a young Rod Stewart on harmonica and vocals. Numbers recorded included *Up Above My Head* and *I Got My Mojo Working.*[42] According to Ottilie this was a Marquee Club event which someone put together and then surreptitiously taped. She recalls the three of them singing around the microphone on *Up Above My Head* with Rod Stewart singing with "the voice of an angel". However a hand-written note from Ottilie made some years later proclaims that she "wouldn't want to hear it now!"

Ottilie is Re-issued and made available to a new public

The advent of the CD format made possible to consolidate a number of Ottilie's significant recordings into a small number of discs. Accordingly Lake issued two major CDs, *That Patterson Girl,* made up of the two Nixa EP s of that title, supplemented with other material, and *The Blues Book and Beyond,* an augmentation of several earlier recordings.

The warm reception given to these new issues shows that Ottilie is today far from forgotten, years after she ceased performing.

One CD reviewer writes

> This outstanding CD presents the opportunity to get the outstanding Ottilie Patterson as centre stage and wallow in one and three quarter hours of outstanding bliss.[43]

Of the *Blues Book and Beyond* CD a reviewer writes

---

[42] See Appendix, 206
[43] Amazon customer review.

The content of this album both endorses Ottilie Patterson's love of the Blues and also confirms her ability to frictionlessly shift to other genres - it is brilliant.

And yet another says

She is remembered with much affection by the fans. It is not simply nostalgia: she chose a notoriously difficult genre and yet sings Blues more convincingly by far than any other of her generation.

Significant though these recordings were, Ottilie would confess that studio recording was far from being one of her favourite pastimes. What she considered the artificiality of the recording studio, with its comprehensive sound-proofing, so comprehensive that she couldn't hear her own voice, was something she grew to hate, at least until they invented new systems providing foldback, whereby you *could* hear yourself as you sang.

The popularity of Ottilie's recordings, both then and now, showed that she was far from being merely a decorative asset to the Barber Band, but was in fact a fine artiste in her own right. She was beginning to live up to and exceed the hype that had surrounded her after that historic debut at the Royal Festival Hall.

America beckons

Just as the Starship Enterprise had been commissioned to boldly go where others had hesitated to go, so the Barber Band set its eyes on the "Final Frontier", at least as far as British musicians were concerned, the United States. In spite of the daunting logistical challenges involved in such a project, in early 1959 the Chris Barber Band with Ottilie Patterson embarked on the first of what would be a series of six major tours of North America.

There is a commonly accepted logic in the idea that if anyone makes it big in Britain, especially in the entertainment world, they must then set out to conquer the USA. The idea was that a British artiste had not really made it unless and until he or she had conquered America. For some artistes, like the Beatles, this strategy worked, whereas for others such as Sir Cliff Richard it (on his own admission) signally failed. But entertainer after entertainer would accept as a basic principle of life that America *has* to be conquered, simply because it is *there*. The fact that a lot of money also happens to be there in America is of course entirely co-incidental. So off to the USA went the Barber Band.

In their new American adventure they were aided by a wonderful piece of good fortune. The 1956 Monty Sunshine recording of Bechet's *Petite Fleur* had been a huge success on both sides of the Atlantic. When they arrived in America therefore, they were not unknowns. They were the band that had produced *Petite Fleur*. Consequently agents and bookers were falling over themselves to book the band on the strength of that record alone.

The tour was a great success. In 40 days they covered 81,000 American miles, with a momentum that the Melody Maker described as "barnstorming". Chris commented, with not a little surprise, that American audiences proved to be pretty much like British audiences in their enthusiasm for their music, and had received them warmly everywhere they went.

Going to the USA would be every jazz musician's dream, not only because it gives the opportunity to play before American audiences, but because of the opportunity it gave to listen to American musicians at first hand. For Chris and the Band "must see" artists included Clarence Williams, Fats Domino and Ray Charles.

The success of this first American tour quickly led to the second, in September 1959. They were booked to play in the prestigious Monterey Jazz Festival on October 2nd, as well as at a number of Californian Colleges.

In case you might be tempted to think of touring the States with a jazz band to be all glory and glamour, it might be as well to read what Chris himself wrote in his travel diary for this second tour:

On our arrival in New York I was surprised to find that our American Road Manager, Dick Turchen, had hired two 1959 Chevrolet Brookwood Estate Cars, one blue and one white, for the duration of our stay. During our previous trip in February he had bought and subsequently sold a Ford and borrowed a 1952 Pontiac Straight Eight. This time we had the use of two absolutely up to date vehicles, with power steering, automatic transmission, radios and heaters (one even had power brakes) for $70 a week, with no mileage charge. Both cars were vast by English standards, but were by no means too big, as we needed every inch of space to accommodate the six members of the band and all their instruments, plus Ottilie Patterson our singer, our road assistants Keith Lightbody, Dick Teuchen himself, and Harold Pendleton, Executive Secretary of the National Jazz Federation, who was responsible for the whole tour.

The double bass is always a problem, but we put it in the back of one of the Chevrolets, with the neck overhanging the rear seat. This meant there could be only two passengers in the back and three in the front, whereas we normally found three in the back and two in the front more convenient.[44]

The itinerary for the tour, to be followed in these cramped conditions, reads like a North American Travelogue: New York - Hamilton, Ontario - New York - Monterey, California - Stillwater, Oklahoma - Iowa - Wisconsin - Minneapolis - Chicago - Austin - Dallas - Chicago - Cincinnati - Indianapolis - New Orleans - Toronto - Buffalo - New York - Pittsburgh - Hamilton - Springfield - San Francisco - Las Vegas - The Grand Canyon - Kansas City - New Orleans again.   All in 6 weeks. Never let it be said that jazz musicians do not suffer for their art!

One of the highlights of this second tour was the concert in New Orleans' Municipal Hall, at which Chris was made an Honorary Citizen of New Orleans.

New Orleans legend Edmond Souchon writes that the 3,500 audience at the event didn't care whether the style was New Orleans, Dixieland, Chicago or New York. They heard music that was good and said so loud and long with the palms of their hands.

For Souchon one of the highlights was the appearance of Ottilie Patterson.

Little Ottilie Patterson was an atom of surprise for which the audience was totally unprepared. Appearing late in the programme, she had to follow Paul Barbarin's great discovery, Blanche Thomas. Blanche had already knocked the audience into the proverbial loop. Then along came Ottilie. She rocked the Municipal Auditorium to its rafters![45]

---

[44]   *On the Band Wagon,* from *The North American Tour of 1959,* printed on the Chris Barber website.
[45]   *Jazz Journal* (February, 1986). Found in the Barber-Purser archives.

The context of Souchon's comments would appear to be whispers he has heard from British jazz fans and the British jazz media about the direction of the Barber band and the dreaded accusation of "commercialism" that dogged them in this period. So he goes on to make this appeal:

> Why cannot British jazz fans wake up to the wonderful jazzmen they have in their midst and, instead of calling them names, call them to their hearts. They have won ours.

Praise indeed from someone based at the home of jazz.

In a recent Radio Ulster interview, the then Band Manager, Harold Pendleton, suggests that the American welcome for the Barber Band while undoubtedly warm, owed as much to curiosity as intrinsic quality.[46] America after all had plenty of Dixieland Bands, all of which were on a par with the Barber outfit. It was the fact that the Barber Band were Limeys, not supposed to be able to play good jazz, that was the attraction for American audiences. In that respect their curiosity was satisfied. But the Barber Band found that winning over American audiences was every bit as difficult as had other British bands had discovered.

Ottilie Patterson was the exception. Everywhere she sang she was greeted with warmth, enthusiasm - and amazement. "You sing just like one of us" was a compliment from a Negro lady in Chicago that she treasured most among the many compliments she received in the course of her career.

A Love Affair

On her first arrival in America it was for Ottilie love at first sight. In her younger days she admitted to having been, like many people, bigoted and prejudiced about the "Yanks". Overpaid, oversexed and over here - we all recall the slogans.

When she arrived she found all her preconceptions well wide of the mark. In her own words she says

> We went by sea, and when the boat docked we went into the building where the customs benches were. I lifted my trunk at the Customs

---

46 BBC Radio Ulster, 19th August, 2012.

Officer, to be greeted by "Hallo, funny face!" I thought. I love this place. When I told others what he had said they replied "what a terrible thing to say." I didn't, I thought it was lovely.

The Americans were much more extrovert than over here, and were really interested to get to know you.

In email correspondence with American writer Scott Yanow Ottilie recalls that all the Big Moments in her life were in America between 1959-1962. Amongst them she includes the appearance with the Band at the Monterey Jazz Festival in 1959; being on the Bill at the Hollywood Bowl with Basie, Armstrong and the celebrated Firehouse Five; the concert at the Municipal Auditorium in New Orleans, in 1959; President Kennedy's 1962 Washington Jazz Festival with Duke Ellington, Dave Brubeck and Gerry Mulligan on the bill, along with great Gospel groups, such as Marion Williams and the Stars of Faith, and what she described as the "utterly marvellous" Staples Singers. Ottilie recalls having missed the chance of a lifetime by merely stammering "I couldn't, I couldn't" when the Staples Singers asked her to record with them, an example of how, beneath the brash, Irish exterior was someone battling with a genuine self-confidence deficit.

On the same tour they played a concert at the Washington Coliseum, with 8,000 in attendance. Chris describes it as "Ottilie's Day" and celebrates the fact that Ottilie got a bigger reception than everyone except Duke Ellington himself, quite an achievement when you consider that Dave Brubeck, Slide Hampton, George Shearing and Tubby Hayes were also taking part.[47]

The unquestioned highlight of Ottilie's time in America was the encounter with Muddy Watwers at Smitty's Corner, a bar/club on the corner of 35th Street and Indiana Avenue, Chicago. Ottilie recalls how, whilst sitting at a table, listening to Muddy's thrilling Blues Band, she was rocked to her socks when Muddy announced, "And here's a little girl from the State of England.......she really know how to sing the Blues", promptly inviting her up to sing! Terrified beyond belief, Ottilie tottered across to the rostrum and, after a brief conference with the musicians, sang a couple of numbers, Big Bill's *Lowland Blues* and Handy's *Careless Love*.

Ottilie afterwards confessed, "I never felt so honoured and accepted in all

---

[47] *Melody Maker*, June 9th, 1962.

my life, especially when, as I went back to my seat, a lady grabbed me by the arm and said, 'lady, how come you sing like one of us?'" Smitty's Corner was in a poor part of Chicago, in what amounted to a black ghetto, so to be described as "one of us" meant that Ottilie had truly identified herself with the poor and underprivileged black people from within whom the Blues had originated. As a Blues singer, Ottilie had truly arrived.

At Muddy's request she went on to sing with him at other venues, such as McKie's DJ Lounge in Chicago, and the Tay May Club in Gary, Indiana. On some promotional photographs taken in Muddy's home, a photograph of Ottilie is seen taking pride of place on the mantelpiece.

Chris and Ottilie were privileged to stay at Muddy's home from time to time, and spend time with him and some of his musical friends. Through this hospitality she met James Oden (St. Louis Jimmy) and Little Walter, amongst many others.

Ottilie recalls the times spent with Muddy and his friends as some of the happiest days of her life. In a note to Scott Yanow, she writes

> I recently saw a photograph of Smitty's Corner. As I looked at
> it memories overwhelmed me, and tears began to flow.

The American tours, while successful in their own right, were decisive moments also for the Barber Band. They had scaled new peaks. The drive for success had taken on whole new dimensions and gathered a whole new impetus. Things would never be the same. Certainly no-one could go through such a moving experience as touring the USA without being changed. It's that kind of country!

Among the discernible lasting effects on the Band was the importing of American elements into the Barber style. The contact with Muddy Waters led Chris to import elements of the Chicago Blues style into his Band's style to the point where it became virtually a predilection. Whilst Mississippi/Louisiana blues numbers still remained within the Barber repertoire, numbers based on the Chicago style began to creep in more and more and become the norm.

This renewed drive for success was not entirely welcomed and would inevitably have its casualties. The most prominent of these would be clarinettist Monty Sunshine, one of the founder members of the professional Band, back in 1954. In time Ottilie herself would follow.

The End of the Trad Boom

The early 1960's saw the collapse of what had come to be styled as "The Trad Boom", a title disavowed by many serious jazz musicians, not least by Chris Barber himself.   In that period large concert halls had been regularly filled by New Orleans-style bands, and individual recordings like *Petite Fleur* (Monty Sunshine), *Midnight in Moscow* (Kenny Ball) and *That's my Home* (Acker Bilk) had soared up the Hit Parade.

Why it came to end is a matter of continuing debate. Reports in the press and in other places would often throw in ideas about scruffy-looking jazz musicians, uncomfortable clubs, poor musical quality and so on. None of these to my mind are adequate explanations.

What is perhaps nearer the mark is the emergence of jazz fans out of a musical ghetto, largely through increasing exposure to American musicians, and the consequent realisation that there was good music being produced by artistes in other musical spheres related to jazz to one degree or another.

On a larger scale, people sometimes talk loosely about the advent of the Beatles as the thing that killed off traditional jazz as a mass movement. Rarely are things as simple as that. If you study the history of the famous Liverpool Cavern Club, the legendary home of the Beatles, you will find (to your surprise perhaps) that it started its days as a *jazz* club, and that all the leading jazz figures played there.   The Beatles themselves started as The Quarrymen, a skiffle/rock outfit, and freely acknowledged their debt to people like Lonnie Donegan. It is not the case therefore that Beatlemania left jazz behind, but that in a very real sense *it took jazz with it*, as the root of much of what the Beatles and others did.   The Beatles did not kill jazz - they absorbed it into a new musical style, recognising the inbuilt flexibility jazz has had since its inception.

This cross-fertilisation is seen even more clearly in the music of the Rolling Stones, an R&B combo in every way that built a very firm bridge between jazz and rock. So rooted in the Blues were they that they brought Muddy Waters out of the jazz enclave to international recognition. Indeed Muddy's song *Rollin Stone* gave the band its name.

The increasing flow of American Jazz Artistes into Britain, as the Musicians Union became slightly more flexible in its approach, had irreversibly opened a floodgate of diverse musical ideas, and set trends in motion that could not be reversed. Barber himself, with his sponsorship of UK tours for American artistes, was partly instrumental in throwing open the stable door.

The musical tide was flowing strongly, and, like all floods, it swept people away, as well as bringing in others. The punters now had an infinitely wider choice of music than they had enjoyed previously. Feeling the strength of the tide, it was no longer easy for traditional jazz bands, even top bands such as the Barber band, to fill the large concert halls, and the move from the Concert Halls to clubs and other smaller venues began.

Like all forms of history, musical history often repeats itself, so that it may simply be the case that, in the natural way of things, a musical movement had run its course, as many had done previously.

As far back as 1961, at the height of the Trad Boom, *Jazz Journal's* Philip Allen questions whether "Trad" was sufficiently rooted as to have made any significant impression on jazz as a whole.

> While it may be that the present fashion for this music (trad) will pass without its having made any impact on the development of jazz as a whole, it is difficult to see how this music can be written off as "not jazz".[48]

Allen raises an important point, one that provokes very different opinions. What can be said with some certainty is that the flirtation with the Hit Parade (although very few trad pieces actually made it to the *very* top)[49], did make this form of the music vulnerable to the variable and changing winds of musical fashion, winds that eventually left it behind.

It was time for jazz musicians to move on. To their credit, Chris Barber, Ottilie Patterson and most of rest did.

Electric Guitars in the Band

Barber is credited with being ahead of the game, and with ensuring the Band stayed at the top (or near the top) by introducing John Slaughter into the Band as his Electric Guitar Blues player. Ottilie would no doubt have been delighted to see Ulsterman Johnny McCallum supplement Slaughter on guitar, as she would have been when Donaghadee's Jackie Flavelle came in

---

[48] *Jazz Journal,* February 1961.
[49] Tunes like *Petite Fleur* and Kenny Ball's *Midnight in Moscow* being notable exceptions.

later on Bass and Bass Guitar.

It was not of course the first time electric guitars had been seen with the Barber Band, Sister Rosetta in 1957 and Muddy Waters in 1958 having used them to great effect on their tours. What was different now was the introduction of the amplified guitar as a regular part of the Barber line up.

If this move were designed to maintain the Barber Band's popularity amongst the guitar-dominated new musical trends, it didn't initially work, as jazz traditionalists saw it as a sell-out to commercialism and an abrogation of all that was good in that musical tradition. John Slaughter was actually booed in his early performances with the band, just because he was there with his amplifier rather than for the quality of his playing.

This (new) experience for the Band contradicts the superficial idea that the electric guitar was brought in to increase their appeal at a time when guitars were the fashion appearing everywhere.[50]

"Keeping ahead of the game" *may* have been Barber's motivation in all these innovations, but it just as easily have been his way of giving expression to the musical ideas he had been inspired to develop by his contact with Muddy Waters. It marked a new stage in the direction of development the Band wished to go anyway, irrespective of what was happening in the Beatles-Rolling Stones-inspired pop world outside.

Banjo and Guitar player Johnny McCallum points out that the combination of banjo and guitar in a jazz band was not in fact all that novel, and that Duke Ellington amongst others had used such a combination in his orchestras. It would not be surprising and unnatural therefore for Barber, a great Ellington devotee, to follow along the Duke's road. Whatever the motivation, it re-ignited the relentless debate over "commercialism", that provided the conversation topic for many a bar at jazz concerts. Commercialism was an allegation that dogged Barber all through those early years of the Band's life.

There is not room to fully debate the issue here. What it is worth saying is that most of us would agree that there is no point in jazz musicians playing music no one wants to listen to or to buy on record! I am not particularly turned on by the sight of Miles Davis (superb trumpeter though he was)

---

[50] I very clearly recall how churches climbed onto this particular bandwagon, spawning coffee bars and guitars in the process. Mind you, as a Lonnie Donegan inspired guitarist myself, I was all for it!

crouched over in the corner of the stage, microphone clipped to his trumpet bell, with his back to the audience. To perform this way is a sure way of killing jazz off completely for all except the aficionados. At the same time, it is important to keep in touch with the musical roots and not sacrifice them in the quest for temporary success and glory.

Those musical roots also embrace the question of the social function of jazz. Some readers may be surprised at the very suggestion that jazz *has* a function in the development of society. In its inception in New Orleans however it certainly did. Jazz was born into very singular situation in the Crescent City, one in which increasingly severe Segregation Laws were causing great social upheavals and threatening the aspirations of the recently emancipated black population. In that context jazz emerged as a very definitely subversive music, enabling young blacks to establish their identity and meet those aspirations.[51] Jazz provided an adhesive that bound musicians of all colours and backgrounds together in spite of the repressive laws. Those laws might restrict what was done out on the streets or in the concert halls, but it could not prevent things happening in back rooms or cellars. And you can't segregate *sound* anyway. If two bands are playing in the same locality, you can't prevent them listening to each other!

So the emerging music offered a way of indirectly breaking down social taboos and also giving black men and women the opportunity to make their way in the world and excel in one department at least. Had this incendiary social mix not been there, it is genuinely questionable whether jazz would ever have emerged.   Its tendency to flout social and political convention is what makes it what it is. It is so much more than mere entertainment. It is counter cultural in its very essence.

It is always going to be a problem transplanting this music from the social context that gave it its birth and character and placing it in another. Can you do that without depriving it of that essential character?   Perhaps that question lies at the root of the split between Barber and Colyer.   Ken might perhaps answer "no" to that, whilst Chris would see jazz as having wider horizons.

Commercialism *per se* will destroy jazz, for it will tear it from its social roots.

---

[51]   This issue is explored in detail in: C.Hersch, *Subversive Sounds:Race and the Birth of Jazz in New Orleans* (Chicago: University of Chicago Press, 2009).

The notion of jazz musicians and composers being observers of and commentators on society must not be lost. Social comment must not be left to the Punk Rockers and their descendants.

Different readers will have different opinions on this. Some will argue that music is music and not social commentary. Others will feel, like me, that listeners must feel that the music to which they listen has relevance to their everyday lives.

My own view, for what it is worth, is that Chris Barber, whilst undoubtedly having one eye on remaining within the public's attention, cannot fairly be accused at that time of cutting cut himself off in the process from his musical roots in New Orleans. Until relatively recently his repertoire would include a whole bunch of New Orleans tunes, not least in his *Bourbon Street Parade* signature tune, a tune that in itself conjures up the colourful traditions of the French Quarter of the Crescent City. Whether the same can be said for his current Big Band, with its obsession with Ellingtonia, is another question altogether, and one to be discussed on some future occasion.

It is worth paying tribute to Ottilie in this context that, apart from occasional divergences, her concert repertoire with the Band was Blues, Blues, Blues. When she did other things, such as performing Irish songs or setting Shakespeare to music, it was often outside the Barber Band setting. She remained true to her self-attribution as a Blues singer, rather than a Jazz singer. The provenance of the music was everything to her.

Monty Sunshine Departs

The transition to electrification was not however without its dissenters and its casualties. The most significant of these by far was clarinettist Monty Sunshine. Monty, recruited from the Crane River Jazz Band, had been a founder member of the Barber Band, back in 1954.

He did see electrification as a move away from the Band's musical roots, in one interview describing the Band as "the poor man's Shadows".[52] The *Daily Telegraph* obituary says that this remark led to him being "fired". The *Melody Maker* reports Monty confirming this, saying furthermore that he did not know the reason for his summary dismissal.[53] If this in fact were the

---

[52] *Daily Telegraph* Obituary.
[53] "Why was I fired ? - Monty Sunshine" headline in *Melody Maker*, January 7, 1961.

case then my natural reaction is one of great sadness, for to my personal ear Monty had played such a key role in the Barber Band's rise to the top. On some of those earlier recordings, particularly the live ones, Monty is *to my ear* sensational, and his inventive and lively playing stands out.[54]

We never fully know what goes on behind the scenes on these occasions, and are often left to guess at the move and counter move involved in leading to these conclusions. It is for example not as simple as saying that Monty didn't like the electric guitar. He had coped very well for example with both Sister Rosetta and Muddy Waters. It had much more to do with musical aspirations in general.

In one real sense Monty's departure was a watershed. Under the ever-increasing pressures of a crowded and highly competitive musical world it was no longer realistic (if indeed it ever had been) to run the Band as a co-operative. However lofty and noble the ideal, the harsh realities of popular music were against it. With Monty Sunshine's departure it was decently buried.

In a less emotional and more reflective mood, Monty would say that the new Barber style was "simply not my music", and that therefore a parting of the ways was inevitable. Certainly there does not appear to have been any lingering acrimony. The Barber/Sunshine relationship did not break down completely by any means, and Monty would reappear in several successful Reunion Tours.

As well as the touch of class Monty gave to the Band's music, Monty is generally credited with being the one that sharpened up the band's visual appeal, not surprising for someone who, like Ottilie, had significant artistic ability. He got the Band out of casual clothes, so characteristic of pokey jazz clubs, into smart suits suitable for the stages of major Concert Halls. So he was not averse to sharp visual presentation as a way of selling the band. He just feared that the sort of things associated with electrification might creep in and spoil the music, which he saw as the reason for the Band's existence.

Another point that had niggled Monty was the huge success of *Petite Fleur* on both sides of the Atlantic. And yet the credits on the label were to "The Chris Barber Band", with no mention of Monty. Newspaper reports

---

[54] As one person commented to me, on the live recordings it could be because Monty was nearer the recording microphone than the other front line players!

concerning Barber would routinely refer to *"his* recording of *Petite Fleur"*.[55] In fact Barber himself did not feature on the recording at all, the bass being played by Dick Smith, guitar by Dick Bishop, with Ron Bowden on drums. In spite of this, none of the royalties from the massive sales of the recording (2.5 million) went to Monty, the solo performer. All he received was the normal session fee for the recording.

The tune's composer, Sidney Bechet, on the other hand, made an absolute fortune on the back of Monty's efforts. To be fair to Bechet, he did send a telegram to Monty thanking him for what he had done with his tune, though I guess Monty would have regarded this as scant consolation!

This was in fact not the first time that this particular issue had arisen within the Barber Band. The 1954 recording of *Rock Island Line* that was an astounding success, earned singer Lonnie Donegan great fame, and launched him secularly on a solo career. What it didn't do was make him rich, Lonnie receiving only the Session Musician's fee of £3.50, for what was admittedly a surprising chart success. As his widow said, as she prepared material for his posthumous biography, it was something that rankled with Lonnie all his life and left a bitter taste in his mouth.

But then the history of jazz itself is characterised by a rather loose and casual approach to the issues of copyright, credits and performing rights. As far back as 1917 there was the celebrated argument between Joe Jordan, writer of *That Teasin Rag,* and Nick LaRocca, who included the piece as the third strain in his Band's arrangement of the *Original Dixeland One Step.* Clarence Williams, in his New York entrepreneurial days, made a fortune out of garnering the rights for a number of pieces the original writers and performers had "forgotten" to copyright. No less a person than Bessie Smith herself was one of the artistes said to have been on the receiving end of Williams' sharp business practices.

What could not be taken away from Monty Sunshine however, was the fame and acclamation that *Petite Fleur* had earned him, something that gave him ready audiences and great success when he formed his own band. A further Barber connection was made when Monty persuaded Nick Nicholls, drummer for the ex-Barber Band's Lonnie Donegan to join him in his new band. This new band went on to great success, particularly in Germany,

---

[55] e.g. *Belfast Telegraph,* 11 November, 1959.

where his albums sold well for many years. Monty discovered there really was life after Barber!

On the other hand, any doubts that the Barber Band would survive without Monty Sunshine were quickly dispelled with the arrival of a more than capable deputy in Ian Wheeler, formerly of the Ken Colyer Band. He added further to the diversity of the Barber Band's instrumentation by bringing with him the alto sax, something which, unlike the electric guitar, had a long pedigree in jazz history.

In these transitional years other stalwarts of the band in front of whom Ottilie had done her early singing also moved on.

Banjo player *Eddie Smith* did not last long at all after John Slaughter - inspired electrification entered the Band. He moved on just four months after Slaughter's debut. Although Eddie maintained a link with Monty Sunshine, apparently even working for a time as Monty's driver, and although he not infrequently sat in with a number of bands, he never again joined a band on a regular basis. Indeed, he would have spells when he would not play at all. One of his friends from the printing industry speaks of him standing his banjo in the corner and stoically refusing to play. Eventually he went to live in Majorca, where he died, somewhat unexpectedly, in 1992.

Bassist *Dick Smith* (no relation), one of the few musicians who had had the distinction of playing with both the Colyer and Barber bands, also moved on. He became frustrated at the amount of time he was having to spend away from his wife and three children because of the demands of touring. He says that whenever he returned home from tour he found the dog biting him and licking the postman! Dick and Kay moved out of jazz altogether, and spent the next 40 years as hoteliers, living now quietly in retirement in Minehead, Somerset.

Interestingly enough, one of Dick's successors on Bass, Ulsterman *Jackie Flavelle*, left the Band in 1977 for similar domestic reasons. He recalls coming to the end of a tour and seeing the other Band members get on a plane for London, whilst he took the plane to Belfast instead. At time of writing Jackie is back with Barber, playing in the Chris Barber Big Band.

Graham Burbridge, a gun enthusiast whose claim to fame, alongside playing drums, was the ability to outdraw Wyatt Earp, went out of the revolving door, to be replaced by Peter York, as he had originally come in to replace

Ron Bowden. Apparently Graham never played at all after leaving Barber.[56]
If there were significant exits from the band in this period, then there were
significant arrivals also, the most significant of which was the addition to the
establishment of the band in the arrival of a second reed player, John
Crocker, in 1968. He was to stay with the Band for some 30 years.

Crocker's longevity in the Band underlined the interesting fact that, in the
period up to the formation of the Barber Big Band in 2001, the Barber back
line had undergone many changes, whilst the front line in contrast had
stayed remarkably stable, Messrs. Crocker, Wheeler, Halcox and Barber
remaining fixtures throughout that period.

So the band to which Ottilie returned after her initial break, would begin to
take on a distinctively new look as the sixties progressed, with familiar faces
missing and new faces present. What never changed was Ottilie's ability to
"electrify" audiences with her performances (excuse the pun) and maintain
the demand for listening to the Band.

In time Monty Sunshine would by no means prove to be the last casualty of
the relentless drive for success that motivated the Chris Barber Band. This
drive would eventually wash away Ottilie herself.

---

[56] You never know when the ability to outdraw Wyatt Earp will come in handy!

Ottilie at 16 months

Thomas Andrews of Comber

Designer of the Titanic

Teenage Ottilie

Kilbroney House, Rostrevor

Barnes Crescent, Ayr

Roxelle Holm Farm, Ayr

Ottilie and the Early Barber Band, 1955

Albert Watt   *The incomparable Bessie Smith*

Ottilie puts George Melly through his paces

Rocking the Gospel with Sister Rosetta Tharpe

Big Bill Broonzy, sketched by Ottilie

Smitty's Corner, Chicago

A Happy Picture, 1966

Ottilie with Sonny Boy Williamson

I'm a Salty Dog

From the Ottilie Patterson Sketch Book

A smiling Ottilie makes a point

5

EASE ON DOWN THE ROAD

Come on and ease on down, ease on down the road
Come on and ease on down, ease on down the road
Don't you carry nothing that might be a load
Come on, ease on down, ease on down the road

The Wiz

The new life that Ottilie was now leading may well have been exciting, but it was a long way from being idyllic. Amongst many other new experiences, she was introduced to the "joys" of touring, one of a number of things which, as we shall see, she never quite got used to.

For one thing, she was a female in an all-male band in a predominantly all-male musical world. To some extent she'd been prepared for that situation through her association with Jimmy Compton and The Muskrat Ramblers. That however had been student fun, whereas in a professional touring band it was a very different and much more serious business.

A constant problem for Ottilie, being a female cuckoo in an all male nest, was that she felt that she was never felt fully integrated into the band, but was regarded often as an "extra". She thought of the other members of the band as being far removed from her, and was never able to get close to any of them.

One practical consequence of this was that she kept getting forgotten when arrangements were made. In an interview for *Just Jazz* she recounted one particular incident in Nottingham:

> We were up quite early, and needed to get something to eat. The band were gathered at the foot of the stairs at the back door, discussing where to go. Eventually they agreed, and arranged to meet back at the foot of the stairs before going. I was carrying a heavy dress and so I said, "Wait until I've been upstairs and hung this up". I flew up the stairs and back down again, to find they'd all gone. The only person

around was the Hall Keeper. He made the helpful suggestion that maybe they'd gone to the nearby Wellbeck Hotel. So, feeling my way nervously through a strange town, I went on to the Wellbeck, to find the buggers, sorry beggars, stuffing their faces. Pat got up and said, "Sorry, we forgot". At least he didn't make a shuffling apology. I always felt like a Jonah aboard the ship.[57]

In one way her childhood had also prepared her for the privations of touring and the cramped conditions of the tiny hotels in which the Band invariably stayed. Because of two brothers and two sisters living in the Comber cottage, she grew up with the idea of two men sharing a bed as being normal, just as Eric Morecambe and Ernie Wise had done in the bedroom scenes of their TV shows.

The normal concert procedure in those early days at most venues was for Ottilie to sit on stage with everyone else, until called up by Chris to do her song, but at other venues it was different. At places such as the White Hart, in Southall, she tells of sitting in the bar, sipping rum and blackcurrants or something, until someone would come in and say "Ot, it's you, you're on". One evening she sat there all night, until someone came looking for her, to apologise for the fact that she had been forgotten completely!

On another occasion she recalls being left on Crewe Station in the middle of a freezing January, guarding the instrument cases. The idea was that they would all go in for cups of tea, and then one would come out to relieve her. Unfortunately no one did come out, leaving an indignant Ottilie to say to herself "stuff this" and march into the café declaring "your band cases are out there!"

Another very practical problem with which Ottilie had to cope was the wide range of facilities in the equally diverse concert venues in which they played. One aspect of this diversity was the problem of widely varying dressing room facilities. These would vary from a broom cupboard with a mirror to a wonderful carpeted room, complete with bath and shower, at the Usher Hall in Edinburgh. Ottilie recalls jumping into the bath immediately, just so she could say she had taken a bath at the Usher Hall!

More seriously from a professional point of view was the problem of

---

[57] *Just Jazz* Magazine, April 2008.

inadequate P.A. systems. In the days before bands started carting round their own systems, they had to cope with whatever the venue provided. Some systems would be totally unfit for purpose. The worst one she recalls was the Schubert Theatre, Chicago, which had a stage with just one single microphone suspended way above the band's heads. Having searched high and low the realisation eventually dawned on them that this *was* the P.A. system!

Growing increasingly fed up with this experience, Ottilie finally asked husband Chris for a monitor speaker, so that she could hear herself on stage. Her not unreasonable request was met with a firm refusal, followed by a long list of arguments against monitor speakers. The argument grew so intense it almost resulted in divorce there and then, as Ottilie recounts. They went off on holiday to Venice with the fall out from the argument still very much in the air. The disagreement apparently cost Ottilie a romantic ride on a gondola!

A tailpiece to that story is that when Ottilie came back from her enforced layoff with vocal cord trouble, she came back to discover huge monitor speakers as part of the band's standard equipment, something she claimed her husband had not got round to telling her about. Pleasure, surprise and exasperation were there in equal proportions at the discovery.

The great consolation of having to cope with Heath Robinson PA systems and shacks-for-dressing rooms is that there was always the next place. These tatty facilities did not need to be endured for too long. In short order you were following the words of the Wiz and "easing on down the road" to the next special adventure. Ottilie discovered that there was something compelling about always being on the move.

One additional problem Ottilie had to face in those early days was the disparity between the basic vocal sound needed for the Blues and her native Ulster accent. Her Ulster vowels were a constant embarrassment to her, though not really, it must be said, to anyone else. She found them alien to the musical genre within which she was trying to sing. They would not "bend" in the way jazz vowels needed to. As was mentioned earlier, her accent became a subject of friendly teasing from pianist John Lewis, although he accepted it as part of the uniqueness of Ottilie's Blues presentation.

Ottilie's Diary
An extract from a note book kept by Ottilie chronicling a visit to Germany in

1989 gives a flavour of what it was like for her to be on the road, or in the air with the Barber Band.

Tuesday

NW[58] arrived lunchtime. Made his dinner. Washed up, NW no help. Took cat to cattery.

As NW was going down to M & S I asked if he would get my prescription and hair mousse, quoting size for packing and the price of the latter. He came back with too large a size, and had forgotten my prescription altogether.

I spent all morning ironing and packing, before making stew for lunch. I went to have hair done at 1.45 p.m., returning at 3.45 p.m. Put on make up and checked the house was OK. Made a coffee, but then had no time to drink it.

Drove to airport and checked in. I carried my dresses over my shoulder, along with my travel bag. NW asked me to carry one of his bags, as it was lighter than mine. I said I couldn't, because of my inflamed joints and tendons.

The food on the flight to Berlin was poor, both in quality and quantity. KH met us off the flight, but even though we waited ages we couldn't get a taxi. Eventually got to hotel and checked in quickly. I decided then I would go straight to the Phil. with KH. NW ambled in, suggesting we should go later instead. I told him to piss off, as I was in a hurry to go with KH, who had a taxi waiting. KH and I drove off, only to find the taxi driver could not locate the Stage Door. We had to find it on foot instead.

We reach the Café/Bar just in time to see CB dash on stage. This is about 9.30 p.m. I am starving and thirsty by this time. As the bar was about to close I grabbed a glass of water and sat down. KH came along with promoter friends. He is eating something I don't recognise, but then I don't feel like eating anything. I hope Berlin will be open for food after the concert. I played a Steinberg in the dressing room during the second half of the concert. Around midnight we get back to the hotel - there is no food, but KH talks the Chef into feeding us. Very late to bed.

---

[58] Norman Watson, Guitarist and friend from Muskrat Ramblers days, now living in America.

Wednesday

Up at 8.30 a.m., very tired. Slept badly and even engaged in sleep walking. Managed coffee, bread and butter for breakfast, more than I can normally manage. Left the hotel at 11 a.m.

Have problems leaving Berlin as NW only has Visitors' Passport. This causes problems at the Checkpoint. Have to observe DDR speed limits to Brauschweig. After stopping for coffee and the loo we arrive in Eschwege, 250 miles later. The hotel is not serving food until 5.30 p.m., but I was able to get bread and butter and a tuna salad.

After the 6.30 sound check I go to dressing room to do hair and make up. That takes me until 9.15. I go on very nervous but sang well. At the end I am soaked in sweat from the skin outwards. The hair is soaked to the scalp. It is now 10.30, and I have to pack up and go back to the hotel, to go to sleep.

However, when I get to the hotel I find there is a reception on. Twice I nearly fall asleep on my plate. Again it is late when I get to bed, and again I sleep badly, managing only 4 hours broken sleep in all.

Thursday

I awake at 7 a.m., and get up at 8. I am packing until 9.15 a.m. I have breakfast in my room, which consists of coffee and bread. I feel sick, ill and tired.

I take two boiled eggs for the journey, as no one ever wants to stop for lunch. Ate eggs in car at 12.30 p.m. Arrive in Nurnberg at 2.15 p.m. to find all the plans changed. We have to play half an hour earlier than had been planned, and I have to sing earlier still. Hair is a mess, but I am too tired and don't have enough time to do it. I sit at the table where we are playing and cry with exhaustion and hunger.

As I realise our gig is in the restaurant of a department store, I think there may be an opportunity to get my hair done, so I make an appointment for 4 p.m. CB and I manage to share a prawn cocktail and raspberry dessert before this.

My hair do needs 2 hours, but the girl takes me out after only 1½ hours. My hair is soaking wet, so I am snookered. I do my sound check at 6 p.m., still hungry.

I discover there is no dressing room, so I have to use the seamstress's room in the department store. There is just one long mirror and wash basin. No table or anything. The band come in and spread themselves between the sewing room and the band room. They change and eat. I have to take my washing stuff to the staff lavatory and wash and change there.

I have to be ready to go on at 8.50. At 8.30 I am a bundle of nerves, but then am told I am not needed until 9.30 p.m., as times have been changed again. I am dressed by this time and cannot relax. My make up is starting to run with heat and sweat.

On stage I sing two songs, but on the third my legs start to give way. I yell for a chair, but have to get it myself as the band can't stop playing. I go on to do a successful show, after which there are autographs to give. By this time it is 11 p.m., but I can't stop to eat as I need to repack everything. Finally I eat the salad given to me at 6.30 - the first meal of the day. I go back to the hotel but am too tired to remove my make up. Too overtired to sleep. Sleeping tablets don't work. I finally sleep from 4 - 6 a.m.

Friday

I know I can't do another performance tonight. I tell CB I am going to stay in bed, and manage to sleep for another hour or so.

I have to get up however and go out for food, as the hotel only serves breakfast. At 4 p.m. I have my first meal of the day, apart from the bread and butter from the breakfast table I have been carrying round all day.

Asked NW to come to my room at 9 p.m. to take me to the restaurant in the Station so I could get supper. Back at the hotel I pack all my cases and dresses ready for the morning. CB stays until 1.45 a.m. and then goes to his room.

I get fully washed and dressed for the flight next morning before falling asleep on the bed at 3.30 a.m. I wake up at 8 a.m., snatch some coffee, bread and butter and then set off for the airport at 9.30 a.m.

I arrive home at 3.30 p.m., but have to go out shopping to make NW's meal. There are still dishes from last week. NW is not much use. He neither brought my dresses in from the taxi, nor carried them upstairs nor helped in any way. He used my phone for 45 minutes to call long distance. He paid, but then later asked for the money back as he said he hadn't enough to go and see his girlfriend. This reminded me of Nurnberg, where I had to carry my dresses, his coat, my shoulder bag, his duty free and his travel bag - because he was away for a drink.

Ottilie makes her own analysis of a typical day for her on the road:

- Car travel en route to venue - 4½ to 5 hours
- Preparation before concert (hair, make up, sound check, lights etc) - 3 to 3½ hours
- Length of concert (including autographs) - 3 hours
- Re-packing personal gear - 1 to 1½ hours
- Unwinding after performance - 2½ to 3 hours

Total time at work - 14-16 hours, excluding:

- Meal times (if any)
- Personal relaxation
- Shopping for necessities
- Sightseeing

Average sleep for OP - 4 hours

Not very much glamour involved in that account !
Amongst the multitude of jottings that Ottilie left behind was one entitled *King of the Road*, written in 1970 as a tribute to a journey on the M1 :

It's not even an hour since we left,
And we've done twenty-five thousand already;
Though HE says we've come seventy-three
He can't fool me,
Because I know
there's Watford Gap to Doncaster still to go.
And that's nearly eighty five million twenty two thousand and forty two miles at least,
By MY count.
And tomorrow we're playing Inverness - oh my God!

Touring was not all bad for Ottilie of course. Inevitably it had its lighter moments. Two of these came in the one concert at the *Samson and Delilah Ballroom* in Norwich on 2nd October, 1959.
In her diary Ottilie recalls being in a good mood (a rare enough occurrence in those days for her to actually mention it) so that she actually made jokes into

the microphone, one of them announcing "this is the interval number and this is Henry Hall speaking"[59]. She tells how this flew out of her mouth, with full Irish accent, before she could stop it.

She recalls also how, at the same concert, she almost shrieked out with laughter during Monty Sunshine's performance of the Sidney Bechet piece, *Si Tu Vois Ma Mere*. The usual procedure was for Monty to play it once through and then for Chris to join in on an off-stage microphone. Unfortunately the design of the Samson and Delilah did not allow for a mike to be used off stage. Chris therefore had to use the room Ottilie was using as a dressing room, which opened onto the hall half-way down and play from behind a curtain over the heads of the audience. Both he and Ottilie were giggling so much it was a struggle to complete the piece. How amused or otherwise the management were we aren't told.

Nothing Like It
If you were to ask Ottilie what kept her going at this pace, and why she kept on doing it, she would simply reply "because there's nothing like it".

> The music itself is so exciting that it is impossible not to get excited yourself (except when feeling ill or exhausted - and an awful lot of my professional life was lived in a constant state of fatigue. It's a very gruelling life unless you've got an iron constitution, which Chris Barber has, but I don't).
> Being principally a Blues Singer, I regard lyrics as tremendously important, and so my mission and my role is to get them across to that audience out there. The communication of meaning and emotion is of paramount importance in my book.
> Performing music itself is an adventure, especially because of the improvisational requirements of Blues/Jazz. Actually some good improvisations even come into being as a sort of defence against the boredom of singing the same thing for nights on end!
> Although travelling was gruelling as far as I was concerned, there was always the adventure of a different venue every night. What would the hall be like tonight? What would the audience be like tonight? What

---

[59] A noted band leader of the time, for whom "This is Henry Hall speaking" was his catchphrase.

programme should I do? How should I do it?

Unfortunately I have a (very) emotional, nervous temperament (must be the Irish/Latvian mix!) and an hour before each performance I would be strung up really tight, and by the time I was waiting in the wings to go on I would be shaking from head to foot. If anyone tried to give me an encouraging word while waiting there, I would have snapped like a twig - or maybe even have been ready to punch the well-wisher. (I don't think I ever actually *did* - but I certainly felt like it sometimes!)

And the strange thing is, that the bigger and more important the concert hall, and the bigger, more important and frightening the occasion, the more I would, if I were on form, enjoy it all.

The music and the Band excite you, and you excite the Band. It goes back and forth between you, and of course with the audience becoming excited as well. Everyone becomes part of one great thrill.

There really is nothing like it! [60]

Health Problems

Nevertheless, in these years the pace at which the Band worked really was phenomenal. The so-called "decline of trad" had meant that the big concert hall performances were now a thing of the past, so that the band's income and position in the musical world could be maintained only by taking an increased number of smaller engagements. So they played almost every night, 48 weeks a year. Ottilie herself used to comment that they had travelled with the Band a greater distance than the Earth to the Moon.

One published tour of Europe for example, in February 1962, included 11 concerts in 13 nights:

> Feb 15 Hamburg (Germany)
> Feb 16 Lubeck (Germany)
> Feb 18 Copenhagen (Denmark)
> Feb 19 Stockholm (Sweden)
> Feb 21 Veldert (Germany)
> Feb 22 Wuppertal (Germany)
> Feb 23 Krefeld (Germany)

---

[60] Email to Scott Yanow, 24th May, 2004.

Feb 24 Wolfsburg (Germany)
Feb 25 Osnabruck (Germany)
Feb 27 Kessel (Germany)
Feb 28 Hanover (Germany)[61]

Gradually Ottilie, highly strung as she was, began to go down under stress of this workload. The eccentricities resulting from her nervous and emotional nature began to take on disturbing proportions. Sometimes her performances brought forth so many emotions that she would scarcely make the dressing room before bursting into tears. She and the Band would work continuously for 25 evenings at a stretch, most of them on the road. It was evident that the workload had become too much.

And yet the Band schedule was King, and had to be carried out. To her close friends Ottilie confided that there was one occasion when there had been a "cat fight" backstage (sadly we don't know with whom). Ottilie appeared at the side of the stage with blood streaking her face, and her emotions in tatters. And yet she had to go on! No concession could be made to the schedule.

Even the visits to her beloved United States became a bitter-sweet memory for her. It is probably true to say that, because of her love affair with the States, she was able to cope with the pressures of touring there more than she was able to tolerate touring Europe. But even in America, the hectic itinerary and the distances necessarily covered became highly problematical for her.

Pat Halcox, in his account of the Third Tour, in September 1960, describes a journey of 500 miles in one go to Toronto, and another, of 450 miles, to Waverley in one go. He refers to coping with temperature extremes of 80 degrees in Los Angeles and 95 degrees in Las Vegas. Moving constantly from one time zone to another proved an additional problem.

Even that which should have been the highlight of any jazz performer's life, the opportunity to perform in New Orleans itself, turned out to be a nightmare for Ottilie, as she was ill almost all the time in the legendary Crescent City.

Anyone who has been to New Orleans, as I have, will scarcely be amazed at

---

[61] *Jazz News*, February 7, 1962.

this, as the heat and humidity can make it a very challenging place at certain times of the year for any visitor not in the prime of physical condition. I well recall on several occasions not being able to see across the street because of an impenetrable cloud of steam rising in the wake of the daily Louisiana thunderstorm!

It is to Ottilie's great credit that she was able to make the kind of impact even there that she did in spite of this persistently indifferent health.

As Ottilie confesses

> I always tell people I've had more doctors and hospital visits than they've had hot dinners. My doctor had made some phone calls to the States for me, and to other places, and flown my tablets out.
>
> I was sick in Brussels, in Germany more than once - in East as well as West - and been to hospital in Yugoslavia.
>
> The pressures of performing were enormous and quite exhausting. I was ill a lot of the time and had six months off with jaundice. In that period I was back at home, being looked after by my mother and sister.

The seed of what would grow into a major problem in time were there. Through no fault of her own Ottilie was finding it difficult to keep pace with a highly-motivated and fast-moving band. Barber himself admitted that in the nine years leading up to Ottilie's breakdown they had only twice spent more than a week in any single place.[62]   The Barber Band were reaching for the stars and going from success to success, and those who could not keep up were liable to be left behind. As Chris commented to me, it required total commitment to survive the course.[63]

Nervous Breakdown

The obviously increasing stress on Ottilie led Chris to decelerate a bit by taking on fewer engagements, and even cancelling some. But in October 1962 Ottilie had a nervous breakdown and had to take two months rest on doctor's orders. It is interesting to note that as early as 1957, during a European Tour with Sister Rosetta Tharpe, Ottilie had previously been ordered to rest by the

---

[62] *Bucks Advertiser*, October 25, 1963.
[63] In an interview at his home, March 15, 2013.

doctor in similar circumstances.

In an early attempt to begin a diary on which her life-story could eventually be written she recalls how

> 1959 has been a very full and busy year, crowded with interest, but for me at any rate spoiled by my illness, which one would suppose was a nervous collapse, since I have been otherwise sound. I never was able to appreciate fully or to enjoy the circumstances I found myself in, as always I was prevented from full enjoyment by the emotional strain I was under.

She battled on through the thousands of miles travelled by the band until in 1963 it all caught up with her and she caved in. In an interview with the Daily Sketch she says:

> I'm completely shattered. I need my batteries recharging, and that's a fact. After my last appearance this weekend I knew I couldn't carry on. In the long hours travelling with the band I took up knitting to pass the time. But it's no good trying to knit at 90 mph - it comes out all lumpy. I don't want to do my knitting at 90 mph - it's got too much for me.

She goes on to describe how she now looks forward to the simple pleasures of life, including being a housewife.

Then, with a comment that is grossly unfair on herself she declares:

> I brought this breakdown on myself. But I hope that with enough rest I'll be swinging again.......... sometime.

She had endured nine years of an unbroken sequence of one-night stands, of living out of boxes, a sequence that she came to refer to as a "nightmare".[64] No-one could justifiably blame themselves for breaking down under such conditions.

Humphrey Lyttleton, a distinguished journalist of course as well as a legendary trumpet player, sees Ottilie's collapse as a symptom of a deeper

---

[64] *Belfast Telegraph*, 25 October, 1963.

problem in the whole entertainment business:

> Speaking unhappily about the nightmare of touring, singer Ottilie
> Patterson has announced that for the time being she must give up
> singing with husband Chris Barber's band. Another show business
> casualty.
> All along the line it is a case of frayed nerves and exhaustion. And in
> *every* case it is the one night stand that is the villain.
> In the current, crazy show biz world it seems that fame and fortune are
> not enough (after all, the Barber Band is still among the biggest earners
> of the jazz circuit).
> The problem of the one-nighters grows more acute as the years go by
> and the pace of life increases. For youngsters in the first flush of
> success touring can seem like one long rave. But sooner or later the
> traffic jams, the squalid dressing rooms, dingy hotels and unrelieved
> diet take their toll.[65]

The Band's life went on of course, and that same Daily Sketch piece quoted
above informs the readers that the Band would go on their tour of Holland
and Germany without her. Never one to let opportunities slip, Barber had
engaged American Blues singer Curtis Jones to join them in Ottilie's place,
initially at a concert in Bournemouth, and then for the tour.

Vocal Cord Damage
Throughout her singing career Ottilie had been plagued with laryngitis, and
would at times be totally unable to speak. Finally the problem was diagnosed
as stemming from damage to one of the vocal cords, damage that had
brought severe enlargement of the cord.
One of the main features of the Ottilie Patterson voice was its strength,
something acknowledged by friend and critic alike. As Ottilie herself
recognised, this strength and individuality came from singing from her
throat, something that characterised all jazz singers, rather than from her
diaphragm, as classically-trained singers do.
It was one thing to recognise this as a problem, but quite another to do

---

[65]   *Sunday Citizen*, October, 1963.

anything about it. Again it was the pace of life that was the villain of the piece. With all the one night stands there simply had not been time, until now, to take lessons and remedy the problem. She had to practise on her own, with just the mirror for company.

Her only guiding principle had been:

If it hurts, I'm wrong - if it doesn't hurt, I'm OK

What was to be the remedy?   Complete silence for three months! Not only was she not to sing, she was not to speak either!   For a naturally talkative Irish girl this was tantamount to torture.   For Chris however, as for any husband, this could be seen as a dream come true!

To help with this she took to wearing a medallion around her neck, advising to whom it may concern,

Under doctor's orders NOT TO SPEAK

To avoid misunderstanding Ottilie took to wearing it wherever she went. She recalls going into the High Street Butcher's one day, with a writing pad she took with her for communication purposes. On reading of doctor's orders the Butcher took the pad from her and wrote on it "poor old soul".

Ottilie's mother, living with them at the time in Hampstead commented that since Ottilie had stopped speaking the house resembled a mortuary.

Clearly, if Ottilie wanted to carry on singing, then arrangements needed to be made to recruit a singing teacher to enable her to make the stylistic adaptations required to ensure the problem didn't recur. Chris had contacts with someone at Covent Garden (where else) and the necessary arrangements were made.

It was in the course of these lessons that Ottilie made an amazing discovery. She had imagined naturally that her native language was the language of Ulster. But she discovered in fact that her native tongue was actually Latvian, the native language of her mother! Her singing teacher observed that she always sang better and more comfortably in a foreign language.   To encourage this tendency the teacher began to feed her more and more material in French or Italian. Through singing in these other languages there was less strain on Ottilie's voice, and she could actually extend her vocal range from one and a half octaves to more than three octaves.

Ottilie observes that

> When I sing in Latvian there is no strain at all, and it all comes
> naturally. But what a Latvian Bessie Smith would have sounded like
> goodness knows!

Apart from taking her singing lessons and making these discoveries, how did
Ottilie cope with these months of enforced silence? Well, not by sitting back
and doing nothing, that's for sure. That would not have been Ottilie. What
she did was to go back to her artistic roots and take up painting and wood
carving once again.

Again, with characteristic self-deprecation she speaks of starting by painting
a bowl of flowers in oils. "I wanted it to be strong and powerful" she
declared, "but it came out looking like the thing from Outer Space." Several
times she tried to paint Chris, but gave up because he wouldn't sit still for
long enough! Brian McAnoy, long-time friend of Ottilie, describes him as
someone who you never felt was really settled, who was always *Pret a
Manger*, "ready to go".

Down On the Farm

Part of Ottilie's recovery time was spent at the Grange, the Henlow Beauty
Farm. Here she enjoyed a regime of facial massage, hand and foot care, and a
paraffin wax bath. The wax bath does not sound very inviting, but is
apparently very good for the figure (I must remember that).

After ten years of one night stands, Ottilie found the Farm the ideal place to
rest and relax. Unlike the standard image of Health Farms as being all carrot
juice and ice baths, the atmosphere of the Grange was so gentle and relaxing
that Ottilie felt an improvement straight away.

Ottilie found the atmosphere at the Henlow Farm so attractive to her -
"swinging" as she put it - that she chose to spend her time there rather than
going on a Mediterranean Cruise with the Band. Apart from admitting to
being no sailor, it was calm and quiet that she needed at this point in her life,
something a working cruise would have denied her. The Farm offered her
everything she didn't have when she was working, and thus gave her the
energy and resources to cope with what was becoming an increasing strain.

First Comeback

The novelty of resting soon wore off, and the urge to perform began to grip Ottilie once again, although it was fully two years before she was given the all-clear by her specialists to go back on stage.

Appropriately her first comeback performance was in Ulster, in Bangor's Queen's Court Hotel.

When the *Daily Sketch* sought her out she said:

> Inside me there's a knot, and I must let it out - I *must* sing.
>
> Other women tell me I haven't lived because I haven't had children. But they haven't experienced standing on stage and giving out to an audience.
>
> When I finished a song at a recent London concert there was silence for a minute. Then the applause came. Now I want to work and work and work. There's a lot of time to make up.[66]

However, undeniably an important stage had been reached in Ottilie's life. A Rubicon had been crossed. She would never be well enough again to sustain the hectic pace of touring that she had maintained in the days before her health collapsed. John Crocker, who joined the Band in 1968, testifies that in the first few years of his time with the Band he saw very little of Ottilie.

Her performances with the Band were irregular and spasmodic. It became a major art for jazz promoters to coax Ottilie to perform for them. She no longer had to sing for her supper, and being in semi- retirement could pick and choose where she performed.

She could also indulge herself in other things outside the orbit of the Band. Drummer Pete York recalled an evening at Birmingham Town Hall for example, when she topped the bill, appearing with Long John Baldry and the Hoochie Coochie Men (which then included one Rod Stewart). The rest of the programme was made up of the Yard birds (with Eric Clapton), Sonny Boy Williamson and the Spencer Davis Group ![67] For Ottilie to be advertised *above* such people gives an indication of just what status she occupied as a star in

---

[66] *Daily Sketch,* June 23, 1967.
[67] John Service, *Ottilie Patterson, An Obituary,* Barber Website.

those days.

What is not generally known is that Ottilie sang the title track for the 1964 film, *Where has Poor Mickey Gone?*, a film starring Warren Mitchell in his pre-Alf Garnett days, and which had the first major role for John Challis, later to become famous as "Boycie" in *Only Fools and Horses*.

Then, in 1969, Ottilie launched out in a totally different direction with her solo album, *Spring Song,* released by Polydor. In many ways this was as far away from Jazz as it's possible to get. *Spring Song* was a pastiche of disparate texts set to music, with arrangements by Richard Hill. There was for example a swinging version of the *Song of Solomon* from the Old Testament; Helen Waddell's version of Ausonius' elegaics to his young wife, from the 4th century; a famous Latin drinking song from the 13th century; texts from Shakespeare's comedies and his Sonnet n.8, as well as a number of Ottilie's own compositions.

A contemporary European newspaper comments:

> In a time when stereotyped success formulas only too often serve as a poor substitute for truly creative art, it is most rewarding to see an artist display new and unexpected talents which offer fresh possibilities of personal expression. Ottilie Patterson has highly interesting and also amusing things to say and she has found a charming and witty way of her own of saying them. [68]

In spite of all this fulsome praise the album did not sell very well, although Ottilie continued right to the end to regard it as one of her best recordings, one of the few, she would say, of which she was not in later life embarrassed.

In those days of the declining popularity of "Trad" Ottilie never made the transition from the concert hall to the small jazz clubs that many bands were forced to make. She preferred the large concert atmosphere to the up close and personal ethos of the jazz club. Besides, for anyone not in the peak of health, jazz clubs could be very unhealthy, smoke-filled places, as was discovered so tragically by entertainer and non smoker Roy Castle. I can recall seeing the Barber Band perform at Birch Hall Hotel near Oldham in

---

[68] *Bund,* (Bern, 11th February, 1971)

1983, in front of a mere 50-70 people. Ottilie was most definitely not with them.

And why should she be? By packing them in at major venues in the fifties and sixties, and helping thereby establish the Barber Band at the pinnacle of public acclaim, to the detriment of her health, she had earned the right to pick and choose.

And while much of the magic was still there, she would never *quite* attain the heights she had scaled before the break. Thus a degree of frustration was added to her already considerable health problems.   She did recover well enough to perform some infrequent and irregular gigs with the Band.

Jazz writer Trevor Hodgett recalls seeing her for the first time in 1972, at Queen's University's Whitla Hall, in Belfast.[69]

> What staggered me, as an eighteen year old, was the audience, which seemed to mainly consist of old guys in their forties[70] who sat beaming with delight throughout the performance and who to a man were madly in love with Ottilie.
>
> And the rapport between Ottilie and this audience came from the fact that they saw her as a down-to-earth, unpretentious Ulster lass who had gone across the water and taken the English scene by storm and yet who had remained unchanged by the fame. - who was still the same uncomplicated, fun-loving girl she had always been.

She was well enough also to accompany the Band on two European tours, to Budapest and to Prague, where she was listed under the name of Ottilie Pattersonova. She recorded six numbers at the Lucerna Hall in Prague in 1970, including her classic *Baby, Won't You Please Come Home?*, with Pat Halcox's eerie off-microphone piano in the background, as well as a powerful version of *Bill Bailey.*

After the Prague concert she spoke to one of her enthusiastic Czech fans. "Why do you enjoy it so much, when you don't understand the words?" she asked him. "Ah," he replied, "we may not know the words, but we know the feeling."

---

[69] C.Harper & T.Hodgett, *Irish Folk, Trad and Blues: A Secret History* (London: Cherry Red Books, 2005), 157.

[70] Charming! If you're considered old at 40, then there's no hope for me.

In the ground-breaking Hungarian visit also Ottilie's English/Irish vocals did not seem to present an insuperable problem. The Hungarian Communist Party Leaders had been previously been suspicious of any musical combination performing overtly decadent Western music, fearing that enjoyment of the music might open a cultural window that would lead to general dissatisfaction with their lot behind the Iron Curtain. What Ottilie and the Band discovered was that this particular window was already wide open, as their audience had been well prepared by listening to the wonderful Radio Luxembourg and Voice of America broadcasts. Ottilie represented no threat to the Hungarian way of life at all, and in the end many of the Communist leaders were the Band's biggest supporters.

Ottilie drops out again

These exciting European ventures proved to be only the calm before a storm, and later in the early nineteen seventies deteriorating health forced Ottilie to cease performing once again.

At the height of their powers Chris had brought a classic Victorian "pile" on the edge of Rostrevor, in County Down, named Kilbroney House. Killbroney made it possible for Ottilie to be near family and friends, and to find a retreat from what had become for her a hectic life.

If buying the house was partly a gesture to Ottilie, so that she could live close to her places of birth and upbringing, it was also part of a contemporary trend whereby big stars tended to buy big houses to display their aura. That last sentence is on reflection a little ungenerous, since the evidence suggests that Chris himself liked Ireland and found it one of the few places where he could genuinely relax.

John Crocker, reed player in the Barber Band for over 30 years, describes it as a house suitable as a subject for the TV programme *The Restorers*, but *before* the restorers had chance to move in and do their transforming work![71] It should be noted that, as he says in the same conversation, that buying the house was typical of Chris' willingness to bend over backwards for Ottilie, to make her illness-plagued life as tolerable as possible.

Sometimes that very worthy enthusiasm overstepped the mark. To a friend Ottilie recounted the story of how one day delivery man turned up at the

---

[71]   In conversation with me at his house on 22nd August, 2012.

door with a huge oak table and 8 chairs. Ottilie explained that there must have been a mistake since they already had dining suite, and she knew nothing of this. Undeterred, the delivery told her that Mr. Barber had ordered it, and promptly brought the furniture into the house, even though Ottilie protested that it was far too big and that there was no room for it in the house. Chris returned from tour a few days later, said "hello" and then sat down to read his paper, ignoring the huge pile of furniture. When Ottilie, in true wifely style, asked him what it was all about, he calmly walked out into the garden, returning with a huge axe. After reducing the new furniture to matchwood, he sat down to resume reading his newspaper, leaving Ottilie, for once, lost for words.

Kilbroney would become a ready-made haven for Ottilie as she began a second major period of recuperation. The problem with the house, as Ottilie's mother herself was later to observe, was that it was off the beaten track as far as Chris and Ottilie's work was concerned. That work was centred on London, not Northern Ireland. It meant inevitably therefore large swathes of time when the recuperating Ottilie was at Kilbroney, whilst Chris was off conquering the world with the Band. With Ottilie at home and Chris on his endless travels, the "haven" tended towards becoming a prison, with Ottilie isolated from almost all the things that had made their life together so fulfilled. Isolation, coupled with continuing poor health, began to drag Ottilie down to the depths.

As had been the case in her first period of recovery, Ottilie did not sit back, but filled the time and space as positively as she could by regularly inviting friends and relatives for the weekend, and thereby putting the house to good use. Some of these visitors would be friends and acquaintances from the early pre-Barber days, such as Brian McAnoy and family. Al Watt, by now of course living in Florida, used to take time to make contact with Ottilie on his occasional visits to the British Isles. On those visits he would of course meet up with Chris also. In telephone conversation with me from Florida, Al remarks that he was always greeted with politeness by Chris, but gained the clear impression that Chris did not have a great enthusiasm for Ottilie's Ulster friends. To him they were part of Ottilie's distant past. The world had moved on.

In the same curious way that young child often assume that ghosts reside in churches, so Kilbroney had a reputation amongst some locals for being haunted. This was never really taken seriously, though visitors do relate a sense of walking past certain spots in the house on a hot summer's day and feeling a distinct chill. I think however that Ottilie would never have stayed there on her own for as long as she did if these rumours were to be taken at all seriously.

Some idea of the size of Kilbroney House may be judged by the fact that it is now a Residential Care Home for the Elderly, with, incidentally, an outstanding reputation.

A Significant Diagnosis

Medically, Ottilie's breakdown proved to be the thin end of a very long wedge. Her relatively slow recovery over the next few years suggested that something more fundamental was wrong besides vocal cord problems and nervous exhaustion. Finally in 1973 it was discovered that she had been suffering from a mild form of epilepsy.

Any reader who suffers from epilepsy or who knows an epilepsy sufferer will know that it is not an affliction to be minimised or treated lightly. One of the implications of this was that there was no way Ottilie could return to life at the pace she had lived before her breakdown. Whilst her voice would certainly get back to a high enough standard to perform with the band and enrapture audiences just as before, she would inevitably have to rein herself in.

The recovering and often isolated Ottilie received a major blow when, in July 1975 her father, Joe, died. He and Julia had bought a bungalow in Chippenham, Wiltshire round about the same time that Ottilie and Chris had bought Kilbroney. Joe died in Bath Hospital, on 26th July, aged 81. He had been admitted on the Monday, and had surgery on the following Thursday. The operation left him very weak, and he passed away in the early hours of Saturday morning. Joe was repatriated to Ireland, and was buried in Movilla Cemetery, Newtownards on 2nd August, 1975.

The isolation of Kilbroney, coupled now with the loss of her father, began to prove more of a hindrance than a blessing on Ottilie's road to recovery. Eventually, in 1977, Ottilie made the move to more manageable accommodation in nearby Bangor, making the further logical decision to bring her widowed mother to live with her.

Julia confesses that she never settled, even though she was now back in Ulster. Ottilie was similarly unhappy, isolated from the jazz community in general and her wandering husband in particular, so that it became a relatively easy decision for her and Julia to move over to England. This was not because either of them had fallen out of love with Northern Ireland - far from it. The move was to get Ottilie in particular close to "the scene", where she could more easily observe the life of her by now estranged husband.

So in 1980 they moved over and set up home in St. Albans, in Hertfordshire. For Julia, moving from place to place was no new experience. After the rigours of moving all the way from Riga to Tblisi in wartime, Bangor to St. Albans in peacetime was not a difficult journey to make. It is a curious and fascinating fact that Julia's diary, which I have had the privilege of reading in part, is full of descriptions of endless comings and goings, journeys long and short. Easing down the road seemed to have been a regular part of her life right from the beginning.

6

MADAME BLUES AND DOCTOR JAZZ

Ottilie began singing with the Band again from time to time in the late seventies and early eighties. In 1979 she appeared at the Magnus Jazz Festival at Wembley.
One jazz critic wrote of the event,

> Ottilie Patterson, the little lady with the big Bessie Smith voice, rescued the first night of the Magnus Records Jazz Festival at Wembley Conference Centre. In her first appearance in the United Kingdom for seven years she dominated the audience, just as she did in the sixties and seventies, sometimes sombre and sometimes just plain gutsy.

John Service recalls seeing her perform at the Usher Hall in Glasgow in 1981, and recalls her voice on that occasion being full of power and conviction. Her fans were delighted at seeing her up and about again.

> How wonderful to hear your fabulous, gutsy, incredible voice once again...good luck in your new ventures. Every best wish from a devoted fan to remarkable lady.
>
> *Mrs. Georgina Sorrell*

> As you know, I have always been a terrific fan of yours and only wish you sang more so that I could have the pleasure of coming to hear you. I loved you singing *Careless Love*. I too wish I were a tiny bird, but I am not quite the right shape!
>
> *George Melly*

In 1982 she performed concerts with the Barber Band in Germany, together with the band of Benny Goodman, and with Ella Fitzgerald and her group. Ella's Bass player in particular loved Ottilie's singing.
A German fan writes:

Thank you for your performance in Eschwege. It was a wonderful concert!

I send you the first report of one of our local newspapers which was published the day after. I hope you can read and understand what the reporter wrote - it is a pure love declaration to you - and it feels right![72]

All the people I talk to in the days after the concert were highly pleased. They admired your engagement, your expression, your style, the voice - sometimes soft and sometimes growing up in tremendous strength.

Believe the voice of the public and trust yourself.

By the way, it never happened in Eschwege before that a concert is mentioned on Page 1.

In love and very sincerely yours,

Wolfgang and Doris Buchbauer

Banjo and Guitarist Stu Morrison comments

> Despite her problems Ottilie still retained her magic. She could step onto a stage and lift the audience by the scruff of its neck into a howling stamping crowd of the sort more often seen at rock concerts. But it was not just her stagecraft. Ottilie's singing was in a class of its own.

The magic had evidently not departed, nor had the mesmeric effect on her audiences. John Warner recalls that what struck him about Ottilie's performances in this period was their intensity, which he attributes to nerves, but which he found rather unsettling.

Chris Harbinson, writing on the Barber website, gives an account of a concert in the Valley Leisure Centre around 1979. After complaining about poor acoustics in the cavernous main games hall, which in his view turned Chris' urbane and witty introductions to the sound of Serbo-Croat, he goes on to complement Pat Halcox, John Crocker, Ian Wheeler and Barber himself for the excellence of their playing.

He then writes, in terms used by many critics before him,

---

[72] German newspaper headline, *Taufrisch zuruck zu den Guten Alten Tagen,* roughly translated, "Back in the Good Old Days".

The emotional high spot of the evening came when Ottilie Patterson joined the Band on stage. This week has seen her returning after a seven year gap, and she obviously relished the occasion. Eyes flashing, tambourine slapping, she launched herself energetically into a version of *Hot Time in Old Town Tonight*.

After a couple more up tempo shouters, she produced her show stopper, a superbly controlled and emotional performance of *Baby, Won't You Please Come Home?*, in which the long drawn out notes showed off the richness of her voice to good advantage.

In that same year Ottilie had scraped enough money together to make some private recordings. Some of the money was taken from her burial fund - as she said "better to sing with it than die with it". In preparation for this and for her planned comeback, she moved from the Irish home to St. Albans in England. She recorded four numbers - *Careless Love, Georgia Grind, Loving You* and a composition of her own, *Make me or Break Me*. What was memorable about these recordings is that they were made, not to the accompaniment of a jazz band, but with the backing of Duncan McKay on synthesiser, an attempt to get a more modern sound. Just the first two tracks were issued but, in spite of some energetic Irish plugging, didn't sell too well.

She did however have more successful side ventures, singing from time to time with the Jim Daley Blues Band in Belfast, as well as appearing at the colourfully named Guinness Jam and Blues Festival in Cork around 1983.

The Grand Canyon
Another indication of a new resolve in Ottilie and a rising spirit of adventure was a holiday she spent in America in 1982 with close friends, including long-time friend Ulsterman Brian McAnoy. The highlight of this trip was a visit to the Grand Canyon in Arizona. After a stay in Las Vegas, they made their way up to Flagstaff, the jumping off point (not literally) for the Grand Canyon. Anyone who has been there, as I have been lucky enough to have been, can imagine the strong impression the sight made on Ottilie. It is an experience beyond words.

Nearby Sedona, and the traditional sites for the Western movies, again aroused her excitement and fascination, as did the history of the Navajo peoples that lived in the area.

Viewing the Grand Canyon is an experience that inevitably broadens a person's horizons. Life is bigger, much bigger, than our little set of circumstances. The vastness and splendour of the Grand Canyon takes a person out of himself or herself. Suddenly anything is possible. Without doubt the experience helped Ottilie come out of herself and prepare for a major comeback with the Band, this time with an enlarged vision.

Accordingly, in the following year Ottilie, back touring with Barber, , gave a series of concerts that were recorded for the album *Madame Blues and Dr. Jazz*, released in 1984. I have the privilege of possessing Ottilie's personal copy on vinyl on what were to be her last recordings.

The album is special in containing several songs that could be said to be quintessentially Ottilie. There are the raunchy numbers *Salty Dog* and *Georgia Grind*. There is a new version of the 1959 classic *Hot Time in Old Town Tonight*, full of life though in Ottilie's opinion not as good as the original 1959 version with Monty Sunshine. There are new versions of the Ann Cole song, *Easy, Easy, Baby* as well as *Stumblin Block*, for which Ottilie owned the arranger's rights. The recording of *Doctor Jazz* includes an all-too-rarely-heard performance of the verse.

The album is a pastiche of recordings made at a series of concerts in 1983 - at Fairfield Hall, Croydon (February), Haywards Heath (May), East Grinstead (May) and Palmers Green (June).

On all the recordings the enthusiasm for the Barber-Patterson combination is very evident. Whatever may have been happening in their private lives, on stage they were the Old Firm, described elsewhere as "Salt and Pepper", back in business. The *Shropshire Star* uses another culinary image in describing Chris without Ottilie as being like "strawberries without cream".[73]

George Melly, in his sleeve notes to the album, describes it like this:

> Ottilie applies herself to each of these songs with that balance of intuition and intelligence which is the hallmark of the true artiste. The Chris Barber Band accompany her with the empathy that comes from a long association with both her and the music itself. They too respect the idiom; they have never been content, not even in the early days, to remained corralled within the "trad" formula.
>
> It is however Ottilie's album. She has never sounded better.

---

[73] *Shropshire Star*, 5th August, 1988.

Many of us who have heard the album would readily agree with George.

Although Ottilie of course did other things in this comeback other than recording this album, it is worth dwelling on it for a while, because it is a window on Ottilie's life in this period.

The first point of interest for me is the voice. It is quite evident that the ravages of laryngitis and vocal cord damage have left their mark. There is a hoarseness, coupled with an inability to access the full vocal range, that is all too evident. And yet in a strange way, to my ear this actually *enhances* the Ottilie sound. The Ottilie of *Madame Blues* has an earthiness, even coarseness, about her voice that is entirely appropriate for a jazz singer.

John Crocker gives an interesting sidelight on the Patterson "come back voice". Every musician knows the damaging effect on performance of a neglect of practice. The musician's mantra is:

> One day without practice *you* notice it
> Two days without practice the *Band Leader* notices it
> Three days without practice *everybody* notices it!

The same is undoubtedly true, if not more so, for a singer. In these performances John sensed a frustration within Ottilie herself that her long lay off, considerably longer than three days, meant that she was unable to scale the professional heights and attain the very high standard she had set before. As we all recognise, the inability to do now what we could once do is one of the great frustrations of later life, and it could well be that Ottilie felt it all too strongly.

To my mind the problem with John's observation is that Ottilie does not actually mention this particular frustration in any of her writings. She is certainly not short of problems and frustrations, but doesn't mention this particular one.

I respect John's point nevertheless to the extent that it is based on his personal observations. Yet I would still want to argue that, whatever the reason for the change in the quality of Ottilie's voice, the sound she produces on these recordings is, to my ears, very definitely the sound of an authentic Blues singer.

As I have said elsewhere, there is something about impurity and jazz that go together and make the music what it is. An operatic diva, perfect as her diction and intonation would be, would not tend to go down well in your average jazz club. In my view it is of the essence of jazz to be impure, irreverent and controversial. Any attempt to sanitise jazz and make it respectable serves to rob it of its true nature.

As Humph says, in a discussion about the ebullient Eddie "Lockjaw" Davis:

> When it comes to the conflict between vulgarity and respectability in jazz, put me on the side of vulgarity every time. At its worst vulgarity has never been more than a minor ailment. Good taste and respectability spell death.[74]

As usual, Humph is right on the mark.

So in my view and the view of others the post-vocal cord damaged and frustrated Ottilie Patterson sounds even more of an authentic Blues singer than she was before, if indeed that were possible.

Divorce from Barber

The performances involved in this latest comeback were for Ottilie different from previous performances and created a greater challenge for her because by the time she made her spectacular comeback she and Chris were separated and, like many others before and since, going through the trauma of divorce.

Chris and Ottilie had always been disparate characters, a living example of the idea that opposites sometimes attract. "Public schoolboy meets girl from lowly community school" could have been an appropriate subtitle for their coming together.

Ottilie was extremely outgoing, full of life and energy and could talk for Ireland, especially about music. She was generous to a fault. Jean Crocker tells of one occasion when the band was off on tour that she took all the band wives out for a slap up meal in Hampstead, at her expense. Kay Smith, wife of Bass player Dick, tells a similar story about another night out with Ottilie and the other band wives.

On another occasion Stu Morrison tells of how, when he had missed the rendezvous time for a trip to Germany, Ottilie came to his rescue and arranged an alternative flight, so he could meet up with the Band without

---

[74] *Melody Maker*, Nov.30, 1957.

causing major disruption to the band schedule.

However, she was an artiste, with the classically unpredictable artistic temperament - and Irish to boot! This double temperament would often reveal itself in typical fashion whenever things were not going well or according to plan, when her language could be almost as colourful as her hair!

Chris on the other hand was unemotional, to the point of a perceived coldness. His mother had been very much a career woman, occupying several high offices in Education, and maybe had not as much time to spend on her son's emotional needs as many mothers would. Whilst having the standard public school training in good manners, he at the same time would struggle to interact socially and make the "small talk" that so often many of us find to be a necessary evil. This shortfall was more than balanced by a straightforwardness, honesty and generosity that, in many people's experience, made him a good person to work with.

Yes, he was always a driven and highly ambitious person - but sensible with it. He has never smoked or drunk beer and spirits. This makes him stand out immediately within the jazz community! He does enjoy a glass of wine from time to time, but is just as likely to be found enjoying a coffee or a soft drink between shows. Looking after himself in this and other ways has bestowed on him a longevity not afforded many jazz musicians.

This coupling together of opposites, initially an attraction, always made the long term prospects for the relationship doubtful. She was emotional and temperamental, he was quiet and unemotional. She had a wicked sense of humour, as her writings reveal, whereas, as a number of people have testified to me, he appeared to have none. It could be said that much of what they were as individuals arose out of this clash of opposites.

The late and much-lamented Pat Halcox summed it up when he said that if Ottilie had married anyone else, she would have been a normal, well-adjusted human being with a very successful career. Drummer Pete York commented along pretty much the same lines. The lack of self-confidence and the epilepsy, coupled with the particularities of Chris' personality made for an unstable mixture that rendered them ultimately incompatible.

This clash of opposites would reveal itself in many ways, not least in their ideas about music, which often differed widely. For it is one of those curious paradoxes that music can simultaneously divide and unite people, as is witnessed by the number of bands that come together with a common enthusiasm for a particular type of music only to break up when they come to varying understandings of that music. The phrase "musical differences" is a short phrase that covers a multitude of things.

Undoubtedly it was the passion for both hearing and performing music that held Ottilie and Chris together, in spite of their personality differences, for so long. However, when events beyond their control prevented them sharing this passion it was perhaps not surprising that problems arose.

The chronic illness that plagued Ottilie created an enforced separation - Ottilie confined at home, with Chris away, still eating up the miles with the Band Schedule. It would be extremely difficult for any marriage to survive, let alone thrive, with this degree of separation. In Ottilie's case the enforced separation was made worse because she felt she could not be sure that he could cope with the many temptations afforded by fans, especially female fans, while away from home.

While it would be anachronistic to use the modern term "groupies" to describe these jazz fans, the term is apt to the point where it tells us there are always some female jazz fans who lack a sense of proportion when it comes to their affection for their idols.

Discussing such a subject is of course of necessity a delicate one, and is complicated by the obvious fact that in such a case reliable information is hard to come by. People are naturally reluctant to talk. But, having looked at this issue quite carefully, I am persuaded that there is enough evidence, evidence that stands on a higher level than rumour, to suggest that Ottilie's fears in this regard were not without foundation. Contemporaries of Chris and Ottilie to whom I have spoken do not line up with great alacrity to dismiss them.

In the end it could simply be that the suspicions Ottilie harboured were only the same suspicions that *any* wife would find plaguing her in the same circumstances. And the delicate state of Ottilie's health would tend to magnify rather than diminish any feelings of having been deserted.

These doubts feature both explicitly and inferentially in her writings, as far back as the early to mid 1960's.

I CARE, I CARE, UBI ES ?[75]
Summer, 1966
You,
My Venus and Mars,
My Moon and My Stars,
And wing-footed Mercury

Say
Oh why is it then,
My god among men,
That your wing-footed feet
Are of clay ?

In yet more graphic style she writes

THE DISCOTHEQUE
7th April, 1967

The legs. O my God, the legs, all talking at once, so that I can hardly make out what they are saying.
Two of them shrieked out at me in a patronising way, and another pair of legs named Angeline slyly breathed that they had communicated with his legs, actually getting in touch. They stated that this was very stimulating for both parties, and that they were in love with each other.
Then there was the hair, all long, slim, prim and proper, looking as if it could hardly say a word, but nonetheless issuing silent, screaming invitations. Sometimes the hair was moderately quiet, and only the legs called out. But the worst times were when the legs and the hair were both shouting at once, and I couldn't hear what they were saying because of myself screaming.[76]

Something that would have come as unwelcome justification to Ottilie for her fears came when Chris suddenly announced that he had now "found a new

---

[75] Translated from the Latin as: "Where are you?"
[76] The work is incomplete. The manuscript is torn off after the last line.

baby" (to quote the song title), in the person of a German girl, one Renate Martha Hillbich, 21 years his junior, and that he had installed her in the Barbers' London flat. Ottilie had fought her way back from epilepsy only to be confronted with, as she put it, "Chris and his girl".

In spite of what we have previously said about Ottilie's emotional ups and downs, she reacted remarkably calmly to this shattering news. She decided that, because of the age difference, this would be a passing fad, and that Chris would get over it. So she stalled on his request for a divorce and gave him twelve months to work Renate out of his system. This proved to be over-optimistic on Ottilie's part, as he rang back after only 8 months to say that he had made his mind up and wanted to be with his new love. "Divorce me or else..." took on the overtones of a demand rather than a request. As Ottilie said,

> Whatever he wants he gets. Chris is a curious mixture of ruthlessness and naivety, and people are always making excuses for him.

Ottilie's problem was that she didn't want to divorce him. In spite of it all, in a way only a woman could understand, she still loved him and hoped against hope he would come back. She was by this time only in her late forties and hated the thought of being alone. She reasoned that half a loaf was better than none, so that she was actually prepared to tolerate Chris having a mistress as long as she could continue by his side as his wife. It should be said that Ottilie was not the first and last wife to come up with such a working compromise on this issue.

If things could possibly be made worse, they were made so by the necessity of Ottilie having to perform in front of her now-estranged husband, as she did in her concerts of the eighties. She would frequently say that a greater than the fear of an epileptic attack was the trauma of getting up on stage with Chris. Her legs would shake even at rehearsal.

It is certainly no coincidence that of all the recordings she made in these concerts the one that stands out as a classic is *Baby, won't you please come home.* To listen to it, with its unfathomable depths of feeling it to have one's hairs standing on end and one's spine tingling uncontrollably.

It is pointed out of course that *Baby* had been part of Ottilie's repertoire for many years, long before the estrangement between Chris and her, and that she always performed it with superb professionalism and great feeling. That may well be the case, but I defy anyone to listen to her performance of the song on the *Madame Blues* album and not see it fitting perfectly into the new context created by separation and divorce.

The song points to another curious paradox. In their personal lives Chris and Ottilie were now miles apart, and yet professionally they were still in close harmony. For "Chris Barber and Ottilie Patterson" the magic was still there, and still pulled them in, whereas for Mr. and Mrs. Barber that magic had disappeared.

In her quiet and dark moments Ottilie would dwell on all this. And as she so often did in those moments, would put pen to paper.

This she wrote as her version of the Old Testament book, *The Song of Solomon:*

THE SONG OF WRONGS
Which is Solowoman's

This is my Beloved,
In whom I am not too well pleased.
Behold he cometh
In Carnaby attire,
Skipping along the City's West End ways
As a young buck after the little deers (dears).

My Beloved is fair and ruddy
- he is ruddy unfair.

His cohorts are as a flock of goats upon the mountain,
Bleating and giving tongue,
Whereof everyone that cometh down to drink
By the rivers of waters,
That, purple from the grape
flow freely from the founts of Mason's Yard.

Yea, this is he,
This is my Beloved,
And I charge ye, O daughters of Jerusalem,
If ye do see my Beloved
Give him a punch up the bracket!

A very understandable part of Ottilie's fear of being left alone is that she did not have children. She had wanted them: Chris had not as Ottilie was often at pains to point out, against occasional calumny. She longed to be a mother, and, as many of her close friends agree, would have made a superb parent.

It is not too difficult to understand that children would not easily fit into the lifestyle that Chris had adopted and the aims and objectives he still had, especially as Ottilie was such a huge part of the band's attraction. One might even accept this, were it not for the facts that many other musicians had managed to balance their marital and professional lives, and that Chris himself went on to have children with Renate, children with whom he continued to have contact even when he and Renate were in their turn divorced.

Of all the issues within marriage that a husband and wife can disagree on, none is so potentially destructive and devastating as a disagreement on the question of whether to have children or not. This fundamental rift ate away at their relationship and was undoubtedly a contributory cause to their eventual split.

As we shall see later, this enforced childlessness was a major factor in Ottilie's later emotional decline and rejection of her past life. She came to feel that she was a failure as a woman, and indeed failure as a person, because she had not borne children.

> Not having children has been the despair of my life[77]

she would later say. All the memories of success she cherished were no substitute for this.

She continued to sing with the Barber Band through these traumatic years, until her final retirement in 1991. Those who heard her in this period got the very real sense that when she sang the Blues she was *really* singing them, because she was singing out of her own experience. Blues had really come to her door, and given her the knowledge of what Jimmy Asman called "the white folks yard".

As we know, what goes around comes around. An interesting tailpiece to this part of the story is that Renate, having provided for the Barber Family

---

[77] *Shropshire Star*, 29 August, 1988.

Tree, suddenly disappeared from the scene. The popular story is that she formed a doubles partnership with a local tennis professional prior to her departure. Fifteen all.

Renate was later to surface with the Barber children in Florida, where she lives today. Relationships between Chris and Renate continue to be good, and Chris is able to keep in contact with his daughters. John Crocker recalls visiting Chris once at his Hungerford home and meeting one of those daughters, finding her a delightful person.

I have not yet discovered any note of what Ottilie said on first receiving the news of Renate's sudden disappearance from the scene, though my imagination leaves me with no shortage of possibilities! Unhappily for Ottilie, however, the break up of his marriage to Renate did not bring Chris coming back to Ottilie, as she might perhaps have hoped. Instead, he took on a fourth marriage to a fourth wife, Kate, to whom he is currently married. I am mischievously tempted to think that, just as most jazz music is four-to-a-bar, that there is something special to musicians about the number 4. Who knows?

A comment that was made to me in all seriousness however was that, whatever the truth might or might not be about Barber as a "Ladies Man" (to use a relatively harmless old expression) he seems to have had a thing about marriage. Scarcely had one ended before he seemed to be ready for another. Naida to Ottilie, Ottilie to Renate, Renate to Kate, with scarcely 16 bars rest in between.

A fact of experience that many readers will testify to is that what goes around come around. This is a common way of describing the Biblical principle of reaping what we sow[78].

Way back in 1957 Ron Bowden departed from the band overnight, being summarily dismissed by Barber (wasn't the band supposed to be a co-operative at this time?). It is difficult to find a rationale behind this in purely musical terms, since it came right at the beginning of the Sister Rosetta Tharpe tour. Bowden's replacement, Graham Burbridge had to be put through a hasty crash (or bang and crash) programme to learn the numbers being done with Sister Rosetta before he could join the tour. Nor was it

[78] "Do not be deceived. God is not mocked. Whatever we sow, that we will reap", *Galatians 6.6, New Testament.*

apparent how style wise Burbridge could contribute anything that Bowden couldn't.   It emerges however that, at a time when Ottilie and Chris were together, but not yet married, Ron's late wife, Mynah, was a close friend of Chris' first wife Naida, as indeed she was with Ottilie. There were therefore open channels of communication between all of them (I hope you're following all this!) Anyone who watches soap operas with any regularity will without too much difficulty detect a critical situation developing here, one that would be relieved by Bowden's swift removal from the Band.   This removal, with no apparent musical rationale, seems to be of the stuff of Eastenders.

If we might be tempted to think that Ron Bowden's sacking from the Barber Band was not straightforward, his subsequent dismissal from the Kenny Ball Band was positively bizarre! In the process of playing *Hawaian War Chant*, a regular part of their repertoire, Kenny would use his mute. In preparation for this he would place it on the floor, just in front of Ron's drum kit. On one occasion, just as he bent down to pick it up, Ron hit his crash cymbal. Kenny decided that this had been a deliberate attempt to deafen him, and terminated Ron's employment on the spot after 40 years! The fact that Ron had been hitting his crash cymbal at that same point in *Hawaian War Chant* for all of those 40 years didn't seem to register with Kenny.

Getting back to Ottilie, it is fairly clear that this latest comeback of hers was conducted under a great degree of stress and difficulty, and put great strain on the professionalism of both Ottilie and Chris. It is my thesis however that this tension proved to be a creative tension, and added immeasurably to the quality of the music. The music was not an accompaniment to life, it was life itself.

Whilst Ottilie remained the consummate professional, there is no doubt that she maintained this level of professionalism at some cost to herself. She had to deny her strong feelings as she stood up again and again to sing intimate love songs next to the husband of 20 years whom she was now divorcing and whom, in spite of all that had happened with Renate and other "conquests" she still loved and longed for to come home. If that is the "Glory of Love" then it is also the pain of love, and many readers will themselves know what that means.

One way of releasing the tension was to pour herself into her songs, especially songs like *Baby won't You Please Come Home* and *Bill Bailey, won't you Please Come Home*, both of which feature on the *Madame Blues* album. The

Daily Mail in particular describes the performance of the first of those as

> Ottilie's singing and Barber's Music intertwining with the intimacy of a lover's kiss

That is a fairly apt description, and the supreme irony is that many Ottilie fans, including me, would regard this performance of *Baby won't You Please Come Home*, taken at slow pace, and with Roger Hill's haunting guitar in the background, as perhaps her finest performance of all, because of the personal depths of feeling it plumbs.

It is probably true to say that Ottilie's ability and professionalism would have enabled her to present the pathos inherent in this song whatever her personal circumstances may have been.   Be that as it may, Ottilie herself was conscious that in their post-divorce situation this song was *special*. It was about Chris and no-one else.

This song truly is the Blues. To listen to it is an emotional experience, and one can only wonder how her ex-husband could be the only one unmoved by it.

7

RETREAT TO AYR

In spite of all her singing, "Baby" didn't come home. Neither for that matter did Bill Bailey, in spite of all those promises about doing the cooking and paying the rent. Continuing indifferent health made Ottilie feel that living in the tension between personal and professional life was no longer worthwhile

.

Final retirement

Partly because of this poor health and partly due to the private circumstances that made it impossible for her to be away from home for any length of time, Ottilie decided in 1991 to stop singing professionally altogether. Not only did she decide to end her performances, she decided that the memories of that career were so painful that she would turn her back on jazz altogether. As far as Ottilie were concerned, her life in music was over. She would henceforth seek fulfilment and contentment elsewhere.

Moving House

Her mother Julia, in her diary, refers often to the lonely and sad life Ottilie was living, and comments that the situation was driving a wedge between her and the one she describes as "my best friend".

So a decision was made to attempt to bring what remained of the family together. In July 1981 Ottilie (now separated from Chris) bought a house at Beechwood Avenue, St. Albans. We can speculate that part of Ottilie's motivation for moving back to England might have been to be nearer to Chris, or at least nearer to the sphere of life in which he now lived.

Julia, living on her own since Joe's death, decided to move from Chippenham, where she had been living, to live with Ottilie. The attraction of this move was partly the chance to be near Ottilie and partly the significant Latvian expatriate community in and around London. It was the latest and final move of the many she had made since her early days in Riga.

Moving to Ayr

Ottilie later confessed that she never really liked St. Alban's, a dislike she impishly points out she shared with scientist/mathematician Stephen Hawking, and therefore had never really settled there. Moving to the Hertforshire city had been basically a temporary expedient, a useful base for operations. Now she decided to make the Big Move. She finally concluded reluctantly that, because of Bill Bailey's reluctance, there was nothing to keep her in St. Alban's. So in 1989 she sold up and moved to Ayr on Scotland's west coast.

Rejection of the Past

"Why Ayr, of all places ?" I hear you ask. "It's so out of the way!" Ottilie would probably have responded that its remoteness represented its main attraction! She wanted to get away - from England and from a life the memories of which were for her only painful.

It is important to recognise that for Ottilie this was not merely a geographical move to a new point on the globe. It was a change of life. It represented a deliberate and conscious turning of her back on her former life in music and everything that had gone with it.

One indication of this emotional separation from her former life is supplied by long-time friend, Ben Hendricks. He tells of how, after a long period without contact with Ottilie he wrote to Lake Records to ask for her current address. Lake Records answered that they would pass on his request, but he was not to be surprised if he received no reply.[79]

Ottilie had been through a lot. She had for years faced up to the ordeal of trying to keep up the impossible pace of touring whilst suffering steadily declining health, the former undoubtedly accelerating the latter.

There was also the bitterness of rejection, being cast aside by a sports car lover chasing after a younger model, a rejection made worse by the fact that she had never stopped loving her sports car enthusiast, and never stopped yearning for him to return. Many might reasonably wonder whether such love and devotion were fully deserved.

---

[79] Hendricks, *Lost in a Jazz Band*, 7.

Childlessness
Above all, there was the devastating knowledge that she had sacrificed the biggest aspiration of her whole life - her longing to have been a mother - to the never-to-be-satisfied thirst for success of the band. In a writing that expresses her dark, despairing rejection of religion and all other value systems, she expresses the reductionist view that the only purpose of life is to reproduce the species. Even in those very limited terms she regarded herself as having missed the mark. "I am a failure" she would say, "I didn't reproduce".

Strictly speaking this was not true, because back in 1956, in the days when the band was making its breathtaking surge up the popularity charts, she had become pregnant. However, as Barber himself had admitted, Ottilie represented a huge part of the band's appeal, so that taking time out to raise a child would have seriously stalled that popularity surge for the band. Maybe it would have stalled permanently, who knows? The opportunity for motherhood for Ottilie had to be sacrificed, as it turned out permanently, on the altar of band success.

The pain of childlessness that Ottilie felt in later life was made worse by guilt, and the realisation that the opportunity had been there and not taken, a pain that was made infinitely worse when her ex-husband went on to have children subsequently with his third wife.

To Trevor Hodgett she confided:

I've had very hard times. The life and music were all jumbled up and they were causing me misery. But the performances were an escape from the misery - so it was a vicious circle. I was trapped. I thought, "where do I go? What do I do?"

It's all on that track from *Spring Song* : "Mrs. Pankhurst, don't emancipate me. I'd rather have my chains. They hurt far less than brains. And in this day and age, I'd rather have my cage". That's what I was writing about.

I didn't know what to do so I just kept on and in the end it was decided for me. I'd been acquired, hired, married and fired. After so long I couldn't even listen to the Blues. I was heartsore.[80]

---

[80]   C.Harper & T.Hodgett, *Irish Folk, Trad and Blues: A Secret History* (London: Cherry Red

It is unfair and untrue to say that Ottilie became a recluse in Ayr, as people sometimes allege. While she did withdraw decisively from was the musical spotlight, that didn't in itself make her reclusive. In her new surroundings she had the same measure of social interaction as did anyone, and when later she moved into a care home, she settled into the community of the home perfectly normally. But what was definite was that "all that jazz" was firmly in the past. She would rarely talk about it (unlike Uncle Albert of *Only Fools and Horses* fame) and after 1991 she would not sing or play for anyone at all.

Ayr was for Ottilie not simply a very pleasant spot on the map. It represented a retreat, a bolt-hole, an escape from everything that had brought her pain and despair. If it is true that she found a measure of contentment in Ayr, it was only because Ayr had helped her escape the stress of her former life.

Other reasons for moving to Ayr

Apart from sister Jessie, Ottilie had no family that were in ready contact with her and who would therefore tie her down emotionally to any particular locality. So in that respect where she lived didn't matter. However Ayr was handy, as sister Jessie was not all that far away, living just down the road in a cottage on the outskirts of Stranraer.

In addition, Ayr was a jumping off point for Ireland. Whilst she couldn't actually see Ulster from her house, as she occasionally mischievously claimed, she did have Glasgow Airport close by, and could easily hop over to the country of her birth should the fancy take her. Whether she could actually see Ulster or not was irrelevant anyway. It was the *feeling* of being close to home that mattered to her.

As Ottilie said in an interview with the local Ayr newspaper:

> If you look back in history we're all mixed up, the North East of Northern Ireland and the South West of Scotland. When the religious troubles were happening in Scotland whole congregations and their ministers would go over and settle in Northern Ireland. And people

---

Books), 162.

still have the same names. I just feel the tribe of Scots are my cousins, and I don't feel a stranger.

She had visited Ayr previously, inevitably on a Band tour, and had gained a favourable impression of it.

On first arrival she moved into a flat above the manse on Fort Street, the main Ayr thoroughfare. No doubt there were times when the music drifting downstairs would have caused the Pastor to wonder about whoever it was had moved in above him! The flat was in fact merely a temporary staging post until she found a house of her own. Eventually she came across the house in nearby Barnes Crescent, a house with rooms large enough to take a piano and do whatever entertaining she had a mind to do. In 1989 she bought it and moved in.

Musical fashions had moved on, as they always do, so that the piano she installed in the house turned out to be an electric piano. The instrument was not exclusively reserved for jazz however, and the music a visitor to Ottilie would hear her play was just as likely to be classical music as the Blues. Contemporary and up to date it might be, but she, like many pianists, found that the electric piano was no substitute for the real thing.

In turn Jessie moved from Stranraer into Ayr, to be near to Ottilie. The question of them actually living together, even though they were both approaching 70, never arose. Although they loved one another dearly, and were in contact on the phone on a daily basis, they could never have actually lived together. There is no doubt skin and hair would have flown!

Like brother John, sister Jessie had not been content to bask in Ottilie's reflected glory, but had been concerned to make her own mark in the world. In Jessie's case it was through championing the cause of adult literacy. At the time she became closely involved in the scheme she was Principal of an English Department in Hertfordshire. A colleague who had begun to teach some adults to read discovered that she had so many pupils on her hands she couldn't cope. She needed help. Jessie provided it and found herself launched into a new and worthwhile career.

She moved up to the Dumfries and Galloway Region, to face the challenge of organising an area that stretched from Stranraer in the West to Castle Douglas. The biggest part of this challenge would prove to be the recruitment of a sufficient number of tutors to provide what was an essential element of the scheme, one to one tuition in the client's own home.

One of the main principles that Jessie held to passionately and sought to hammer home in the course of her campaigning was that the inability to read effectively did not imply a lack of intelligence. She sought to emphasise that people with literacy problems were, on the contrary, often highly intelligent, ran their own businesses effectively and contributed fully to society, though not as fully as they would be able to do were they able to read well.

Ottilie's health, as well as her moods, was up and down, and while it was good to have Jessie nearby, for someone who in her previous life had been everywhere and met everybody it clearly was not enough to meet her needs. The remedy was provided by Jessie herself. Jessie was on the way home from shopping one day with her carer, Lisa Watson. On this occasion, instead of actually going straight home, Jessie insisted on a detour, to take Lisa round to meet her sister in Barnes Crescent.

On arrival Jessie sought out Ottilie with the command:

Ottilie, Ottilie, come and meet Lisa. Everyone should have a Lisa!

First impressions were good, and Lisa began going to care for Ottilie every other day, an arrangement than soon progressed to involve a daily visit. With increasing age and infirmity, greater dependence on Lisa soon developed.

In 2002 Jessie died, which was the signal for Ottilie to go into a really serious decline.   This decline was triggered by the realisation that with the loss of Jessie she literally had nobody. Lisa more than filled the gap left by Jessie's passing, and over the years she and Ottilie became closer and closer. Over time Ottilie came more and more to regard Lisa as a daughter rather than a carer.

Ottilie goes into care

Ottilie's circumstances were to undergo a further change. One day in 2007, Lisa called early at Barnes Crescent to tell Ottilie that her visiting time would have to be altered because she had to attend a funeral that day. On entering the house her calls to Ottilie were not returned. On further searching Lisa was horrified to find a pool of blood on the floor - but still no Ottilie.

Fearing the worst, she rang the Police (after all Ottilie was from Northern Ireland) and was both relieved and further mystified when they knew nothing of any incident involving her.   A further call to the local hospital revealed that Ottilie had been taken there, and was currently in the Intensive Care Unit.

The story was that Ottilie had not waited for Lisa to arrive, but had got up and begun to make her way downstairs in her dressing gown. At the bottom of the stairs she had slipped on the kitchen floor. A cup she had been carrying shattered on impact, and the fragments had gone into her face.

In the ICU she developed a water infection which temporarily affected her mental stability. For three weeks the staff had to listen to tales of gun-running for the IRA, as well as a recurring nightmare of guards hiding behind a wall. It was difficult to make sense of - but definitely exciting to listen to!

Discharge from hospital meant admission to a respite hospital where for 17 weeks she was treated with antibiotics. Her condition improved, but the infections had left their mark, and the ability to make the sort of decisions necessary to live any sort of independent life had gone. She could not go home, even with the superb daily care Lisa had been providing.

Ottilie would have dearly liked Lisa to move in with her and live with her. That, however desirable from Ottilie's point of view, was simply not practicable. Lisa was a mum, with a teenage daughter, Ashley. Teenagers do what teenagers do - play loud music, slam doors, and bring their livewire friends round, sometimes in large numbers. To have Ashley constantly tiptoeing around because of Ottilie would clearly be unfair, as Ottilie understood.

So a case conference was set up at the hospital, with Ottilie, Ottilie's solicitor, a social worker and Lisa coming together to consider the options. The particular role of the lawyer was to determine whether Ottilie would be mentally competent to make any far-reaching decisions about herself and her care that would prove necessary. The outcome of the conference was that a suitable Care Home would be found, ideally one at which Lisa could continue to visit and care for Ottilie.

Eventually they discovered Rozelle Holm Farm Private Care Home, a beautiful modern home situated in the outskirts of Ayr. Ottilie liked it, and agreed to go in on one condition - that Lisa would be there all the time. Lisa understood this. Their relationship had grown so close that Lisa had become unhappy at the thought of someone other than her looking after her "mum". The solution to this particular dilemma was found by Lisa taking a job at the Home, and starting to gain qualifications as a Care Nurse. The Home accepted this, though many privately assumed the arrangement last only as long as Ottilie was around, and that once she were not Lisa would quietly fade away. This proved not to be the case however and Lisa is there still, having over the years progressed from novice to Senior Carer status. Meeting Ottilie had started a whole new life for her.

Rozelle Holm is an interesting place. The philosophy of the home is that it should be furnished with exactly the sort of things that the residents would have had in their own homes. This has led to some of the most exotic things you could imagine being seen in some of the rooms.

The most exotic thing I saw on my visit to Rozelle was a series of cabinets containing (full) whiskey bottles. The owner of the home is apparently a "Whiskey Connoisseur", a passion shared, from a practical aspect at least, by many of his fellow countrymen. However, before readers all rush out to reserve a place at Rozelle, you should know that all these cabinets are kept locked! The best that the Scottish residents can do is sit and look at them. The thought that struck me immediately was that to allow a Scot to view a bottle of whiskey but not be able to touch it is, I reckon, something that should be referred to Amnesty International![81]

So Ottilie settled in to another home and another phase of her life, the last move. One is reminded of the song she used to duet with Lonnie Donegan, *When I Move to the Sky,* and it's line "that will be the last move for me".

In Rozelle, surrounded by love and care, Ottilie found a great measure of contentment. But as we have previously said, it was contentment found at a price. She was content because she had excluded music and performing from her mind. There was peace because there was no music. Sadly she could not find consolation in the quality of her recorded work, constantly and wholly unfairly expressing discontent with almost everything that she had ever recorded.

The Dark Moods

I deliberately referred to Ottilie finding a *measure* of contentment only, because she would go through excessively dark moods, and at those times it would take all Lisa's efforts to bring her through.

From the point of view of the interested reader, it is very useful that in these

---

[81] Only joking, of course!

moods of black depression Ottilie would write, allowing her feelings to spill out through her pen, and sometimes dissipate in the process. Here is an extended sample of one such piece of writing, written in hospital in May 1989. It is not by any means a great piece of literature, but does reward the patient and persevering reader, illustrating as it does the depths into which Ottilie sometimes sank:

Jailhouse Blues, a place from which mother would never be able to rescue me again.

Only it's worse, because he is still alive. He has abandoned me utterly, truly, and - worse still - in preference to another "baby". He has abandoned me - condemned me - to the world of infantile incomprehensibility and the derangement of the external and internal worlds, where reality has to be learned and acquired.

Before you are born you are part and parcel of your mother's world. You are indivisible from her. Then, horror of horrors, you are born, brought out into a flashing, roaring blinding place. HELL. You are now exposed to sensations the like of which you have never previously encountered., the myriad stimuli of the external world. It's unbelievable and unendurable, and you cling to your mother like blazes, to be incorporated into her, to be assimilated to her skin and warmth. You are by no means separate yet.

This brightness, this light, with the harsh, unmuffled noise is everywhere - all around you, interminably, eternally, infinitely stretching all around you. The world has exploded and been blown apart into a blinding, roaring vastness. THIS IS NOT YOU. YOU NOW HAVE NO CONFINES. YOU HAVE BEEN EXPANDED INTO INCOMPREHENSIBILITY (Ottilie's capital letters) and are now without shape or boundaries.

This must be non-existence. What has happened to you ? What is this awful coldness all over your skin that you have never ever felt in your whole existence from conception until now?

Thank God I wasn't *born* in hospital, otherwise I doubt whether I would be sane enough to be writing this to you now.

And worse - I was born two months too soon. I wasn't ready or prepared for this catastrophe - I hadn't been FINISHED.

You have no substance around you. You have been changed into a large, noisy blinding dimensional madness. You have died - exploded - changed into something so vast it is beyond your understanding. Nothing is familiar, everything is alien. YOU are alien. Your skin shrieks and your brain screams. They don't belong to you any more. You have lost them in this explosion. You have lost yourself in this explosion. You have been stretched to infinity - you have been BORN.

Jailhouse Blues - the utter terror, the fear and incomprehensibility of it all. Last night, at the table I thought the sense of desolation, grief and despair would be unendurable if I allowed myself to feel it. (Sometimes I think life consists of bearing the unbearable).
The terror is, at 57, as frightening to me know as if I were a year old. It is undiminished, undiluted. As Chris used to say, you can't argue with emotions or the senses. Even though I know I can't be hurt any more, the terror remains, and is as vivid as if it were actually now.
Of course Mummy's death in 1987 didn't help. When I was a child I worried about how old I would be when Mummy died, and whether I would be able to bear it. Would I be big enough and grown up enough not to cry? If she died at 70, I would be 35. Would I manage not to feel the awful loss of it all?
NO MOTHER - the thought chills me to the bone.
I cried a bit when we got the news that she had died. But it was normal adult crying. Jessie and I felt as though we had been cast adrift. It was awfully sad, but not unbearable - *then*. I suppose all the panic attacks I'd been having in 1988 could be put down to losing Mummy. The child in the hospital in 1933 woke again, to find no mother, in a world of unspeakable fear and terror, a fucking great hospital.

This is all very difficult to express in words, since words are the least effective method of communication except for cake recipes or programming video recorders! Anyway, they are my attempt to describe how my (lack of) personality felt at being prematurely ejected from the womb. My cry has often been "I wasn't ready, I wasn't finished. Maybe, maybe, maybe…"

In even darker moods Ottilie would become extremely nihilistic and negative:

"Straighten up and fly right"

Where ? With whom?

You're on your own. That's the trouble.

A beautiful day, a beautiful world, and nobody in it but me. Me and my brain, the only thing in life that I possess, the only luggage I brought into the world. I won't be taking it out with me - it will be dead. Poor lonely brain. All that thinking and struggling all your life to make sense of existence, and then "curtains" - how sad.

All very pointless.

You've solved your puzzle of birth, blues and existence. Now it's just a case of going on living until you die. Not much mystery about that. You just hang on while life washes over you, kindly or not, according to the weather as it were. Just like the rest of nature.

You are now sane, or what people call "sane". No great shakes this mental stability, is it?

Life is just a matter of breathing after all. On you go, breathe in, breathe out, until one day you don't breathe any more. Bleak, isn't it?

We did invent God. God was our Birth Power. We never quite forgot it, and invented him in our image. Ridiculous when you think of it : all the churches and temples built in God's honour. Power -worship. Our power, our huge, monstrous, infantile Ego - God. Sad, isn't it?

And Jesus the Loser, the sad one, the tragic one. Symbol of the love we all need. But love and power are inimical. In love versus power, love will suffer.

Jesus the Loser - our need for love and gentleness. But that way we will lose our skins and our hides in a survival struggle, for love is self sacrifice. Power fears love, and doesn't understand it. So what it fears it destroys. Love gives way, power doesn't. Even God sacrificed Jesus. The mighty win, the gentle lose. In a dog eat dog existence, the passives lose. The weak go to the wall, the powerful send them there.

Unfortunately more people love to be powerful than be loving. That's why I am a pessimist. I love to love, but love has no place in a materialistic world, where it is needed most of all.

The need for power is actually a misconception, or mis-perception that goes way back.

Actually, we are nothing, just a bundle of senses and instincts, trying to adapt to our existence and environment. No big deal.

There is no special role for us except to stay alive, mate, reproduce and die. That is our destiny - no more, no less.

And I did nothing except manage to stay alive. I didn't fulfil my natural role, just an unnatural one. I went against the dictate of nature. I didn't reproduce. I only became an artist. I only reproduced songs. A deviant, I.

Just a defence-mechanistic role I invented for myself to try to cope with the incomprehensible painful world I was born into. And when denied reproduction by my mate, it was all I could use against the pain.

Which brings us back to the beginning.

The brain.

The brain and me.

That's all anybody really has.

All else is self - deception.

In such moods she would go through spells of destroying pages and pages of personal documents, especially ones that related to her relationship with Chris. Whatever relief this may have brought Ottilie, it has caused great frustration to anyone trying to write her biography! I have diaries belonging to Ottilie with page after page torn out. These destructive rampages are simply a measure of how low she had sunk and how far she had turned her back on the old life.

To be sure, she would tinkle on the piano in the Home when nobody was around. As soon as she discovered someone listening however she would immediately stop. To suggest she might entertain her fellow residents was to invite a withering look and probably an blunt Irish oath as well. Ottilie the public performer was very definitely a figure of the past.

Longing to go back

And yet there is the nagging question - would she *really* have refused to go back had the opportunity arisen?

In an interview for the local Ayr Newspaper she described her hideaway as a cruel exile.[82] The weekly phone calls from Chris were an agonising window on a world to which deep down she longed to return.

---

[82] *Ayr Advertiser*, 19 October, 1989.

> Without singing life is awful. Without working on stage it is like death.
> I can live on stage. There is no substitute - it's my fix.

At the same time she recognised that time had moved on, and the ravages of ill health had taken their toll. Practising on her own at home, after a performance gap of years, told her that it was unlikely that she could attain the same level of performance as before. And the ultra-professional Ottilie would have settled for nothing less. It would be all or nothing. Half measures were of no interest to her. Gradually it crept up on her that probably it would have to be "nothing".

The trauma of the divorce has eased somewhat, and she was able to maintain a level of friendship with her ex-husband. Not a lot of people will know that at the end of 1995 a binary star in *Ursa Major,* the Great Bear, was designated "Ottilie and Chris" by the International Astronomical Society in Geneva.[83] A note from Ottilie tells us that this was put to the Society as a gift to Chris from her. In a very real sense then their destinies were truly written in the stars.

However, that was one thing. Any opportunity to sing with the band would have been quite another, and would have had to come from him. He was very definitely the boss - as many others had found over the years. But she gives more than a nod and a wink that she might well have done under certain conditions - the main one being that the invitation to return came directly from Chris himself.

As a man I claim solidarity with my fellow men in finding the ways of woman often unfathomable. Although simultaneously she hated Chris for what she felt he had done to her, yet he remained the love of her life until her dying day. The thought of marriage to someone other than Chris and relationships never entered her head. He was *her* man. She was Frankie and he was Johnny, and in her heart she stuck with him. In the words of the 1956 song, recorded by Lonnie Donegan, *Love is Strange.*

So the answer to the paradox presented above is probably that, while there were many aspects of her former life such as touring she would not have

---

[83] For the anoraks the Star is classified as "Ursa Major A11h25m135-D44 SYMBOL 176 \f "Palatino Linotype" \s 1150'A7B."

touched again with the proverbial barge pole, she would undoubtedly have gone back, if asked, to *Chris*.

As Lisa says, had Chris come knocking at the door and said, in the words of the Shakespeare sonnet, "Come away my love", she would have been off like a shot. Riddled with arthritis as she was in her later years, she would still have gone, reckoning the arthritis as a problem to be resolved later.

Sadly for Ottilie that knock on the door never came.

8

OTTILIE'S PLACE IN THE STORY OF JAZZ

St. Luke begins his Gospel by saying "inasmuch as many others have taken it in hand to write an account of what has recently happened among us......so it seemed good to me also".[84]   The same could be said of Ottilie Patterson. A number of others before me have considered or even begun the effort of writing up her life, without that effort reaching full fruition. Those attempts have been made because people shared with me the burning conviction that Ottilie was worth writing about. She had a story that needed to be told. She was not someone to be allowed to disappear into the mists of time without some worthy tribute to her memory that would inspire and encourage others to follow in her steps. Whether this present volume will be worthy to achieve that lofty purpose only the readers can judge, those readers especially who knew Ottilie and are proud to be called her friends.

In this penultimate part of the work it is time to try and sum up what it was that made Ottilie so special to those who now treasure her memory.

Impact

Just as people talk about where they were when JFK was shot, so people are keen to share the memory of when they first heard and saw Ottilie live.   She had many qualities, and chief among them was the ability to make an immediate and lasting impression on her audiences.   From experienced, hard-bitten jazz critics like George Melly, to humble teenagers like myself, people were captivated by the contrast between the slight, diminutive frame of this provincial Irish girl and the strength of the voice that issued forth from it.

That is the first point to note, and the first lesson Ottilie teaches us. Big sounds don't come exclusively from big people. You don't have to possess colossal proportions to be a good Blues Singer. What matters is not the size

---

[84]   Luke 1.1

of your body, but the size of your heart. And Ottilie's heart for singing the Blues *was* colossal.

Review after review of band concerts speak of how the atmosphere of the concert hall was lifted as soon as Ottilie came on stage. Stu Morrison reflects that Ottilie, petite and pale, was not a glamorous person in herself (something Ottilie herself would have agreed with), but she could *project* glamour onto the stage. She had a personal magnetism that could make the audience believe they were watching a film star. Stu observes that no-one could turn an audience from passivity into wild excitement quite like Ottilie. At the end of the day this ability to bring about such transformation is inexplicable – it is pure gift.

Bursting with Talent

Ottilie was the classic role model for those of humble origins who come to believe that anything is possible. She was simply bursting with talent. She was an amazing artiste, and could very easily have made her name in the world of the visual Arts. Both her casual doodles, some of which are included in this book, as well as her more formal compositions display a skill way beyond that of the enthusiastic amateur.

We also recall that, prior to her being bitten by the Blues bug, her musical training had been in the field of classical music. Once again, she had the talent to have made a classical pianist, had providence not guided her in a different direction. Ottilie was one of those multi-talented people who make ordinary mortals like myself feel desperate about our own limitations.

It is worth noting that this love of the classics was by no means abandoned when she took up singing the Blues. As Brian McAnoy told me, when she was in one of her more relaxed and positive moods in Ayr and could be persuaded to sit at the piano and play for others, what she would play was just as likely to be Bach and Rachmaninov as it was to be Jelly Roll Morton or her beloved Albert Ammons.

A Positive Personality

Sadly, In our highly competitive world of today talent is not always enough. Many a genius from a humble background has gone unrecognised by the wider world, either because the opportunity to express the talent has not come along, or because the talent has not been encouraged or nurtured. It may be also that individual concerned has not had sufficient ambition and thrust to follow the path their talent marks out.

Here the contrast between Chris and Ottilie surfaces once again. Coming from a relatively privileged background Chris failed to make it as an actuary, only to find the path to the Guildhall School of Music opening up for him[85]. Whilst full allowance and credit is due to Chris for his determination to succeed in his chosen field, it is undeniable that the early part of the path to success had been eased for him somewhat by his family background and circumstances.

Ottilie on the other hand, whilst certainly blessed with loving and supportive parents, did not have the financial resources required to make doors swing open for her automatically. She needed to push and push hard for the opportunities she needed. Had she fled in tears from those early evening rebuffs at that Soho Club, the opportunity to sing the Blues in public may never have arisen. Thankfully, as we know, she persisted, until she found the way in through pianist Johnny Parker. Perhaps it's Johnny we should thank for being the key to Ottilie's success!

Once Ottilie had set her sights on what she wanted to do, she summoned all her strength and determination to carry on until she achieved it. Nothing would stop her. This is all the more remarkable because of the lack of musical antecedents in Northern Ireland. Compared to England, and London in particular, Ulster was a relative desert in terms of playing and listening to jazz.[86] Even Ken Smiley, one of Northern Ireland's leading exponents of jazz, found the lack of opportunities in Ulster driving him along the trail to London that others had established. This same path Ottilie was determined to follow.[87]

Those same personal qualities of determination and strength were to serve her well many times over, as she entered the turbulent and highly competitive world of the Blues singer. That she was able to see off all her musical competitors and get to the top is a tribute again to the aforementioned combination of abundant talent and personal strength.

---

[85] Reismann, 213.

[86] The development of jazz in Ulster is however well charted in the works of Brian Dempster and Trevor Hodgett. It is a rich and noble tradition. My point is that it is *in comparison to the English scene* that it appears thin.

[87] As we have already pointed out, Smiley's work as a journalist was the main reason for his moving to London.

One of the characteristics of the jazz world of that time was that it was a predominantly male world. To be sure there were other accomplished female artistes such as Cleo Laine, Beryl Bryden, Kathy Stobart and Annie Ross, but the vast majority of members of jazz bands were male. Hard drinkers, smokers and womanisers abounded. Language that would make sailors blush was standard. It was not a world for shrinking violets.

But then Ottilie was no shrinking violet. If her appearance gave the idea that butter wouldn't melt in her mouth, then, as John Crocker commented to me, people pretty soon discovered that it would! Her language, as well as her hair, could be exceedingly colourful at times. But then, many would argue that this was understandable, and that many of the brash characteristics Ottilie developed were essential for her survival.

Part of Ottilie's armoury was a dry, wicked sense of humour. This comes out in her copious writings, a number of which appear at different stages in this book. Her passion for crossword puzzles stemmed from a love of words and word plays, so that the style of humour that appealed to her most was that which involved the clever use of words:

> Paranoia, paranoia,
> How can anyone enjoia,
> Who the dickens will emploia
> When you suffer paranoia?

If Ottilie herself were writing this she would very likely say that the Mezz Mezzrow book that was so inspirational for her in her youth had left her with no illusions about the world of jazz that she was entering. Mezzrow himself, though an energetic campaigner for racial integration in jazz bands, was far from being a paragon of virtue. He became as well known for his drug-dealing than for his music. So much so that, in his heydey "Mezz" actually became slang for marijuana, finding a reference to it in the Stuff Smith song, *If You're a Viper.*

He was also known as the "Muggles King," the word "muggles" being slang for marijuana at that time, a little known fact declared in the title of the 1928 Louis Armstrong tune *Muggles.*

The Masks of Janus
Hanging over the Proscenium Arch in many theatres are the twin masks of

Janus, twin faces that look in opposite directions. One face is smiling, the other is crying, reminding theatregoers that drama, and therefore life, is about *both* triumph *and* tragedy, about both laughter and tears.

In many ways Ottilie was the embodiment of that paradox. Triumphs she undoubtedly had in abundance, just reward for her prodigious talent. But those triumphs had to go hand in hand with tragedy - the tragedy of the persistent illness that dogged her footsteps all through her professional career, the tragedy of a failed marriage, and the desperate tragedy of unrequited love. When she smiled on stage, it was the smile on the painted face of the clown, a mask hiding the heartbreak within.

Ottilie was a person who lived in a state of constant emotional tension. Sometimes this tension would build up to a peak just before performances, so that what she described as "the walk to the microphone" became a walk of courage and determination, as her nerves were first controlled and then overcome. Once she reached the microphone it was of course a completely different story. There the richness of the material she was performing, and all the history that material stood for, drove everything else out of the picture.

I have a pet theory about this. I have in fact "pet theories" about many things, entirely my own devising and not endorsed by any recognised authority. My theory is that it is same high dose of nervous energy that makes performers sensational on the one hand, and at the same time unbearable on the other.

Why are many big stars apparently so temperamental? Well, it is not necessarily because they are difficult people by nature, though some undoubtedly are. The answer lies in their nervous energy, in both positive and negative forms. Channelled into their professional performances this energy lifts them above the average and the ordinary; channelled in the opposite direction, into their personal lives, it often makes them awkward and unbearable. *And you simply cannot have one without the other.* That's my theory anyway - not so original perhaps, but undoubtedly true.

John Crocker makes the interesting comment that much of Ottilie's later behaviour was occasioned by her response to her relationship with husband, boss, then ex husband Chris. Her heartbreak at first losing him, followed by the frustration of vainly hoping for him to return was undoubtedly a major factor in the downward spiral on which her emotional life went, as Ottilie's personal writings abundantly indicate.

In a way however it was Ottilie's very emotional instability that kept her on top in her performances. Without the constant emotional turmoil she felt she would scarcely have been the wonderful singer that she was. She would certainly not have been the *Blues* singer that she was. She was an authentic Blues Singer in every sense. Her experience may not have been the same as Bessie Smith's "white folks yard", but it was an authentic Blues experience just the same. We have already made mention of *Baby Won't You Please Come Home* as being grounded more and more in Ottilie's experience as time went on. Incidentally, it is worth emphasising in passing that "Blues Singer" was the description Ottilie preferred to that of "Jazz Singer". Although the two descriptions are obviously related, the former is more appropriate as describing what Ottilie was about. It was the *Blues* in particular that first grabbed hold of Ottilie, via Bessie Smith, and not jazz in general.

Really the Blues
Part of the appeal of the Blues to Ottilie and other artists was that they represented an integral part of the history of the Black people of the South, as Big Bill Broonzy had demonstrated. The origins of the Blues is usually traced to the songs of the cotton fields, field hollers, etc. as a music that expressed the feelings of the people. In this respect they were closely linked to Gospel music, which contributed the idea that people's aspirations and miseries would be dealt with, though not in this world. It could be said that the Blues were the secular equivalent of Gospel. Many artistes, including Ottilie, included both in their repertoire.

The precise link between the Blues and jazz is actually not easy to determine since the earliest jazz musicians such as Buddy Bolden, King Oliver and Louis Armstrong were city men, and would have had little or no first hand experience of what had gone on in the cotton fields. The essentially rural blues came to them second hand at best.

When we come to ask what Ottilie's main achievement was, then undoubtedly it was to explode the myth once and for all that only
black people can authentically sing the Blues.[88] Americans seeing Ottilie for the first time, having listened to her records only, expected to see a huge

---

[88] When I use the term "Black" People I am of course referring to African Americans, descendants of the slaves moved from West Africa to New Orleans and the surrounding areas. To refer to them simply as "Black" is intended as shorthand only, and in no way geared to causing offence - which I sincerely hope it will not.

Bessie Smith type "Mama" coming on stage, and were quite astonished to see a petite, white Irish girl emerge into the spotlight.

Stu Morrison correctly points out that many, many European women have made the attempt to grasp or emulate the spirit and style of the Afro American blues and gospel singers, with varying degrees of success. He goes on

> Janis Joplin tried and, some say, succeeded, in doing so, but I am not making comparisons here. All I know is this: I have worked with American blues singers – Howlin' Wolf and Sonny Boy Williamson, to name but two – and I think I may be permitted to say that no-one else of European extraction came as close to doing it as Ottilie did.

As we have mentioned, the compliment Ottilie treasured most of all was the one from the lady from the audience at Smitty's Corner who acclaimed Ottilie's singing as "like one of us". Ottilie sang the Blues with a lusty clarity and innate grasp of the idiom that swept away all objections.

To be sure, Ottilie had paid her dues. She had immersed herself in the world of Ma Rainey, Bessie Smith, Leroy Carr, Robert Johnson and of course her beloved Big Bill Broonzy and others, so that she knew what the Blues were all about. Her singing was authentic in that it was rooted in the historical and sociological origins of the Blues. She knew her stuff.

But she also realised that, as was the case with jazz itself, Blues performers must pay proper allegiance to Blues origins, while not necessarily being confined to them. At the end of the day the Blues represented a *feeling*, a response to bad circumstances, and a way of protesting against those circumstances.

So the Blues originated as a response to the situation of negroes in the Post-Civil War Southern States of America, where they were legally free but on the receiving end of economic enslavement and harsh legal repression in the form of the new segregation laws.

But are injustice and repression confined to the American South? Have they never occurred anywhere else before or since? Of course they have. Have men had their hearts broken by faithless women only in Mississippi and Louisiana? Of course not. And because of that Blues becomes a legitimate response to the low points of life wherever they occur.

At the Monterey Jazz Festival in 1959 Ottilie was introduced to the audience by jazz vocal trio Dave Lambert, Jon Hendricks and Annie Ross in the following way:

> I've heard the Blues in Mississippi.
> Alabama, Georgia, North and South Carolina, Florida and Tennessee,
> But when I heard of Blues in Ireland, That was really news to me.
> But the Blues sure do get around,
> Oh the Blues do get around.
> They even made the scene with the Wearers of the Green,
> Yes the Blues do get around.
> And here's Miss Ottilie Patterson, straight from Belfast Town.[89]

The American Press and jazz going public were beginning to see that the Blues were not something to be closely confined within geographical and cultural boundaries. This was not an easy admission to make, as jazz was coming to be seen more and more as an essential part of what defined American culture.

The Blues ain't nuthin' but a poor workin' man feeling bad

Lonnie Donegan sings in his version of the Blues *Rocks in My Bed*, tying together poverty and misery in the precise combination that characterises the Blues.

Ottilie was therefore a pioneer, a trailblazer, one who widened musical horizons, and who found her version of Black music accepted by Black People themselves.

Characteristics of Ottilie's Voice

Students of the History of Jazz in New Orleans will know that one of the pioneers of Jazz in that city was the legendary Buddy Bolden. They will also know that there are no extant recordings of him by which we might know what he was like as a musician. We have to rely on the reminiscences of those who knew him and heard him, people like Bunk Johnson and Louis Armstrong. While these reminiscences diverge at many points, they agree on

---

[89] Sleeve notes from *Chris Barber's Blues Book, Vol.1*, 1960.

two things - Bolden was a genius, and Bolden was *loud*. Part of the legend was that on a still night he could be heard playing clear across the Mississippi, in Algiers.

We have said enough about Ottilie to confirm her genius as a performer. She resembled Bolden also in the strength of her performance. She was not a trained singer, something she herself ruefully admitted when she developed vocal cord problems in the early sixties. Her sound came therefore from her throat, rather than from her diaphragm as it should have done. She did undertake singing lessons after this initial health breakdown, but by then the damage had been done and the horse had well and truly bolted.

Ottilie's voice *was* strong. It made an impression because its strength stood in dramatic contrast to the slenderness of her frame. This contrast was the first thing to strike George Melly at the Royal Festival Hall in 1955. The contrast would go on to astonish many people subsequently.

I attend many jazz events. At these events I hear a significant number of female jazz singers. In the past ten years of attending these events I have not heard anyone who comes even remotely within touching distance of Ottilie. These girls, sometimes unkindly referred to as "singing housewives", do their best and give their all, and I am certainly not going to belittle their efforts or criticise them. But the ones I have heard lack the two chief characteristics that made Ottilie's voice what it was - strength and authenticity. Listening to these girls only serves to remind me (if I needed reminding) of just how good Ottilie actually was.

Harold Pendleton rightly describes her as the "best jazz singer this side of the Atlantic - a natural". He is of course perfectly correct as far as he goes - but we might suspect that Ottilie really merited a high ranking on *both* sides of the Atlantic.

Memories of My Trip

What of the assessment of her ex-husband, bandleader Chris Barber? More than once we have seen him generously admit that Ottilie gave the wow factor to the Band, that something special that helped to lift the Band above their contemporaries.

Things changed of course, and because of her health problems the Band had to make its way in the jazz world, in a post-Trad Boom without her at the front. This it unquestionably succeeded in doing, but one suspects the magic was not quite there once Ottilie had moved out of the picture.

In 2011 Chris released a landmark CD entitled *Memories of My Trip*, designed to highlight the great variety of artistes who had appeared with Chris over his 60 year career. Rather than a biography in music it was intended as a bridge between the older American Blues artistes such as Big Bill Broonzy, Sonny Terry and Brownie McGhee and younger British counterparts such as Van Morrison, Eric Clapton and Mark Knopler who had taken on the mantle of the Blues.

Where would Ottilie feature in such a musical kaleidoscope? The answer turned out to be on just 4 of 31 tracks, only 2 of which feature solo performances, and only one of which, *St. Louis Blues*, was a typical Ottilie feature. Criticisms were made of this apparent playing down of Ottilie, to the extent that Chris was forced to defend himself in the Letters Page of the *Herald Scotland*.

I was pleased to read your coverage of Ottilie Patterson, who deserved all the praise you gave her for her remarkable ability. As you noted, she and I were married (until long after the touring schedule which a band such as mine needs to undertake in order to survive in a competitive world).

Not only was she loved for her singing here in the UK but, most importantly she was completely accepted by the American blues public when we performed in the United States at such widely varied places as Smitty's Corner, where she sang with the band of Muddy Waters and brought the house down.

She was equally warmly received at President Kennedy's first Washington jazz festival in 1962, when there were 15,000 people (mostly black since Washington was still then a segregated town). Among her fellow performers were the Staples Singers. They were so impressed with Ottilie's singing they asked her to join in with them for a recording.

I was however hurt by your suggestion by implication that I joined in with others who did not take enough notice of Ottilie's talent when programming our new CD.

This CD was not produced to be the story of my 60-year career but rather to be of many hitherto unreleased recordings of significant importance to our happily successful campaign to persuade British people to care for the Blues as much as we did.

Almost all of Ottilie's recordings are copyright releases belonging to various major labels, so my choice of Ottilie's songs for the new CD was very limited.

But, wonderfully fortuitously, we found a live recording from a 1962 concert in Cologne that was taped by the British Forces Network.

It contains the best Blues I ever heard Ottilie sing, a magnificent version of *St. Louis Blues* featuring clarinettist Edmond Hall, former sideman of Louis Armstrong.

I know that she meant every note of it, and it is on Track One, Disc Two of our *Memories of My Trip* on Proper Records.

Whether anyone else remembers and values Ottilie, rest assured that I certainly do.

Chris Barber writing to the Herald, Scotland, July 5th, 2011.

Leaving aside the issue of the subtle promotional plugs scattered throughout the letter, the reader will make his or own mind up as to the adequacy of the word "value" at the end of the letter to describe someone who had been such a major part of both Chris' professional and personal life.

9

EPILOGUE

The combination of constant nagging illness and the reluctant acceptance that her situation in relation to Chris and everything associated with him was not going to change eventually sent Ottilie into terminal decline. Like King Ahab of Old Testament fame she turned her face to the wall and shut out the world with all its memories.[90]

The world was finally decisively rejected. Everyone was excluded - except her precious Lisa. Lisa, Ottilie's "adopted daughter" was the only one allowed to intrude on those final dark days. On June 20th, 2011 Ottilie passed away peacefully with Lisa by her side.

Part of Ottilie's rejection of her past life was the insistence that news of her death should not be released until after her repatriation to Ulster and her funeral.

This wish was respected, so that the funeral in Movilla Cemetery, Newtonards was a low key affair, with a rota minister, a small handful of friends and what remained of Ottilie's family. So low key was the funeral that getting any information from local funeral directors about the arrangements at all proved an extremely difficult task even for a determined clergyman researcher!

Many of Ottilie's devout fans may have regretted not having the opportunity to pay tribute in the time-honoured way by saying farewell to her. But once they have entered into Ottilie's mindset in those final days, the decision to keep things low key becomes entirely understandable and reasonable. Her life in music had brought her unbelievable high points - but it had also plunged her into the depths of despair, and in those later, illness-ridden days it was inevitably the low points that filled her mind. Those same fans would get their opportunity to pay their tribute in due course.

The news leaks out
Eventually the news leaked back across the water. I can remember being in a

---

[90] 1 Kings 21.4.

session at a Jazz Festival in Dove Holes, Derbyshire, when it was announced from the stage that Ottilie had passed away. A respectful silence fell over the audience, followed by a buzz of quiet conversation as people began to share their memories of her with those sitting near them. Others will talk of similar moments on other jazz occasions when news of Ottilie's demise was solemnly announced.

Eventually tributes began to flood in. All the national daily papers carried obituaries of her, many of which have provided source material for this study. That her death should feature so prominently in the top dailies is significant in itself and a fitting tribute to her top place in the history of music, especially when we reflect that New Orleans Jazz does not usually figure very highly if at all in such eminent publications!

Personal tributes were also made. John Service, native of Ayr but now resident in Switzerland, recalls that one of the first things he did on hearing was to phone Chris Barber. He recalls that Chris's usual upbeat, machine gun delivery was absent and that they were, for several minutes, two sad elderly men sharing their thoughts and memories. Stu Morrison speaks of having had a very similar conversation with him.

The Blue Plaque

We have noted that whatever Ottilie had achieved, and wherever she had travelled in the world, she never lost touch with her Ulster roots. Although the initial journey from Newtownards to London and the world of Jazz was essentially on a one-way ticket, she had been a regular visitor back to Ulster, and had spent significant periods of her life in residence there. Even the choice of Ayr as her twilight residence was dictated emotionally at any rate, because it enabled her to be near the place of her birth.

It is equally true to say that the people of Ulster were proud of her. In all the reports of her early meteoric rise to fame, especially in the Irish press, were very quick to highlight the link with Northern Ireland. She was very much "the Comber Lass", or "the Girl from Newtownards", and to that extent she had forever put this quiet part of County Down on the map.

It is only appropriate therefore that the leaders of the local community should wish to mark Ottilie's passing in some way. Without wishing any disrespect to anyone, part of the feeling was that it would be good for Comber to be remembered for something other than an ill-fated cruise liner.

And so Comber community leaders John Andrews and Erskine Willis teamed up with Ards Council to organise the erection of a Blue Plaque on 26, Carnesure Terrace, Comber. On 23rd February 2012 it was duly unveiled by the Mayor of Newtownards, Mervyn Oswald.

The crowd of around 100 represented appropriately a cross section of the community, with Father Martin O'Hagan, member of the internationally acclaimed trio of vocalists, *The Priests,* along with Protestant clergy, the Rev. Ian Gilpin and Canon Jonathan Barry. Ottilie would certainly have approved the joint representation of the two Church Communities.

The Tribute Concert

To celebrate Ottilie's life without providing music would of course have been quite unthinkable. And so the unveiling was followed in the evening by a Gala Concert in the La Mon Hotel, Gransha, Castlereagh, just outside Comber.

Again, John Andrews and Erskine Willis were the prime movers in the organisation of the concert, along with help from Drew Hogg and local Jazz broadcaster, Walter Love.

The Linley Hamilton band were booked to provide the music, and Patsy Malarkey charged with the (nigh impossible) task of singing in the Ottilie Patterson style.

Whilst a number of the people who had played significant roles in Ottilie's life were naturally invited along, including Lisa Watson and Brian McAnoy, others turned up totally unexpectedly, including famous Ulster-born singer Van Morrison.

The most memorable thing about the evening was the attendance. The organisers started out very tentatively, wondering if anyone at all would turn up. After all, it was more than 30 years since Ottilie had lived in Northern Ireland. They need not have worried. To their amazement more than 500 turned up. The La Mon had never known anything like it, and was creaking at the seams.

It was a great night, and evokes strong memories for all who were there. But it was not all about the past. The occasion was used as an opportunity for encouraging the jazz scene in Ulster, being used as an opportunity to launch Brian Dempster's Book, *Tracking Jazz - The Ulster Way.* Again, the indomitable Madame Blues would have wholeheartedly approved.

Ottilie's story is a story, often echoed in the jazz world, that triumph and disaster often do go hand in hand, that life for all of us can often follow the path of the roller coaster. Her life scaled the highest heights, while at the same time plumbing the deepest depths. It is a reminder that whether we hit heights or plumb depths is not always within our control, and can be decided by the behaviour of others around us and the circumstances we find ourselves in.

Above all it is an inspiration to us to recognise that big things do sometimes come in small packages, that anything is possible when determination is allied to talent. Ottilie had both qualities in abundance, and rightly justifies her high ranking in the history of jazz.

It is a story of what might have been, had fate and health been kinder to her. As she herself put it:

> When I look in the Mirror, what do I see?
> All them blues - and they's all me.
> When they Began the Beguine I wasn't there;
> I miss everything.

Ottilie Patterson (1983)

OTTILIE PATTERSON
DISCOGRAPHY

compiled by Gerard Bielderman
Zwolle, Netherlands

(Reproduced by kind permission)

Abbreviations:

acc	=	accordion
as	=	alto saxophone
b	=	string bass
bj	=	banjo
cl	=	clarinet
co	=	cornet
d	=	drums
g	=	guitar
hca	=	harmonica, mouth organ
p	=	piano
sou	=	sousaphone
ss	=	soprano saxophone
tb	=	trombone
tp	=	trumpet
ts	=	tenor saxophone
vo	=	vocal
wb	=	washboard

CHRIS BARBER'S JAZZ BAND	Live, Royal Festival Hall, London - 9 January 1955

Pat Halcox (co), Chris Barber (tb), Monty Sunshine (cl), Lonnie Donegan (bj,vo), Jim Bray (b), Ron Bowden (d), Ottilie Patterson (vo).

DR20146 St. Louis Blues (OP-vo)	Decca DFE6252; London 820 878-2*; JazzWorld JW77036*
DR20147 I Hate A Man Like You (OP-vo)	Decca DFE6303; London 820 878-2*
DR20149 Reckless Blues (OP-vo)	Decca DFE6303; London 820 878-2*; JazzWorld JW77036*

CHRIS BARBER'S JAZZ BAND	London - 3 March 1955

Pat Halcox (co), Chris Barber (tb), Monty Sunshine (cl), Lonnie Donegan (bj), Jim Bray (b), Ron Bowden (d), Ottilie Patterson (vo)

Poor Man's Blues	Nixa NJE1012; Lake LACD30*

CHRIS BARBER'S JAZZ BAND	London - 8 March 1955

Pat Halcox (co), Chris Barber (tb), Monty Sunshine (cl), Lonnie Donegan (bj), Jim Bray (b), Ron Bowden (d), Ottilie Patterson (vo)

Trouble In Mind	Nixa NJE1012; KAZ CD13*
Make Me A Pallet On The Floor	Nixa NJE1012; KAZ CD13*
Careless Love	Nixa NJT500; Knight KGHCD103*, KGHCD202*; Castle Com munications MBSCD413/4*

These 3 titles also on Lake LACD30*.

CHRIS BARBER'S JAZZ BAND	London - 9 March 1955

Pat Halcox (co), Chris Barber (tb), Monty Sunshine (cl), Lonnie Donegan (bj), Jim Bray (b), Ron Bowden (d), Ottilie Patterson (vo)

Ugly Child (PH out)	Nixa NJT500; Lake LACD30
Sister Kate	Nixa NJE1012; KAZ CD13; Lake LACD30

CHRIS BARBER'S JAZZ BAND	(BBC British Jazz) London – 14 March 1955

Pat Halcox (co), Chris Barber (tb), Monty Sunshine (cl), Lonnie Donegan (bj), Jim Bray (b), Ron Bowden (d), Ottilie Patterson (vo).

Trouble In Mind (OP-vo)	Lake LACB235
Sister Kate (OP-vo)	unissued
Reckless Blues (OP-vo)	unissued

OTTILIE PATTERSON with CHRIS BARBER'S JAZZ BAND	London - 16 March 1955

Ottilie Patterson (vo), Pat Halcox (co), Chris Barber (tb), Monty Sunshine (cl), Lonnie Donegan (bj), Jim Bray (b), Ron Bowden (d).

DR20148 Nobody Knows You When You're Down And Out (PH/MS out)	Decca F10621,DFE6303
DR20149 Weeping Willow Blues	Decca F10621,DFE6303

| CHRIS BARBER'S JAZZ BAND | (BBC Jazz Club) London - 18 April 1955 |

Pat Halcox (co), Chris Barber (tb), Monty Sunshine (cl), Lonnie Donegan (bj,vo), Jim Bray (b), Ron Bowden (d), Ottilie Patterson (vo).

When I Move To The Sky (LD/OP-vo) Bear Family Records BCD15700-8 HI*,
Timeless Traditional CDTTD586*

Ottilie Patterson (vo), Lonnie Donegan (g), Dickie Bishop (g), Chris Barber (hca), Jim Bray (b).

Please Get Him Off My Mind Timeless Traditional CDTTD586*

| CHRIS BARBER'S JAZZ BAND | (BBC Jazz Club) London - 9 May 1955 |

Pat Halcox (co), Chris Barber (tb), Monty Sunshine (cl), Lonnie Donegan (bj,vo), Jim Bray (b), Ron Bowden (d), Ottilie Patterson (vo).

See See Rider Timeless Traditional CDTTD586*

| CHRIS BARBER'S JAZZ BAND | (BBC Jazz Club) London - 1 August 1955 |

Pat Halcox (co), Chris Barber (tb), Monty Sunshine (cl), Lonnie Donegan (bj), Micky Ashman (b), Ron Bowden (d), Ottilie Patterson (vo).

Jailhouse Blues Timeless Traditional CDTTD586*

| CHRIS BARBER'S JAZZ BAND | London - 16 September 1955 |

Pat Halcox (co), Chris Barber (tb), Monty Sunshine (cl), Lonnie Donegan (bj), Micky Ashman (b), Ron Bowden (d), Ottilie Patterson (vo).

I Can't Give You Anything But Love Nixa NJL1; KAZ CD18*; Lake
LACD30*; Ronco CDSR056*

| CHRIS BARBER'S JAZZ BAND | London - 25 September 1955 |

Pat Halcox (co), Chris Barber (tb), Monty Sunshine (cl), Lonnie Donegan (bj), Micky Ashman (b), Ron Bowden (d), Ottilie Patterson (vo).

New St. Louis Blues Nixa NJL1; Philips 832 593-2*;
Lake LACD30*;Prima Musik 0533-2*

| CHRIS BARBER'S JAZZ BAND | London - circa November 1955 |

Pat Halcox (co), Chris Barber (tb), Monty Sunshine (cl), Lonnie Donegan (bj), Micky Ashman (b), Ron Bowden (d), Ottilie Patterson (vo).

Jelly Bean Blues Timeless Traditional CDTTD586*
Can't Afford To Do It Timeless Traditional CDTTD586*

| CHRIS BARBER'S JAZZ BAND | London - circa December 1955 or January 1956 |

Pat Halcox (co), Chris Barber (tb), Monty Sunshine (cl), Lonnie Donegan (bj), Micky Ashman (b), Ron Bowden (d), Ottilie Patterson (vo).

How Long Blues Timeless Traditional CDTTD586*

Back Water Blues	Timeless Traditional CDTTD586*

CHRIS BARBER'S JAZZ BAND — London - 27 March 1956

Pat Halcox (co), Chris Barber (tb), Monty Sunshine (cl), Lonnie Donegan (bj), Micky Ashman (b), Ron Bowden (d), Ottilie Patterson (vo).

Reckless Blues	Timeless Traditional CDTTD586*

OTTILIE PATTERSON with CHRIS BARBER'S JAZZ BAND — London - 9 July 1956

Ottilie Patterson (vo), Pat Halcox (co), Chris Barber (tb), Monty Sunshine (cl), Dick Bishop (bj), Dick Smith (b), Ron Bowden (d).

Beale Street Blues	Nixa NJE1023; KAZ CD13*; Castle Duet DCD CD214*
Jailhouse Blues	Nixa NJE1023; KAZ CD13*; Prima Musik 0533-2*
Tain't No Sin	Nixa NJE1023

Ottilie Patterson (p,vo), Dick Bishop (g), Chris Barber (b).

Shipwreck Blues	Nixa NJE1023

These titles also on Lake LACD30*.

CHRIS BARBER'S JAZZ BAND — Live, Royal Festival Hall, London - 15 December 1956

Pat Halcox (co), Chris Barber (tb), Monty Sunshine (cl), Eddie Smith (bj), Dick Smith (b), Ron Bowden (d), Ottilie Patterson (vo).

Mean Mistreater	Nixa NJL6

Ottilie Patterson (p,vo-1), Johnny Duncan (g), Chris Barber (b).

Bearcat Crawl	Nixa NJL6; Lake LACD30*
Lowland Blues (1)	Nixa NJL6; Lake LACD30*

These 3 titles also on Dormouse DM23CD* and Lake LACD55/56*.

CHRIS BARBER'S JAZZ BAND — London - early 1957

Pat Halcox (co), Chris Barber (tb), Monty Sunshine (cl), Eddie Smith (bj), Dick Smith (b), Ron Bowden (d), Ottilie Patterson (vo).

I Wish I Could Shimmy Like My Sister Kate	Timeless TTD517/518
Goodtime Tonight	Timeless TTD517/518

Note 1: These tracks were originally recorded for the British Transport Commission advertising film "Holiday". They make up the complete soundtrack of this film with a spoken commentary by the actor Robert Shaw.

Note 2: The dates given by Timeless are not correct.

Note 3: All titles also on Timeless CDTTD517/518*.

OTTILIE PATTERSON with CHRIS BARBER'S JAZZ BAND   London - 26 August 1957

Ottilie Patterson (vo), Pat Halcox (tp-1), Chris Barber (tb-2), Eddie Smith (bj), Dick Smith (b), Ron Bowden (d).

I Love My Baby (1)	Nixa 7N15109; Lake LACD30*
Kay-Cee Rider (2)	Nixa 7N15109; Lake LACD30*

CHRIS BARBER'S JAZZ BAND   **London - 12 September 1957**

Pat Halcox (tp), Chris Barber (tb), Monty Sunshine (cl), Eddie Smith (bj), Dick Smith (b), Ron Bowden (d), Ottilie Patterson (vo).

When The Saints Go Marching In	Nixa NJT508; Marble Arch CMACD113*
	EMI CDB7 97492 2*; Savanna SSLCD205*
Just A Closer Walk With Thee	Nixa NJT508; Pickwick PWK054*;
	Lake LACD30*

OTTILIE PATTERSON with CHRIS BARBER'S JAZZ BAND   London - 23 January 1958

Ottilie Patterson (vo) with Pat Halcox (tp), Chris Barber (tb-1,vo-backing-2), Monty Sunshine (cl), Eddie Smith (bj), Dick Smith (b), Graham Burbidge (d).

Trombone Cholly (1,PH/MS out)	Nixa 7NJ2025; Lake LACD30*
Lawdy, Lawdy Blues (2,PH out)	Nixa 7NJ2025; Lake LACD30*

CHRIS BARBER'S JAZZ BAND   **Live, Town Hall, Birmingham - 31 January 1958**

Pat Halcox (tp), Chris Barber (tb), Monty Sunshine (cl), Eddie Smith (bj), Dick Smith (b), Graham Burbidge (d), Ottilie Patterson (vo).

a	Lonesome Road	Nixa NJL15; KAZ CD13*
b	Moonshine Man	Nixa NJL15

(a) also on Dormouse DM23CD*.
(b) also on Dormouse DM24CD*.
Both titles also on Lake LACDD55/56*.

CHRIS BARBER'S JAZZ BAND   **Live, The Dome, Brighton - 1 March 1958**

Pat Halcox (tp), Chris Barber (tb), Monty Sunshine (cl), Eddie Smith (bj), Dick Smith (b), Graham Burbidge (d), Ottilie Patterson (vo).

Pretty Baby (CB out)	Nixa NJL17
Georgia Grind	Nixa NJL17; KAZ CD13*
Careless Love	Nixa NJL17
Strange Things Happen Every Day	Nixa NJL17

These titles also on Dormouse DM24CD* and Lake LACDD55/56*.

CHRIS BARBER'S JAZZ BAND   **(BBC Broadcast) London - 28 April 1958**

Pat Halcox (tp), Chris Barber (tb), Monty Sunshine (cl), Eddie Smith (bj), Dick Smith (b), Graham Burbidge (d), Ottilie Patterson (vo).

	Moonshine Man	unissued
a	How Long Blues	Black Lion BLP12124/25

I Love My Baby (CB/MS out)   .   unissued

    (a): Sonny Terry (hca), Brownie McGhee (g) added.

CHRIS BARBER'S JAZZ BAND   **(BBC Broadcast) London - 5 May 1958**

Pat Halcox (tp), Chris Barber (tb), Monty Sunshine (cl), Eddie Smith (bj), Dick Smith (b), Graham Burbidge (d), Ottilie Patterson (vo).

Tain't No Sin	unissued
Strange Things Happen Every Day	unissued
Sobbin' Hearted Blues	unissued

CHRIS BARBER'S JAZZ BAND   **(BBC Broadcast) London - 12 May 1958**

Pat Halcox (tp), Chris Barber (tb,vo), Monty Sunshine (cl), Eddie Smith (bj), Dick Smith (b), Graham Burbidge (d), Ottilie Patterson (vo).

	Weeping Willow Blues	unissued
	Sister Kate (+CB-vo)	unissued
a	When Things Go Wrong	Black Lion BLP12126/27

    (a): Sonny Terry (hca), Brownie McGhee (g) added.

CHRIS BARBER'S JAZZ BAND   BBC Broadcast) London - 26 May 1958

Pat Halcox (tp), Chris Barber (tb), Monty Sunshine (cl), Eddie Smith (bj), Dick Smith (b), Graham Burbidge (d), Ottilie Patterson (vo).

I Can't Give You Anything But Love	unissued
Pretty Baby (CB out)	unissued
In My Home Over There	unissued

MUDDY WATERS   **Live, Free Trade Hall, Manchester - 26 October 1958**

Muddy Waters (vo,g), Pat Halcox (tp), Chris Barber (tb), Monty Sunshine (cl), Otis Spann (p), Eddie Smith (bj), Dick Smith (b), Graham Burbidge (d), Ottilie Patterson (vo).

She's Got Dimples In Her Jaw (MW+OP-vo)	Krazy Kat KK7405

OTTILIE PATTERSON   **London - 14 November 1958**

Ottilie Patterson (vo), Norman Connor (acc), Chris Barber (b), Martin Fitzsimmons (d), George Campbell / Gerard Dillon / Madge Campbell / Ron Cunningham / Dixie Fisher / Jessie Patterson (vo).

Accordion Medley	Pye NPL18028
Hallo Patsy Fagan (OP-vo)	Pye NPL18028
Captain Fisher (OP-vo)	Pye NPL18028
The Stack of Barley	Pye NPL18028
The Colleen Dhas	Pye NPL18028
The Mapgpie (OP-vo)	Pye NPL18028
The Oul' Man From Killyburn	

Brae (OP-vo)   Pye NPL18028
The Ould Lammas Fair (OP-vo)   Pye NPL18028
Eileen O'Grady (OP-vo)   Pye NPL18028
I Know My Love   Pye NPL18028
Let Him Go, Let Him Tarry (OP-vo)   Pye NPL18028
The Inniskilling Dragoon (OP-vo)   Pye NPL18028
Accordion Reels   Pye NPL18028
The Valley of Knockanure   Pye NPL18028

All titles also on Pye Golden Guinea GGL0242 and Marble Arch MAL648.

OTTILIE PATTERSON with CHRIS BARBER'S JAZZ BAND London - 20 January 1959

Ottilie Patterson (vo), Pat Halcox (tp), Chris Barber (tb), Monty Sunshine (cl), Eddie Smith (bj), Dick Smith (b), Graham Burbidge (d).

There'll Be A Hot Time In The Old Town Tonight   Columbia SEG7915; Teldec 8.26525*; Chris Barber Collection CBJBCD4001*

CHRIS BARBER'S JAZZ BAND   London - 29 January 1959

Pat Halcox (tp), Chris Barber (tb), Monty Sunshine (cl), Eddie Smith (bj), Dick Smith (b), Graham Burbidge (d), Ottilie Patterson (vo).

Darling Nelly Gray   Columbia 33SX1158/SCX3277; Teldec 8.26525*

OTTILIE PATTERSON with CHRIS BARBER'S JAZZ BAND London - 3 February 1959

Ottilie Patterson (vo) with Pat Halcox (tp), Chris Barber (tb), Monty Sunshine (cl,ss-1), Eddie Smith (bj), Dick Smith (b), Graham Burbidge (d).

How Long Blues   Columbia SEG7915; Chris Barber Collection CBJBCD4001*
Well, Alright, O.K. You Win (1)   Columbia SEG7915; Teldec 8.26525*; Chris Barber Collection CBJBCD4001*

Ottilie Patterson (p,vo).

Squeeze Me   Columbia 33SX1158
Squeeze Me (alt.take)   Chris Barber Collection CBJBCD4001*
Tain't Nobody's Business   Columbia SEG7915; Chris Barber Collection CBJBCD4001*

CHRIS BARBER'S JAZZ BAND   Live, Deutschland Halle, Berlin - 23 May 1959

Pat Halcox (tp), Chris Barber (tb), Monty Sunshine (cl), Eddie Smith (bj), Dick Smith (b), Graham Burbidge (d), Ottilie Patterson (vo).

Easy Easy Baby   Columbia 33SX1189/SCX3282 Chris Barber Collection CBJBCD4002*

The following titles from this concert, sung by Ottilie Patterson, remain unissued:
Salty Dog - Nobody Knows You When You're Down And Out - Darling Nelly Gray - Trouble In Mind - Down By The Riverside (OP-vo) - Come

Along Home To Me

CHRIS BARBER'S JAZZ BAND   **Live, Monterey Jazz Festival - 2 October 1959**

Pat Halcox (tp,vo), Chris Barber (tb,vo), Monty Sunshine (cl,vo), Eddie Smith (bj), Dick Smith (b), Graham Burbidge (d), Ottilie Patterson (vo).

There'll Be A Hot Time In The Old Town Tonight	unissued
Careless Love	unissued
Come Along Home To Me	unissued

OTTILIE PATTERSON with CHRIS BARBER'S JAZZ BAND London - 8 December 1959

Ottilie Patterson (vo) with Pat Halcox (tp), Chris Barber (tb), Monty Sunshine (cl), Eddie Smith (bj,g-1), Dick Smith (b), Graham Burbidge (d).

Let Him Go, Let Him Tarry	Columbia SEG7998
The Real Old Mountain Dew	Columbia SEG7998
The Little Town In The Old County Down (1,CB/MS out)	Columbia SEG7998
The Mountains Of Mourne (1,CB/MS out)	Columbia SEG7998

These titles also on Chris Barber Collection CBJBCD4001*.

OTTILIE PATTERSON with CHRIS BARBER'S JAZZ BAND   **London - 3 sessions in July 1960**

Ottilie Patterson (vo) with Pat Halcox (tp), Chris Barber (tb), Monty Sunshine (cl), Eddie Smith (bj), Dick Smith (b), Graham Burbidge (d).

a	Bad Spell Blues	Columbia 33SX1333/SCX3384;
	Kid Man Blues	Columbia 33SX1333/SCX3384
	Four Point Blues	Columbia 33SX1333/SCX3384
b	Back Water Blues (CB/MS out)	Columbia 33SX1333/SCX3384
	Kansas City Blues	Columbia 33SX1333/SCX3384
	It's All Over	Columbia 33SX1333/SCX3384
a	Tell Me Why	Columbia 33SX1333/SCX3384;
	Mama He Treats Your Daughter Mean	Columbia 33SX1333/SCX3384
	Can't Afford To Do It	Columbia 33SX1333/SCX3384
	Blues Before Sunrise (PH/MS out)	Columbia 33SX1333/SCX3384
	Trixie's Blues	Columbia 33SX1333/SCX3384
	Me And My Chauffeur (PH/CB/MS out)	Columbia 33SX1333/SCX3384

(a) also on Chris Barber Collection CBJBCD4001*.
(b) also on Philips 838397-2*.

CHRIS BARBER'S JAZZ BAND   **Live, Palladium, London - 31 March 1961**

Pat Halcox (tp), Chris Barber (tb), Ian Wheeler (cl), Eddie Smith (bj), Dick Smith (b), Graham Burbidge (d), Ottilie Patterson (vo).

Too Many Drivers   Columbia 33SX1346/SCX3392
Squeeze Me (PH/IW out)   Columbia 33SX1346/SCX3392

        Both titles also on Chris Barber Collection CBJBCD4002*.

CHRIS BARBER'S JAZZ BAND with OTTILIE PATTERSON   London - 22 Sept. 1961

Pat Halcox (tp), Chris Barber (tb), Ian Wheeler (cl), Eddie Smith (g), Dick Smith (b), Graham Burbidge (d), Ottilie Patterson (vo).

I'm Crazy 'Bout My Baby   Columbia 45DB4760
Blueberry Hill   Columbia 45DB4760

        Both titles also on Chris Barber Collection CBJBCD4001*.

Ottilie Patterson (vo), Keith Scott (p), Alexis Korner (g), Eddie Smith (bj-1), Dick Smith (b), Graham Burbidge (d).   <u>same session</u>

Only The Blues (1)   Chris Barber Collection CBJBCD4001*
Lawdy Lawd (It Hurts So Bad)   Chris Barber Collection CBJBCD4001*

CHRIS BARBER'S JAZZ BAND   London - 6 October 1961

Pat Halcox (tp), Chris Barber (tb), Ian Wheeler (cl), Eddie Smith (bj), Dick Smith (b), Graham Burbidge (d), Ottilie Patterson (vo).

Tain't What You Do   Columbia 33SX1401/SCX3431
                         Chris Barber Collection CBJBCD4001*

CHRIS BARBER'S JAZZ BAND   London - 16 November 1961

Pat Halcox (tp), Chris Barber (tb), Ian Wheeler (cl), Eddie Smith (bj), Dick Smith (b), Graham Burbidge (d), Ottilie Patterson (vo).

When The Saints Go Marching In   Columbia 45DB4817,33SX1412;
                         Philips 832593-2*
Down By The Riverside   Columbia 45DB4817,33SX1412;
                         Philips 832593-2*

CHRIS BARBER'S JAZZ BAND   London - 9 January 1962

Pat Halcox (tp), Chris Barber (tb), Ian Wheeler (cl,as-1), Eddie Smith (bj), Dick Smith (b), Graham Burbidge (d), Ottilie Patterson (vo).

Basin Street Blues (1)   Columbia 33SX1401/SCX3431
                         Chris Barber Collection CBJBCD4001*
I Can't Give You Anything But Love Columbia 33SX1401/SCX3431
                         Chris Barber Collection CBJBCD4001*

CHRIS BARBER'S JAZZ BAND   London - 4/16/19 April 1962

Pat Halcox (tp), Chris Barber (tb), Ian Wheeler (cl), Eddie Smith (bj), Dick Smith (b), Graham Burbidge (d), Ottilie Patterson (vo).

Come On Baby (1)   Columbia 45DB4834; Philips 838397-2*

I Hate Myself For Being Mean To
You (1'58)   Columbia 45DB4834; Philips 838397-2* I
Hate Myself For Being Mean To
You (1'45)   Philips 838397-2*
Till We Meet Again   Philips 838397-2*

CHRIS BARBER'S JAZZ BAND   **Budapest - 7/8 July 1962**

Pat Halcox (tp), Chris Barber (tb), Ian Wheeler (cl,as-1), Eddie Smith (bj), Dick Smith (b), Graham Burbidge (d), Ottilie Patterson (vo).

Mountains of Mourne (CB/IW out)   Qualiton LPX7195
Mama He Treats Your Daughter
Mean (1)   Qualiton LPX7195
This Little Light Of Mine   Qualiton LPX7195

These titles also on Storyville STCD408*.

CHRIS BARBER'S JAZZ BAND   **London - late September 1962**

Pat Halcox (tp), Chris Barber (tb), Ian Wheeler (as), Eddie Smith (bj), Dick Smith (b), Graham Burbidge (d), Ottilie Patterson (vo).

Weeping Willow Blues   unissued
Come Along Home To Me   unissued

OTTILIE PATTERSONOVÁ & CHRIS BARBER'S JAZZ BAND   **Prague - 29 March 1963**

Ottilie Patterson (vo), Pat Halcox (tp), Chris Barber (tb), Ian Wheeler (cl,as-1), Eddie Smith (bj), Dick Smith (b), Graham Burbidge (d).

Strange Things Happen Every Day (1) Supraphon 0197
See See Rider (PH/IW/ES out)   Supraphon 0197

OTTILIE PATTERSONOVÁ & CHRIS BARBER'S JAZZ BAND   **Prague - 30 March 1963**

Ottilie Patterson (vo), Pat Halcox (tp), Chris Barber (tb), Ian Wheeler (cl,as-1), Eddie Smith (bj), Dick Smith (b), Graham Burbidge (d).

I Love My Baby (CB/IW out)   Supraphon 0197
Freight Train Blues (1)   Supraphon 0197

OTTILIE PATTERSON   **London - 26 August 1963**

Ottilie Patterson (vo), Arthur Greenslade (p), Judd Proctor (g), Jim Sullivan (g), Lennie Bush (b), Kenny Clare (d), The Ivor Raymonde Singers (vo).

Jealous Heart   Columbia DB7140
It Won't Be Long   Columbia DB7140

OTTILIE PATTERSON   **London - 23 December 1963**

Ottilie Patterson (vo), Sonny Boy Williamson (hca), Arthur Greenslade (p), Judd Proctor (g), Jim Sullivan (g), Lennie Bush (b).

Baby Please Don't Go   Columbia DB7208

I Feel So Good   Columbia DB7208

CHRIS BARBER'S JAZZ BAND — London - 28 February 1964

Pat Halcox (tp), Chris Barber (tb), Ian Wheeler (cl), Eddie Smith (bj), Dick Smith (b), Graham Burbidge (d), Ottilie Patterson (voice-1,melodica-2).

Banks Of The Bann (1)	Decca PFS4070
Streets Of Laredo (2)	Decca PFS4070
On Top Of Old Smokey (1)	Decca PFS4070

OTTILIE PATTERSON with LONG JOHN BALDRY & THE HOOCHIE COOCHIE MEN — London - 4 March 1964

Ottilie Patterson (vo), Long John Baldry (vo), probably Rod Stewart (vo,hca), Brian Auger (org,p), unknown (g), unknown (d).

Up Above My Head	unissued
Don't Tell Me Nothing About Blue	unissued
What'd I Say	unissued
I Got My Mojo Working	unissued

OTTILIE PATTERSON with THE CHRIS BARBER BAND — London - 8 May 1964

Ottilie Patterson (vo), Pat Halcox (tp), Chris Barber (tb), Ian Wheeler (cl), Johnny Parker (p), Eddie Smith (bj), Dick Smith (b), Graham Burbidge (d).

Tell Me Where Is Fancy Bred	Columbia DB7332
Ah Me What Eyes Hath Love Put In My Head	Columbia DB7332
Blow Blow, Thou Winter Wind (PH/IW out)	Black Lion BLP12126/7
When In Disgrace With Fortune	unissued

Probably Johnny Parker omitted.

Stumblin' Block	unissued
I Just Want To Make Love To You	unissued

CHRIS BARBER & OTTILIE PATTERSON — London - 25 May 1964

Ottilie Patterson (vo), Pat Halcox (tp), Chris Barber (tb,vo), Ian Wheeler (cl), Eddie Smith (bj), Dick Smith (b), Graham Burbidge (d).

Hello Dolly	Columbia DB7297

SONNY BOY WILLIAMSON & THE CHRIS BARBER BAND — Live, Free Trade Hall, Manchester - 31 May 1964

Sonny Boy Williamson (hca), Pat Halcox (tp), Chris Barber (tb,vo), Ian Wheeler (cl), Eddie Smith (bj), Dick Smith (b), Graham Burbidge (d), Ottilie Patterson (vo).

This Little Light Of Mine	unissued

OTTILIE PATTERSON   London - c. May 1964

Ottilie Patterson (vo), Sonny Boy Williamson (hca), Eddie Smith (bj), Chris Barber (b), Graham Burbidge (d)

      Where Has Poor Mickey Gone   film sound track

          Note: Made for an advertising film for Watneys Brewery.

THE CHRIS BARBER BAND   London - 5 or 6 August 1964

Chris Barber (vo), John Slaughter (g), Eddie Smith (g), Dick Smith (b), Graham Burbidge (d), Pat Halcox & Ottilie Patterson (vo-backing).

      If I Had A Ticket   Columbia 33SX1657; EMI CDB 7 97492 2*

OTTILIE PATTERSON with THE CHRIS BARBER BAND London - 16 September 1964

Ottilie Patterson (vo,+p-1), Ian Wheeler (hca-2), John Slaughter (g), Eddie Smith (g), Dick Smith (b), Graham Burbidge (d).

      Bad Luck Blues (2)   Columbia 33SX1657; EMI CDB 7 97492 2*
      Frankie And Johnny (1,2)   Columbia 33SX1657; EMI CDB 7 97492 2*
      When Things Go Wrong (1,2)   Columbia 33SX1657
      Back To The Country (3)   Columbia 33SX1657

          (3): Pat Halcox / Chris Barber / Ian Wheeler (vo-backing).

OTTILIE PATTERSON   London - 9 December 1964

Ottilie Patterson (vo) with (probably) John Slaughter (g), Stu Morrison (g), Dick Smith (b), Graham Burbidge (d).

      Roll Back Jack   unissued
      I'm Going Where I Belong   unissued

OTTILIE PATTERSON with THE CHRIS BARBER BAND   London - 15 April 1965

Ottilie Patterson (vo,+p-1), Ian Wheeler (hca-2), John Slaughter (g), Stu Morrison (bj,g), Dick Smith (b), Graham Burbidge (d), Chris Barber (vo).

      Frankie And Johnny (2)   unissued
      When Things Go Wrong (1,2)   unissued
      Back To The Country   rejected
      I Met My Baby (+CB-vo)   rejected
      Bad Luck Blues   rejected

THE CHRIS BARBER BAND   London - 20 July 1967

Ottilie Patterson (vo), Pat Halcox (tp), Chris Barber (tb), Ian Wheeler (cl,as), John Slaughter (g), Stu Morrison (bj), Jackie Flavelle (b), Graham Burbidge (d).

      Star Of The County Down   unissued

OTTILIE PATTERSON   London - November 1968

Ottilie Patterson (vo) with an orchestra directed by Richard Hill, incl. John

Wilbraham (tp,piccolo), Roger Coulan (org), Sheila Bromberg (harp), Jim Sullivan (g), string section led by John Georgiadis.

Spring Song	Marmalade 608011
Sonet No. 8	Marmalade 608011
It Was A Lover And His Lass	Marmalade 608011
The Bitterness Of Death	Marmalade 608011
Latin Drinking Song	Marmalade 608011
Hey Ho The wind And The Rain	Marmalade 608011
Please Accept My Apologies Mrs. Pankhurst	Marmalade 608011
Why So Pale And Wan, Fond Lover	Marmalade 608011
The orphan	Marmalade 608011
Song Of Solomon	Marmalade 608011
Ad Uxorem	Marmalade 608011
The Sound Of The Door As It Closes	Marmalade 608011
Helen Of Kirkconnell	Marmalade 608011

CHRIS BARBER SE SVYM ORCHESTREM   Live, Lucerna Hall, Prague – 22 October 1970

Pat Halcox (tp,p-1), Chris Barber (tb,vo), John Crocker (cl,as-2), John Slaughter (g), Stu Morrison (bj), Jackie Flavelle (b), Graham Burbidge (d), Ottilie Patterson (vo).

Trixies Blues (PH/JC out)	Panton 11.0273H
Doctor Jazz	Panton 11.0273H
Baby Won't You Please Come Home (1,JC out)	Panton 11.0273H
Star Of The County Down	Panton 11.0273H
Bill Bailey (2)	Panton 11.0273H
When The Saints Go Marching In (+CB-vo)	Panton 11.0273H

OTTILIE PATTERSON with THE CHRIS BARBER BAND Live, Jazz Festival, Ljubljana - 3 June 1971

Ottilie Patterson (vo), Pat Halcox (tp), Chris Barber (tb), John Crocker (as), John Slaughter (g), Steve Hammond (g), Jackie Flavelle (b), Graham Burbidge (d).

Bill Bailey	Suzy LP303

OTTILIE PATTERSON   London - 6/7/11 April 1972

Ottilie Patterson (vo) with orchestra directed by Richard Hill.

Johnny I Hardly Knew You	unissued
Bigatory Ballad (2 takes)	unissued

THE CHRIS BARBER BAND with OTTILIE PATTERSON   Live, Magnus Jazz Festival, Wembley - 16 October 1979

Pat Halcox (tp), Chris Barber (tb), Ian Wheeler (cl), John Crocker (ts), Roger Hill (g), Johnny McCallum (bj,g), Vic Pitt (b), Norman Emberson (d), Ottilie Patterson (vo).

There'll Be A Hot Time In The Old Town Tonight	unissued
Doctor Jazz	unissued
Darling Nellie Gray	unissued
Baby Won't You Please Come Home (PH/CB/IW/JC out)	unissued
Come Along Home To Me / I Got My Mojo Working	unissued
Bill Bailey (PH/CB/IW out)	unissued

OTTILIE PATTERSON   **London - November 1982**

Ottilie Patterson (vo), Duncan Kaye (p), remainder unknown. Directed by Richard Hill.

Georgia Grind	Fat Hen FM001
Careless Love	Fat Hen FM001
Make Me Or Break Me	unissued
Loving You	unissued

OTTILIE PATTERSON with CHRIS BARBER Live, Fairfield Hall, Croydon - 8 May 1983

Ottilie Patterson (vo), Pat Halcox (tp), Chris Barber (tb), Ian Wheeler (cl,as+hca-1), John Crocker (ts), Roger Hill (g), Johnny McCallum (bj,g), Vic Pitt (b), Norman Emberson (d).

Georgia Grind	Black Lion BLCD760505*
There'll Be A Hot Time On The Old Town Tonight	Black Lion BLCD760505*
Baby Won't You Please Come Home (A)	Black Lion BLCD760505*
Doctor Jazz	Black Lion BLCD760505*
Darling Nellie Gray	Black Lion BLCD760505*
Bill Bailey	Black Lion BLCD760505*
Easy Easy Baby (1)	unissued

(A): Ottilie Patterson (vo) acc. by Roger Hill (g), Vic Pitt (b), Norman Emberson (d).

OTTILIE PATTERSON with CHRIS BARBER   **Live, Clair Hall, Haywards Heath - 8 May 1983**

Ottilie Patterson (vo), Pat Halcox (tp), Chris Barber (tb), Ian Wheeler (cl,as+hca-1), John Crocker (ts), Roger Hill (g), Johnny McCallum (bj,g), Vic Pitt (b), Norman Emberson (d).

Salty Dog	unissued
Darling Nellie Gray	unissued
Doctor Jazz	unissued
Baby Won't You Please Come Home (A)	unissued

191

There'll Be A Hot Time On The Old
                  Town Tonight   unissued
Easy Easy Baby (1)   unissued
Stumblin' Block   Black Lion BLCD760505*

(A): Ottilie Patterson (vo) acc. by Roger Hill (g), Vic Pitt (b), Norman Emberson (d).

OTTILIE PATTERSON with CHRIS BARBER	**Live, Adeline Genée Theatre, East Grinstead - 31 May 1983**

Ottilie Patterson (vo), Pat Halcox (tp), Chris Barber (tb), Ian Wheeler (cl,as+hca-1.as-2), John Crocker (ts), Roger Hill (g), Johnny McCallum (bj,g), Vic Pitt (b), Norman Emberson (d).

Salty Dog (RH out)   unissued
Darling Nellie Gray (RH out)   unissued
Doctor Jazz   unissued
Baby Won't You Please Come
                  Home (A)   unissued
There'll Be A Hot Time On The Old
                  Town Tonight   unissued
Easy Easy Baby (1)   Black Lion BLCD760505*
Stumblin' Block   unissued
Bill Bailey (2)   unissued

(A): Ottilie Patterson (vo) acc. by Roger Hill (g), Vic Pitt (b), Norman Emberson (d).

OTTILIE PATTERSON with CHRIS BARBER	**Live, Intimate Theatre, Palmers Green - 10 June 1983**

Ottilie Patterson (vo), Pat Halcox (tp), Chris Barber (tb), Ian Wheeler (cl,as+hca-1.as-2), John Crocker (ts), Roger Hill (g), Johnny McCallum (bj,g), Vic Pitt (b), Norman Emberson (d).

Salty Dog   Black Lion BLCD760505*
Darling Nellie Gray   unissued
Doctor Jazz   unissued
Baby Won't You Please Come
                  Home (A)   unissued
There'll Be A Hot Time On The Old
                  Town Tonight   unissued
Easy Easy Baby (1)   unissued
Stumblin' Block   unissued
Bill Bailey (2)   unissued

(A): Ottilie Patterson (vo) acc. by Roger Hill (g), Vic Pitt (b), Norman Emberson (d).

❑ ⌘ ❑ ⌘ ❑ ⌘ ❑ ⌘ ❑ ⌘ ❑

CD TITLES

Bear Family Records BCD15700-8 H: Lonnie Donegan / More Than 'Pye In The Sky'

Black Lion BLCD760505: Madame Blues & Dr. Jazz

Castle Communications MBSCD413/4: 18 Jazz Classics Volume 4
Castle Duet DCD CD214: Barber, Ball and Bilk / Jazz Jamboree

Chris Barber Collection CBJBCD4001: Ottilie Patterson Back In The Old Days
Chris Barber Collection CBJBCD4002: The Classic Concerts 1959/1961

Dormouse DM23CD: Chris Barber In Concert Volume 1
Dormouse DM24CD: Chris Barber In Concert Volume 2

EMI CDB 7 97492 2: Jazz Band Favourites

JazzWorld JW77036: Greatest Hits

KAZ CD13: The Essential Chris Barber

Knight KGHCD103: A Golden Hour of Trad Jazz
Knight KGHCD202: A Golden Hour of Trad Jazz

Lake LACD30: Ottilie Patterson with Chris Barber's Jazz band
Lake LACD55/56: The Chris Barber Concerts 1956/1958

London 820 878-2: Chris Barber's Jazz Band Live in 1954/55

Marble Arch CMACD113: Barber, Ball & Bilk

Philips 832 593-2: The Entertainer
Philips 838 397-2: Trad Tavern

Pickwick PWK054: All That Trad

Savanna SSLCD205: Barber, Ball & Bilk

Storyville STCD408: Chris Barber in Budapest

Teldec 8.26526: The Traditional Jazz Scene Vol.2

Timeless Traditional CDTTD586: Chris Barber 40 Years Jubilee

A few more songs, not issued: Heavenly sunshine / Moan you moaners / Sporting life / Don't fish in my sea / Honeysuckle rose / Southbound train / Ain't we have fun / You'll be razzling till the wagon comes / Hit the road Jack / My baby / On a Christmas day / I gotta love somebody / All by myself / Salty dog / Irish black bottom / Cake walkin' babies.

SELECTED WRITINGS
OF
OTTILIE PATTERSON

When childhood was my weak and helpless state,
(called innocence by Old Men in their fond and foolish way)
The seeds of future harvests and the outcome of my fate
Already had been sown and taken root
Which, in maturer years would grow to bear a bitter fruit.

My childhood days were golden with the sun
(called summertime by Old Men in their dreamy, smiling way)
And I would play with all the gold till night, when gold was done,
But soon to golden morning would awake,
And think the sun was mine and that its gold was mine to keep.

One day I woke to find my sun had gone
(called faith by Old Men in their simple, witless way)
And I who played with sunshine and who called the sun my own
Grew wild with sorrow and with disbelief,
And wept for the sun, who thought its gold alone would cure my grief.

Wet eyed at last I looked upon the world
(called many names by Old Men in their sage and toothless way),
And seeing all its tarnish and its tawdriness unfurled,
I wept afresh for all I'd lost and loved,
While in the dark the seeds of future harvests moved.

Written sometime between 1960-63

TWICE TIMES TABLE

My husband has an IQ of one hundred and sixty five,
He is in M.E.N.S.A.
My IQ is not nearly so high;
I am Sub-MENSA,
Paralytic that is

(For the non-Classicists, "mensa" is the latin word for "table")

1963

MAN OVERBOARD

Penzance,
Land's End,
Wits end,
End of my tether.

Romance,
The Cruel Sea,
He and She,
Together.
And as for me-
All, all at sea.

A single glance
And she
Beguiled:
Caught by chance
As she smiled
Now He

Is in love with love,
And tangled in Romance
At his wits' end
At the end of his tether.

While for me
It is Land's End,
Love's End
And wits end
All together.

Man overboard.

Penzance, July 1965

LABOUR OF LOVE

How effortless to praise a lover!
Pleasure, laughing mocks the task;
Lovers' pens find easy labour,
Writing words of honey flavour,
Clover blooms among the grass.

Oh how easy lovers sing
Tunes of sworn fidelity!
For lovers' love in early Spring,
Mocks the song the cuckoos sing;
But where the singer, where the song,
That sings of winter's loyalty?

July, 1966

TALE TOLD BY A MINI-SKIRT
(With apologies to Maurice Chevalier)

Every little breeze seems to whisper 'blue knees'
Birds in the trees seem to shiver 'blue knees',
Candidly blue,
All winter through,
Fluorescent crescents.

Woollen stockings I've had to where to survive,
(not that I'm old, I'm just thirty five)
Long knickers too,
Candidly who
Would love me in these?

Winter 1966-7

THE GRAFTENBERG SONG

I hate the f---ing English,
They're cold as friggin' ice,
And when life is unbearable
They say "isn't it nice!"

God help the bleedin' English,
For when I say "hello"
They shrug their English shoulders
And just don't want to know.

You know that I'm half Irish,
A fact I mustn't mention,
For you can tell by how I yell
And scream to get attention.

My other half is Latvian,
Mixed with a touch of German,
While Patterson's a Scottish Name,
From way beyond Dunfermline.

Oh I'm a hale and hearty girl
And know just what I'm worth;
And rough the diamond I may be,
But salt I am of earth.

So stick that up your snobby nose,
You cold blood English creature,
O self-controlled you well may be,
But ice cold are by nature.

I'd rather be the way I am,
And feud and fuss and fight,
At least I know that I'm alive,
And not half dead from fright.
So pity on you English folk,
With all your high-bred notions;
For you can keep your upper lip,
And I'll keep my emotions.   *January, 1969*

INSTRUMENTS OF TORTURE

Sometimes it happens I get sick of jazz,
Sick of the crazy sounds the music has;
Cacophony that shrieks within my brain,
Again, again, again and yet again.

Have you heard the way the yellow trumpet screams?
As played by ghoulish fiends in ghostly dreams;
It's burning brass goes screaming through my brain,
Again, again, again and yet again.

The heavy trombone snarls an angry growl
That changes to a high, despairing howl,
Whose melancholy madness sweeps my brain,
Again, again, again and yet again.

The clarinet, with weeping, sickly tone,
With stuttering cadences and drooling moan
Goes piercing through my tired and aching brain,
Again, again, again and yet again.

Tonight I hear them and my nerves vibrate
As the instruments of torture shriek and grare,
Tomorrow I shall hear it all again,
Again, again, again and yet again.

Undated

UNTITLED

When you were a song
I was an instrument;
When you were a sonnet,
I was the rhyme.
When you were eighteen
I was sixteen
When you were a man,
I wasn't the woman.
                    - S-otto voce

When you were the sunshine
I was the flower;
When you were the morning
I was the sky;
When you were the summer
I was the rainbow;
When you were the winter
I froze
                    - Moriendo

April, 1983

FANTASY FIGURE

I was a Fantasy Figure
In someone else's life,
But I didn't find God.

I am a Fantasy Figure
In the minds of the audience,
And when they go home
I don't exist.

I am a Fantasy Figure
Singing in a musical group;
And when the music ends
So do I.

April, 1983

POST PERFORMANCE BLUES

Take all the roses from your hair,
The party's over - who's to care?
You're left there, hanging in the air
As I am.

The applause you heard is dead and gone,
The show is over, they've gone home;
You lie awake all on your own
As I do.

You do your act, you sing your song,
You Queen it there, nothing goes wrong;
Yet you can't sleep the whole night long,
As I can't.

O Love, what good is anything?
Applause to make the rafters ring
Is nothing - love is everything
And I've none.

I sing of love and feel the pain,
Words O so simple, song so plain,
My love is yours, and that's your gain,
But my loss.

April, 1983

THE COMING OF THE WEE MALKIES

Not written by Ottilie, but by Scottish dialect poet, Stephen Mulrine.
Kept by Otilie as one of her favourites, as being very much in tune with her own sense
of humour.

Whit'll ye dae when the wee Malkies come,
If they dreep doon affy the wash-hoose dyke
And pit the hems oan the sterrheid light,
An play keepie-up oan the clean close-wa'
Missis, whit'll ye dae?

Whit'll ye dae when the wee Malkies come,
If they chap yir door and choke yir drains,
And caw the feet dae yir sapsy weans,
An tummle thur wulkies through yir streets,
Missis, whit'll ye dae?

Whit'll ye dae when the wee Malkies come,
If they chuch their screwtaps doon the pan,
An stick the heid oan the sanitary man;
When ye hear thum shauchlin doon yir loaby,
Chantin, "Wee Malkies! The gemme's … a bogey!"
Haw, Missis, whit'll ye dae?

THE REPLY

"Haw, Missis, whit'll ye dae?" they say

Here's whit I'll dae when the wee Malkies come;
I'll wallop their lugs and skelp their bum.
I'll blouter their nebs on the clean close wa'
And gie them a tast o' heid the ba'.

I WONDER, HONEY

Looked out of my window and I thought I saw rain,
But it was only my teardrops on the window pane;
And I wonder honey,
Do you think of me
As I think of you?

The day I met you I never knew
That one day, baby, I would fall in love with you.
And I wonder honey,
Do you think of me
As I think of you?

I go to the window, I go to the door,
Just hoping to see you ass by once more,
And I wonder honey,
Do you think of me
As I think of you?

The Summer's over and now it's Fall,
I wonder did you ever love me at all?
And I wonder honey,
Do you think of me
As I think of you?

Now winter is coming with all it's ice and snow,
Without you, baby, Where can I go?
And I wonder honey,
Will you ever miss me
As I miss you?

October, 1998